FAME, FATE, and the FIRST KISS

Books by Kasie West

Pivot Point
Split Second

The Distance Between Us
On the Fence
The Fill-In Boyfriend
P.S. I Like You
By Your Side
Lucky in Love
Love, Life, and the List
Moment of Truth
Listen to Your Heart

FAME, FATE, and the FIRST KISS

KASIE WEST

HARPER TEEN
An Imprint of HarperCollinsPublishers

HarperTeen is an imprint of HarperCollins Publishers.

Library of Congress Control Number: 2018952752
ISBN 978-0-06-285100-0

Typography by Torborg Davern
19 20 21 22 23 PC/LSCH 10 9 8 7 6 5 4 3 2 1
❖
First paperback edition, 2019

To my Donavan, who has a big heart, a curious mind, and a contagious laugh. You make life better and I love you!

Dancing Graves

INT. THE GRAHAM MANSION—NIGHT.
SCARLETT, seventeen-year-old daughter to
wealthy estate owner and zombie hunter
LORD LUCAS GRAHAM, paces her bedroom,
a fire glowing in the fireplace. She
nervously awaits the return of her father
and BENJAMIN SCOTT, the man she hopes to
marry, from a hunt.

                    SCARLETT
Where are you?

EXT. A FOREST—NIGHT
In the forest surrounding the mansion, on
horseback LORD LUCAS and BENJAMIN SCOTT,
nineteen-year-old suitor of SCARLETT
GRAHAM, fight off a horde of angry
zombies.

                    LORD LUCAS

Only kill if you must! There is still
hope for them. The cure is closer than
ever.

                    BENJAMIN

There are too many!

                    LORD LUCAS

Retreat!

ONE

"Your face is falling off."

I reached up to my chin, where Grant's eyes were glued, and felt the long piece of fake skin that the makeup artist had adhered to my real skin hanging by a thread.

"My face is supposed to be falling off. I'm a zombie." I was a zombie! Acting in my very first movie role alongside Grant James. Superstar Grant James. We'd been on set for a week now, but I still couldn't shake the excitement of that thought.

"I don't think it's supposed to look like that," he said.

"My face is falling off," I said, turning toward Remy,

the director. He was behind a camera and a monitor with about ten other people.

The boom operator to my right groaned and moved the pole to his shoulder. This was at least our twentieth take of the scene; his arm was probably sore.

"Makeup! Leah!" Remy called. "We need a face fix!"

Even with the large light box blocking the direct rays of sun from the scene, the heat still radiated off the soil around us. It was hot in Los Angeles for September. We were shooting in a graveyard today, and if we were out here much longer, I knew I'd start to feel like an actual zombie, slowly melting away.

Leah hurried forward with her bag of supplies and got to work on my face. Remy stepped into the shot as well. "I need you both to add some chemistry to this scene. I'm not feeling anything."

"I'm not either," Grant mumbled.

We weren't projecting chemistry? We'd had plenty of chemistry when we auditioned for the part. Guess my becoming zombified wasn't helping.

I could fix that. I may have been the newbie on this set, but I wasn't new to acting. I had been in a few commercials, a dozen high school plays, and had made four guest appearances in *The Cafeteria*, a long-standing television show. Sure, approximately three people remembered me being in the show, but that didn't mean I wasn't good.

This movie was my big break. And my first real chance to prove I was star material.

I stayed perfectly still while Leah poked and prodded at my chin. Grant paced behind her, stepping over mounds of dirt and around fake headstones. He mumbled his lines, completely forgetting two. I didn't say anything. That was Remy's job.

Leah took a step back, gave my face a once-over, and said, "Perfect."

I smiled. "I look pretty?"

She swatted at my arm playfully and then took her place behind the monitor again.

"Okay," Remy said. "Places, everybody."

Three hours later, Remy yelled, "Cut. That's a wrap."

Leah stepped forward to remove a premade section of my zombie face that she never let me take off myself (too valuable, she once told me). I started to say something to Grant, when, past the lights and monitors, I noticed my dad weaving his way through the crew, his eyes glued to Remy. I shook my hands, hoping that would help Leah move quicker. The second she was done, I rushed to intercept my father. I wasn't fast enough. By the time I got there, my dad was talking about the appropriate number of breaks for an underage actress. Remy's expression was unreadable.

"Dad," I sang out. "You're here. Again."

He didn't miss a beat. "I've been here for two hours, and there wasn't a single break."

"We'll keep that in mind," Remy said.

"Thanks, Remy," I said. "I'll see you tomorrow." I hooked my arm in my dad's and forced us both toward my trailer.

"Lacey," Dad said. "I wasn't quite finished."

"Didn't you have that talk with him yesterday?"

"And obviously nothing changed."

"Dad, I feel great. We had plenty of breaks, I promise. Half the time, we're just standing around waiting for the lights to get moved anyway." We had at least two more months of filming. This could not keep happening.

"That's not the same as an off-set break," he said when we stopped in front of my trailer. He looked at the door, then back at me. "Aren't you coming home right now?"

Right. Home. I was underage, which meant that I was the only lead cast member who wasn't living in my provided trailer, which was towed to each location along with the rest of the equipment. I had to trek at least forty minutes (depending on where we filmed for the day) home every night to my dad's apartment . . . a place that didn't feel like home at all. It had been seven years since I'd lived with my dad full-time, and we were still getting used to it. When he'd offered to move down to LA with me, I thought he was finally supporting my acting career. What I didn't realize until we were down here was that he just wanted to micromanage it.

"I need to get some homework done first." I opened the trailer and stepped inside. He followed me.

"That reminds me—why did you tell Tiffany to stop coming?"

I sat down on the couch and unlaced my boots. "Who?"

"Tiffany. Your tutor."

"Oh, right. I didn't tell her to stop coming. She quit."

"Really?"

She had . . . after having to wait two hours for me for the third day in a row. My daily call sheet may have spelled out my schedule, but sometimes we got behind.

"Yes, really. Besides, Father dearest, I don't require a tutor," I said in an English accent. "I can work on homework packets on my own." My dad had found a school close by to sponsor my home studies. The semester started three weeks ago, before we began filming. When I was done, I would finish out my senior year back home with my mom and friends. That was probably why I wasn't super invested in the homework or the weekly emails I got from my sponsor teacher.

"You're right. A tutor wouldn't be required if you actually finished the packets and turned them in all by yourself too," he returned in his own English accent. I smiled. My dad was a bit of a nerd, who always dressed in khakis and actually parted his auburn hair to one side, but with a little effort, he could pull off a leading man. He nodded toward my homework on the table. "That's why I hired you another one. Someone who I will keep updated on your schedule. Even when it changes."

I dropped the accent. "What? No, Dad. I'll get to my homework, I promise. I don't need a babysitter. This is the biggest opportunity of my life. I'm focusing. Channeling my zombie nature. Zombies do not do independent study packets."

He gestured to my zombified face. "Somehow I don't think that *this* is the biggest opportunity life will afford you. And the amazing thing about school is that finishing it makes it so when opportunities get ruined, you have something to fall back on." He held up my barely started homework packet. "He'll be here tomorrow."

"He? You hired a man to tutor me? That's going to be weird hanging out with a strange man in my trailer."

"He's not a man. I hired a student this time, from your sponsor school. It will be good for you to hang out with someone your own age."

"Don't you think a guy my own age will be more of a distraction?"

"You think of the most creative ways to get out of

things. No, I don't think that. I know how your mind works. Boys will get in the way of your big dreams; I don't remember the last time you gave one the time of day."

"I'd give one the time if he asked."

There was a knock on the trailer door, and Aaron, the director's fifteen-year-old son, poked his head in. "Can I get you anything, Lacey?"

I smiled. "I could use a cold bottle of water, please?"

"Lacey can get her own water," Dad said.

"It's okay. I'm here to help." Aaron walked to the little fridge in the kitchen area. "I stocked your fridge with drinks this morning." He pulled one out and handed it to me.

"You're the sweetest. Thank you!"

He looked down, his cheeks going pink.

My phone buzzed on the table. We weren't allowed phones on set, so there was a list of notifications from the day. I entered my passcode and quickly looked through my texts. They were mainly from Abby and other friends back home.

"Anything else?" Aaron asked from beside me.

"Oh, no. I'm good." I held up my water. "Thank you."

He nodded, then backed out of my trailer, shutting the door.

"When did you get a water fetcher?" Dad tugged on

the leaf hanging off the stem of one of the roses my mom had sent over my first day of filming. Seven days later, they were now droopy and wilting. "I thought Faith was your assistant. You need two?"

I unscrewed the cap on my water bottle and took a sip. "Dad, Faith is the assistant director. And that was Remy's son. Don't call him a water fetcher. I think he wants to work on movies when he grows up."

"So he gets your drinks?"

"No, he just kept following me around, asking me how he could help. I tried to tell him I didn't need anything at first, but he seemed really sad about it. So I ask him for things now and again. It's easier this way." I set my water on the table and unlaced some ribbons from my hair, hanging them on a rack of clothes in the corner.

"I see," Dad said, even though it didn't seem like he understood at all. "So how *did* things go today? Do you want to quit yet?"

I scrunched my nose at him. "You will be the first to know if I ever want to quit. Try not to gloat too much if that happens."

He put his hand on his chest as though deeply offended. "You know I would never gloat."

"No, you'd just be so happy that your head might explode."

"You know it's not about me."

"I know, I know. It's about your deep concern for my fragile ego."

"I just think there's nothing wrong with being a kid before you have to grow up. This industry can do crazy things to people."

"Those people don't have you, Dad." I wrapped him in a hug. The only one driving me crazy right now was him, but he was my dad, and I was pretty sure that's what dads were supposed to do, so I'd forgive him for it. Not even my overbearing dad was going to take away the excitement of where I was and what I was doing.

His shoulders rose and fell again. "This is how you talk me into things."

"Besides, I'm far from a kid." I peeled up a corner of latex from my cheek and pulled it off slowly. "Daaadddd, help me! My face is falling off."

"Did you seriously just do that after claiming you weren't a kid?"

"You're right. My timing was off." I walked to the vanity and dropped the piece of latex there, then picked up a Q-tip and dipped it in some sort of magical makeup dissolving solution Leah had given me on day one. It made the fake skin come off easier.

"So I'll see you back home at ten with a finished homework packet," he said, his hand on the door now.

"Yep."

He left the trailer with a click of the shutting door.

I sank down into a chair and immediately regretted it as the corset I wore dug into my hips and ribs. I stood and loosened it. The makeup I had to endure may have been atrocious, but the wardrobe was gorgeous. Historical zombies knew how to dress. I ran my hand down the tattered sleeve of the billowy blouse.

I threw my corset over the rack, then picked up my phone.

Abby answered after three rings, "Hey, movie star."

"Hi! I got your one thousand texts today."

"I know you said you can't check during filming, but it's just habit now."

"I understand. I miss you too!"

"When do you get a break to come visit your not-so-cool Central Coast friends?"

I felt a twinge in my chest. There wasn't a second that I regretted accepting the role of Scarlett, but it was hard not to feel a little homesick. I felt a million miles away from all my friends, who were doing all the things that we used to do together, like meeting up at the diner after school and planning our weekend. "My Central Coast friends are the coolest, but filming seems like it's going to be pretty nonstop for the next few weeks. Especially since things aren't going that well. Apparently Grant and I have lost our chemistry."

"Why?"

"Probably because I look like maggot-eaten death most days." I grabbed a wipe and began scrubbing at the residual makeup and adhesive on my skin. I'd need a long shower tonight. My hair, normally red and curly, was straight and streaked with dirt, making it look mostly brown.

"I still don't understand why his character is supposed to want to kiss your character in that state."

"Because true love transcends all. What you really should be worried about is why *my* character wants to kiss *him*. I'm a zombie. Sure, a partially cured zombie, but still, shouldn't I just want to eat his brains? I guess things don't have to make complete sense in movies."

"It makes sense. True love really does transcend all. It's kind of sweet, actually."

I laughed. "Spoken like a woman in love. How is Cooper?"

"Amazing."

"So the whole best-friends-turned-lovers thing is something you'd recommend, then?"

"Absolutely. Why? Do you have a best friend you're looking to turn into more?"

"Ha! I have no friends. I just moved here, live with my single and very-much-out-of-the-social-scene dad, and am on a movie set every day."

"I didn't realize you were the only person acting in this movie."

I pursed my lips. "You're right. I'm being antisocial."

"Which is very weird to me. You are the queen of parties here. You throw one for every occasion."

I ran my hand along the clothes hanging on the rack as I walked by, feeling the silky material drift through my fingers.

"You still there?" Abby asked.

"I'm feeling a little pressure. This is such an amazing opportunity, and I'm terrified of messing it up." It was the first time I'd admitted that out loud. This was probably why I was feeling off, why Remy felt no chemistry between Grant and me. I needed to relax. I breathed in and then out slowly.

"I'm sorry," Abby said.

"Enough about me. How's your art? Have you posted any more paintings online that I can drool over?" Abby was going to be a world-famous painter one day, I was sure of it.

"No. School is taking all my free time."

"School is a poacher of time, that's for sure. Speaking of, I have at least half of an independent study packet to complete by ten o'clock tonight. I better run."

"Okay. Good luck," she said.

"Tell Cooper I say hi."

"Have fun working on your chemistry with Grant James. He may not be feeling it, but one look at his face and I'd think you wouldn't have a hard time at all," she said. "Is he as hot in person as he is on the big screen?"

"Hotter." And the entire cast and crew knew this, including him.

She laughed. "It's a tough job you have, Lacey Barnes. Super tough."

"I know. Some of us are called on to sacrifice for the greater good. And some must pay good money to watch those who've heeded the call."

"Talk to you later."

We hung up, and I grabbed my independent study packet. I worked on it for a solid five minutes before my mind drifted back to what had happened on set today. What I really needed to be studying was Grant James. Abby was right, I had some chemistry to work on, and I knew how to do just that.

Dancing Graves

INT. THE GRAHAM MANSION—MORNING
BENJAMIN and SCARLETT talk in the study
with Scarlett's friend EVELIN, twenty-
year-old longtime acquaintance of the
family, as chaperone, reading a book in
the corner but really listening to every
word they say. Scarlett doesn't know, but
Evelin has feelings for Benjamin.

                    SCARLETT
Are you okay? Did you come to any harm
last night?

                    BENJAMIN
We managed to drive them back, barely. I
worry your father is too concerned with
saving them when we should be more concerned with the living.

SCARLETT

They are the living, Benjamin. You shall
see; Father will finish his cure and
restore them.

BENJAMIN

I hope you are right. For their sakes.

EVELIN

For all of our sakes.
**A loud crash sounds as a stone is thrown
through a window and lands with a thud on
the carpet just behind Scarlett. Benjamin
rushes the women out of the room.**

BENJAMIN

Hide! And don't come out until I tell you
it's safe!

TWO

Grant James and I needed to be friends off set. That was all there was to it. It's not like we didn't talk between takes and goof around a little, but that was obviously not a big enough bond. If we were friends off set, as ourselves, we'd have a better flow and connection on camera. We'd been filming for only a week, but I should've thought of this before now.

It was close to eight o'clock, so I had about an hour and a half to secure Grant's friendship before my dad would expect me home. As I wove through the remaining crew putting away lights from that day's shoot, I had to stop for a moment to take it all in. I was on an actual movie set, making an actual movie. I had dreamed of doing this for as long as I could remember and now it was finally happening. *Happiness* was not the right word to describe how I felt. Maybe *euphoric* or *alive*. Like everything I had worked for my entire life had led me to this.

A couple of security guards were stationed in front of a row of barricades that surrounded Grant's trailer. His trailer was set apart from the rest of them. As if he couldn't mingle with the common actors.

The guards were older, maybe midforties. I waved.

"Hello, Ms. Barnes," the guy on the right said.

"Hi, just here to see Grant."

"Does he know you're coming?"

"No, but I thought we could run lines."

"If you'll just wait here, I'll check with him." He freed his walkie-talkie from his shoulder and relayed my presence to someone else. I had no idea why there was the need for a middleman. I could literally see Grant's trailer behind them with its lights on. All they needed to do was walk twenty steps and knock. Apparently the guards didn't have clearance for his cell phone . . . or his front door. We all stood there in silence, me and two guys three times my size.

"Do you have to stand here all night?" I asked when the silence stretched longer than a minute.

"Yes, we do. We have the graveyard shift."

"I'm Lacey, by the way," I said, but then realized he had said my name.

"Yes, we know who you are."

I smiled. "Social custom dictates that this is the time when you tell me your names."

"Oh, right." The one who'd been doing all the talking so far said, "I'm Duncan, and this is Phil."

Duncan's walkie-talkie crackled, and a female voice came on. "Send her back."

"Let me guess," I said. "I can go back?"

Duncan smiled and stepped aside. "Go on back, Trouble."

"You're not the first person who's given me that nickname," I said.

"I have no doubt about that."

I patted Duncan on the shoulder as I walked by him. When I reached Grant's trailer, I knocked.

"Come in," he said.

I pulled on the handle and hopped up the two metal steps. His trailer was much bigger than mine. That was the first thing I noticed. A long couch on one wall, a table on the other, a flat-screen television, an amazing kitchen, a closed door in the back that I assumed was his bedroom. The second thing I noticed was him. He sat on the couch, eating a protein bar. He wore sweats that he'd rolled up to his knees and a T-shirt. It had been awhile since I'd seen him in street clothes. I was used to his blousy shirts, neck scarves, and vests. He looked more like his nineteen-year-old self like this. He met my eyes with his bright blue ones. Yes, he had a reason to be vain.

"Hey," he said. "I almost forgot what you looked like without all the makeup."

"I sensed you did." I put my hands under my chin as if putting my face on display. "Commit it to memory for tomorrow."

He gave me a half smile and held up his protein bar. "Want one?"

"No, thank you."

"I thought you went home," he said.

"No." I pointed to an open cushion next to him on the couch. "Can I sit?"

He moved his leg, which had been sprawled across the center cushion, down to the floor and said, "Sure."

"Soo . . ." I sat and looked around. Instant friendship wasn't exactly something I aimed for very often. I didn't have a problem making friends, but then again, I didn't normally feel like my career was riding on having a connection with someone. Apparently that was enough to make me forget how I normally talked to people. I spotted a book sitting on the table across from us. "You like to read?"

"Sometimes."

His phone chimed. He checked the screen and typed something into it. I reached over and picked up the book. It was *Dancing Graves*, the book the movie we were filming was based on. I'd read it right after I got the part. His bookmark was about fifty pages in. "You haven't read it yet?" I asked, kind of surprised.

"I'm working on it."

"Don't you feel like books give you a more in-depth version of your character that you can work with?"

"I like to bring my own spin to a character."

There was a knock on his door.

"Come in!" he called.

Amanda came walking in. She played Evelin, my best friend, kind, brave, and in love with my fiancé. She got to wear clean dresses and keep her beautiful brown skin free of any distortion makeup. In real life I knew even less about her than I knew about Grant.

She carried two bottles of beer in her hands. Her eyebrows went up when she saw me. "Hello."

"Is one of those for me?" Grant asked.

"Yes, sir. I thought you could use one after your talk last night about your tight neck." She looked at me. "I didn't know you'd be here or I would've brought another."

"Oh, that's okay. I'm only seventeen." As if I needed to

get caught drinking here. That would be excuse enough for my father to rip up my contract and send me back to my mom's.

"Oh, right," she said. "That's why your dad is always hanging around."

Grant laughed and opened the bottle. I knew Grant was only nineteen, but I was sure normal rules didn't apply to him. I had no idea how old Amanda was.

"I keep forgetting what you look like without makeup on," Amanda said to me.

Grant kicked his foot in Amanda's direction. "That's exactly what I just told her."

"And the dirt highlights are awesome too," she said.

I ran my hand through my hair. Or tried to—it was nearly impossible. "It's one of my better looks."

She patted Grant on the knee. "Make room for me."

He scooted down the couch, and she wedged herself between us. I was glad she'd come. Having an extra person here would make conversation easier. "Are you two dating?"

Grant laughed. "No. But great friends." He tapped his bottle against hers.

"Did you know each other before this?" I asked.

"No," Amanda said. "But we've been hanging out."

If I had been able to stay here on location twenty-four seven, I'd probably be more bonded with them.

"So what were you guys doing before I got here?" she asked.

"I'm not sure," Grant said. "Lacey just showed up. Did you need something, Lacey?"

"No, I wanted to hang out for a little bit. Remy mentioned our chemistry today, and I thought this might be good for us."

Grant and Amanda exchanged a look. "Yeah, could help," he said.

"What is it? Is there something I should know?" I asked, because they'd obviously talked about this.

"No, not at all," Amanda said. "You'll get there."

"I know," I said. Just because I was young didn't mean I didn't know how to act. I sighed and looked around the trailer. This wasn't working. It felt forced, awkward. We needed to do something. "Let's play a card game. Do you have a deck?"

"Uh . . ." Grant pointed to a drawer by a sink. "Try there."

I stood and slid open the indicated drawer. Toward the back, past a pad of paper and some opened mail, I found a deck. I freed it and held it up. "Let the games begin."

"What are we playing?" Amanda asked. "Go fish?"

"Funny." I sat down at the table and shuffled the deck. "So here's the game: It's like war—high card wins the hand. But in this game, low card has to divulge some-thing about themselves. Whoever has all the cards in the end wins." This would not only help me get to know Grant better, but competition always livened up a room. And when people were having fun, they bonded.

I patted the table in front of me. "Come on, you two, the night isn't getting any younger."

"Not any younger than you," Amanda said with a smile, but she stood anyway and took the seat across from me. I wasn't sure if she was trying to be funny or if she was trying to dig at me for some reason. Either way, I knew how to hold my own.

She looked at Grant, who had his phone out again. "Don't be boring. Play with us."

He maintained his seat on the couch. "This game is pointless. Everyone already knows everything about me."

"Grant," Amanda said in a warning voice.

He gave an annoyed grunt and joined us.

I dealt the cards. "Keep them on the table facedown and we all reveal them at once. Are you ready?"

They both nodded.

"Okay . . . go."

We flipped. I had a jack, Amanda turned up an eight and Grant came in low with a three.

"And we have our first loser," I said.

"Of course," he said.

"I've never seen a loser look so much like a winner," Amanda said.

Oh. That was the problem. She may not have been dating him, but it was obvious she liked him. She liked him and thought I was here trying to take him from her. In a few weeks I was going to have to kiss him on camera, but I had no interest in him off camera. He was nice to look at, but he was not worth stalling my career over.

"Okay, Grant," I said. "Hit us with something interesting about you that we haven't already read online."

"Maybe it would be easier to correct some of the things you've read about me online."

"That works too," I said. "It's something new either way."

"Okay, I do not, in fact, have a cat named Buddy. His name is Bucky."

"Boo," Amanda said. "Give us something interesting."

"You'll have to win more than one hand for those," he said.

"No," I said. "That was fine. The key to this game is speed, so someone shares a fact and we immediately do another round." I rested my hand on top of my deck. "Also, I didn't know you were a cat person. How come you don't bring him to live in the trailer with you?"

"He lives with my parents when I'm filming."

"Next," Amanda said, and we all flipped our cards.

"Amanda," I said, when she got the lowest. I snapped my fingers. "Speed."

"Yes, I like to drive fast."

I rolled my eyes, but we all flipped again.

Grant drummed the table with two fingers. "I used to play."

"The drums?" I asked. "Were you good?"

"Why do you think I became an actor?"

I laughed. "Much more practical."

The next flip I lost. "I can eat an entire large pizza by myself." Although I hadn't done that lately. Lately, I'd been watching nearly everything that went in my mouth.

"Gross," Amanda said as we flipped again.

Now the game was picking up.

"I have watched every single animated Disney movie," Amanda yelled out.

"Impressive," I said.

"I used to run track," Grant said after he lost. "I like to run."

"I hate animals," I said for the next round. "They stink and leave fur all over stuff."

Grant gasped, and Amanda laughed.

"I can sleep for twelve hours straight," Amanda said. "I would beat anyone in a sleep-off."

"My weakness is carne asada french fries," Grant said. "I spend an extra hour in the gym daily so I can eat them."

"I have acted in three different soap operas," Amanda said.

"Nice," I said.

"And now I'm in a movie," she said.

"You are?" Grant asked. "Which one?"

"The best one in the world," I said.

Grant laughed, and Amanda yelled out, "Hear hear!"

I lost the next round. "I like to sing," I said.

"Ooh, you two can start a band," Amanda said.

"I don't want a second-rate drummer in my band."

Grant shoved my shoulder. Amanda collected the cards in the center of the table for winning that round.

Grant lost next. "I once proposed to a girl, and she said no."

Amanda paused as she was reaching for the cards. "What?"

"You're only nineteen," I said.

"And we were only five at the time."

I blew air out between my lips and threw a card at him.

"I'm keeping this," he said adding it to his stack.

We finished out the game a few rounds later, with Amanda winning. "Let's go again," she said.

"Wait," I said, noticing a clock on his wall. "Is that the actual time or is it off?" The clock said ten to ten.

"Uh-oh," Amanda said. "The little girl has a curfew. Are you going to turn into a pumpkin?"

"Pulling out the Disney references," I said.

"You know it."

"I have to go. This was fun." I stood.

"This *was* fun," Amanda said. "See you on set tomorrow."

"Remember my face," I said, giving Grant a wink.

He smirked.

I hopped down the steps and onto the asphalt, feeling okay about how that went. It stayed fairly surface level, but that was to be expected for the first round.

I'd only made it a few steps before I heard the door open behind me. I looked back to see Amanda.

"Hey, can I talk to you for a minute," she said.

"Sure."

She glanced over her shoulder at the shut door and led me a little farther away from the trailer. "I know Grant said we weren't together, but I'd like to be."

"Okay." I had figured as much.

"I wanted to put that out there."

I held my hands up. "He's all yours. I don't date."

"Okay, I just . . . wait, what? You don't date? Like, *at all*?" Her dark eyebrows were down in confusion. "For religious reasons or something?"

I laughed. "No. For career reasons. I don't need the distraction. I need to focus."

She smiled. "Okay." Then she nodded back toward Grant's trailer. "I need to focus too."

"Have fun. See you tomorrow."

She took two steps back, then stopped and said, "So if you don't date, how are you feeling about the kissing scene coming up? Do you . . . uh . . . know what you're doing?"

"I've kissed guys before." Though only when I was performing.

"Well, if you need some pointers on chemistry or the kissing scene, I'm kind of known for that. I *am* the soap opera queen, after all."

"I think I'm okay. Thanks though. I just needed a little bonding time with Grant, and we had that."

"Yes, we did. We'll have to all do this again some time."

"For sure," I said. Even though I'd gone into it with a goal in mind, I'd actually had a lot of fun. "And, hey, I may not date, but I'm a notorious matchmaker. If you need help with a plan on how to land Grant James, I'm your girl."

"Yeah?"

"Absolutely."

"I'd love that," she said.

"It's a deal, then. We'll talk soon."

She practically skipped back to the trailer. This whole night had turned out better than I had hoped. It surprised me. Now maybe my dad would surprise me and not get mad at me for being late.

THREE

"You're late," Dad said when I walked through the door.

"Hey, Dad. Nice to see you." I walked into the small living room that was adjacent to the small kitchen. My dad had come to LA a couple of months before me to find us a decent place to live. He was a graphic designer and did most of his work from home, so he assured me it wasn't too big of a sacrifice on his end, but I knew it wasn't the easiest thing in the world to pick up his whole life and move either, even if only for half a year.

"Are you late because you were so wrapped up in your schoolwork that you didn't notice the time?" he asked.

I patted a stack of boxes three-high to the right of the television. "Did I learn my procrastination from you? How long have you been here? Two months? What's even in these boxes? Obviously not anything pertinent to our survival." I tried to pry open the top one, but it was taped shut.

"Lacey," he said in a warning voice.

"I know it might not seem like I was doing homework, but I really was."

"Packet."

"I don't have it. I left it in my trailer."

"I don't know what to do with you right now. I don't know whether to talk to your director about this or—"

"Please don't. Please. Everyone already thinks I'm this little girl on set. As if no lead role in the history of Hollywood has ever been played by a seventeen-year-old."

He stared at me for a moment, a long unnerving moment. Then he said, "There's lasagna in the fridge if you're hungry." He turned around, walked down the very short hall, and shut himself in his room.

I sank to the couch and put my face in my hands. The learning curve of living with my dad was a steep one. He was stricter than my mom, and I was trying to figure out how to deal with that. I'd only ever lived with him one weekend a month and two weeks every summer. In between, we kept up with each other via email, texts, or phone calls. We were both discovering that living with one another full-time was something else altogether.

I started to stand, and my hand met the hard cover of the laptop. Now, in my post-confrontation guilt, probably wasn't a good time to google my name on the computer. I was already feeling down, and reading comments on the internet wasn't a good way to change that. But the combination of time and access to the internet always seemed to draw this desire out of me. I typed my name into the search engine.

It used to be only a few hits came up, mostly related to *The Cafeteria*. Now everything that came up was related to Grant. The first headline I saw read, "Just who is this unknown starring alongside superstar Grant James?"

"Just a nobody," I said. Worse than the entertainment articles were Grant's fans. They were brutal. Social media was full of mentions about who they wished had been cast as the lead instead of me. Like Natalie Mendoza, another big-name movie star. Did they really think this indie film could afford two big stars? I wasn't sure how it afforded the one. This had to be a major pay cut for Grant.

As I scrolled through more pages, an image came up. I gasped. There were pictures of me online, of course—my headshots and stills from the commercial I'd been in and the TV show. But this was awful. Me arriving on set in my sweats, zero makeup, and a sour look on my face. The caption below it read: *Save Grant James from the undead.*

"Stay off the internet, Lacey," I said, shutting the laptop. "Not helpful at all." I dragged myself to bed.

A huge spread of food was always available at craft services, and I made my way to the covered tent the next morning after makeup. Amanda, wearing a long black drape to protect her wardrobe, was standing at the food table, dishing cantaloupe onto her plate. She looked over when I walked up, and startled a little. Then she laughed.

"If I were a zombie hunter, you'd be the first to go," she said.

I put my hand to my chest. "I'm hurt that I mean nothing to you."

"Death."

I bared my teeth at her, and she smiled and took a step back. I grabbed a banana. "Did you and Grant do another round of that game after I left?"

"Actually, we did."

"Did you learn anything interesting about him?" It had been fun, but we had shared only basic facts the night before. I still felt like I didn't know him very well.

"About Grant James?"

"Did someone else show up?" I peeled the banana

and ate it in small pieces.

She plucked a piece of granola out of a bowl on the table and threw it at me with a smile. "No, but it's Grant James. He's been in the public eye since he was six. Nothing he told me last night, including the drumming and carne asada fries thing, was new. Pretty sure everything you'd ever want to know about him is online somewhere."

"Online," I mumbled in disgust.

"Yes, you need to stay off the internet for at least the next eight weeks. That will not help you. It doesn't like you for stealing its boyfriend."

"You've googled me?"

"I was curious about who this nobody starring alongside *my* boyfriend was." She winked at me. I liked Amanda; she seemed to say whatever she thought.

"Yeah, yeah. So . . . about Grant," I said. "I didn't know those things he revealed last night. The only things I've read about him are that his parents divorced when he was ten; he has one brother, who's adopted; he owns three houses; and his favorite person is his grandma."

"You read the *People* article too?" she asked.

"Did someone say something about my grandma?" Grant asked, walking by the food table and swiping a doughnut as he did.

"We weren't talking about you," I said, then under my

breath added to Amanda, "Tell him we were."

"We totally were," Amanda yelled after him, and he smiled at her over his shoulder. She nudged me with her elbow. "You're good."

"Didn't I tell you?"

Noah, the first assistant director, peered around the corner with the scowl he seemed to always wear. "Lacey, they're ready for you."

"More, later," I said to Amanda.

She waved a fork with a piece of cantaloupe on it at me. I followed Noah.

Grant was already in the graveyard, standing on the pile of dirt next to the hole of a newly dug grave. His hair was styled to perfection. His eyes looked extra blue under the lights.

"Hey," I said, stepping in front of him. "Doesn't it feel weird that we're filming at an actual graveyard? I'm surprised we haven't gotten any complaints." I nodded my head toward the group of people beyond the fence who had been absent when I arrived but were now pressed up against the chain-link. They held big signs. None of the signs were angry protests. All of them were variations of *We Love Grant James*. I wondered if he could go anywhere without being recognized. I smiled. Was that my future? I could get used to people holding signs for me.

He popped the last bite of doughnut into his mouth,

then tamped on the dirt pile with his foot. "It's because we're in the back half of the graveyard. Nobody is actually buried here."

"I know, but still."

"How is all this graveyard appreciation coming from a girl who hates animals?"

"You do know graveyards and animals aren't even close to the same thing, right?"

"Right . . . graveyards aren't living things. Do you really hate animals? All of them? Even kittens? Who can hate kittens?"

"Have you been analyzing this since last night?"

Remy joined us on the dirt pile. "Hi, guys, how you feeling today?" He held the shot list in his hand with the scenes that we'd be filming that day.

"Good," I said.

"This girl doesn't like kittens," Grant said.

"Kittens are tolerable," I said.

"Hmm," Remy said. "Maybe we should have your character eat kitten brains for a shot."

My mouth dropped open.

Remy gave Grant a head tilt. "Turns out she likes kittens more than she was letting on." He glanced at his clipboard. "Besides, audiences wouldn't forgive us for that. We better stick to humans." He clapped us back to business. "Okay, we have extras coming in this afternoon for some zombie fighting scenes, but this morning it's just the two of you. So lots of pining. This is the graveyard you might have to be buried in if this cure doesn't work. It's a heartfelt scene. Sad eyes, loving looks, the works."

"Sounds good," Grant said, and I nodded my agreement.

"Quiet on set," Noah called as Remy backed out of the shot. Everyone went silent, even the birds, it seems. The boom operator placed the microphone in place, hovering over our heads.

The guy with the slate came forward.

"Slate in, sound rolling, camera rolling," Noah called out.

"Scene eleven. Take one," the guy who held the slate said.

"And action," Remy said.

FOUR

There may have been lots of supposed pining, but I could tell, even after six hours, that the scenes Grant and I had shot weren't working for Remy. Apparently our chemistry was still off.

"Is her hair red?" he'd called out at one point, referring to me. "It's too bright. It's clashing with all the blood. It needs more mud or something." And so more mud was added to my hair.

Now I was standing by a light, filthy hair, surrounded by zombies. I felt hot and a bit claustrophobic. Someone tripped next to me, and I reached out to keep them from falling, when a huge light began to tip. I grabbed the pole, but it didn't help, the light crashed to the ground, bulb shattering and breaking with a burst. Someone screamed. Several members of the crew rushed forward and immediately began brushing the scattered glass into a pile.

"What just happened?" Remy yelled, staring right at me.

I held up my hands. "It just fell." I wasn't sure what had happened. Had the tripping zombie knocked into it? I was just glad nobody seemed hurt.

It was then that my advocate on set stepped forward and said something to Remy that I couldn't hear. Probably that the underage star with a special contract was going over her allotted hours for the day because Remy said, "What happened to hiring thirty-year-olds who look seventeen?"

Grant laughed next to me.

I scrunched my nose at him. "You could've had a thirty-year-old as a costar."

"That's hot," he said.

"Really?"

He shrugged and laughed again.

"That's a wrap for the day," Remy called, surprising me. Really? We were ending early? With my dad not breathing down his neck, I thought Remy could fix the light and talk down the advocate. He'd done it before.

As Leah removed the premade section on my face I asked her under my breath, "Should I be worried? Does he think I knocked over that light?"

"No, that was an accident. You did great. He's just a big bear. Sometimes he forgets a movie becomes a movie during edits."

"You've worked with him before?"

"Lots of times."

"Leah!" the big bear said.

"Yes?"

"I want more . . . more . . . something on the zombies. Let's chat."

"See," Leah said. "This is his filming persona. He'll be happy in the end." She tucked the section she'd taken off my cheek into a red plastic case.

"Red for blood?" I asked, nodding to the case.

"Don't forget guts. Blood and guts." She gave me a smile and left to go discuss makeup with Remy.

Grant was talking to some guy who I had seen on set before. He was tall, wearing shorts and flip-flops, and didn't seem happy. I waved goodbye, but Grant didn't see me.

I started peeling off wardrobe layers as I walked toward my trailer. Suddenly Aaron was at my side. "Are you okay?" He was looking at my hands like he'd find them bloodied up.

"I'm fine. Was your dad mad about the light?"

He rolled his eyes. "He's always mad. You did great today. I like the way you glare at Grant. I think it's very zombieish. My dad liked that part too. He gave a happy grunt."

I held in my laugh because I could tell he was trying to give me good feedback. Being a director's son, he'd probably been on a million sets throughout his life. "You're going to make a great director one day."

His eyes shot to the floor. "Thanks. Do you need anything?"

"I'm good. Thank you."

He nodded and left me to myself. I slipped off my blouse. I was down to my tank top and ripped-up skirt by the time I closed myself inside my trailer.

A guy around my age sat on the couch, one of his feet propped up on the coffee table, his backpack open beside him. He was the most clean-cut-looking guy I'd ever seen in my life. Had he come straight from singing in a church choir? His dark hair was cropped short on the sides and a little longer on top. He wore a collared shirt and black pants.

I backed out of my trailer, pretended to check the

name on the door, then entered again. "I didn't order a cute boy today. Did I?"

The guy pulled a pencil from the open backpack, took his foot off the coffee table, and leaned forward without even the hint of a smile.

"Are you here to run lines?" I asked. Maybe this was why Remy hadn't put up a fight about ending the day—he'd sent a coach. I headed for the cabinets in the corner where I stored my script.

"I'm Donavan, your new tutor."

I did a one-eighty and walked to the hanging rack instead. I hung up my blouse and corset. "Ah. I didn't order one of those either."

"Your father told me you'd say that. And he told me to tell you that it's this or his having a long talk with your director."

Remy would hate that.

"Did he also tell you how to deliver that message? Because you're channeling him very well. Although your scowl is a little on the heavy side. Maybe tone it down a notch."

"Do you need to get ready before we start?"

"Ready? Do you have some brain warm-ups for me?"

His eyes scanned my face, unruffled by my teasing.

"Oh. You mean my makeup. Am I scaring you?"

44

"Not at all. I found your packet and see you've done only about half."

"I've done half? Nice." I sat on the couch next to him. "But here's the problem. I can't do homework with a stranger. Tell me your five-minute history."

"My five-minute . . . what?"

"Your . . ." Wait, he was a stranger. Remy may not have sent me a coach, but that didn't mean this guy sitting next to me wouldn't make a good one. "You can help me."

"Yes, exactly. Do you want to start with math or English?"

"Chemistry."

He flipped several pages on the packet. "Do you even have chemistry this year?"

I began taking everything between us and putting them on the coffee table: my packet, a binder, a pencil, his phone. "You have never seen me without makeup on." Sure, I was missing the big section on my cheek that made me look even creepier, but I knew what was left still wasn't a pretty sight.

"Your dad also told me you would be very creative at finding ways to get out of this." He reached for the stuff on the table.

I grabbed both of his arms and turned him to face me. "I'll do your packet in a minute."

"It's your packet."

"Whatever. Just help me real fast, and then we can work on that."

He sighed. "I am setting my phone timer for five minutes. When it goes off, we start on the packet."

I crinkled my nose. "You really are a choir boy, aren't you?"

"Five minutes." He picked up his phone.

I smirked a little. He could hold his own. Most boys let me get my way. "Fine."

He clicked a few buttons, then set it back on the table. "So what do you need me to do?"

"Just sit there and tell me when you feel something." For many auditions I'd had to go from meeting complete strangers to performing a scene with them in seconds. This was a little different, since he wasn't an actor, but he'd be fine.

"Are you ready?" I asked.

"Yes."

I lifted my hand slowly, then ran a finger along his shoulder while I stared into his eyes. He had nice eyes—chocolate brown with thick lashes.

He jerked back. "Wait, I thought you were going to try to scare me."

"You'd think, right? No, I need to know when you feel a spark."

"I don't even know you."

"I'm not trying to form a lasting connection. I just need to know how to create chemistry with all this on." I pointed at my makeup.

His eyes traveled over my face. Had Grant's eyes been traveling my entire face today too? Maybe he needed to concentrate on the one thing the makeup artist didn't touch—my eyes.

"Hey . . ." I realized I'd forgotten his name.

He realized I'd forgotten too. "Donavan."

"Right. Sorry. Donavan, don't look anywhere but in my eyes."

"Okay." His eyes went back to mine. It was obvious he was feeling nothing but uncomfortable at this point.

I needed to change that. I kept my hands to myself and twirled my hair while locking eyes. I tried to make mine soft and vulnerable. My dirty hair crunched as I twisted it around my finger, and I held back a sigh. This was the problem—I was relying on the tactics I normally fell back on in a romantic scene, things that wouldn't work in my current makeup-ed state. I inched closer to him on the couch. He smelled like mint gum. If he had a piece in his mouth, he wasn't chewing it. He was perfectly still.

I reached for his hand that was resting on his knee and slowly laced our fingers together. His fingertips were slightly calloused, and I wondered what he'd done to earn those. Yard work? Building? I used my thumb to draw circles on his palm.

His body relaxed, sinking into the couch more, leaning closer to me. I leaned in as well, until my right shoulder touched his left. Then I let my eyes flicker over his face. He had tan, clear skin. His lips were a bit chapped but full.

The phone alarm went off, causing him to jump. His cheeks went pink as he reached for his phone.

"Perfect," I said, backing away. "You felt something, right?"

"Um . . . sure."

I knew he had. He wouldn't have blushed otherwise. "And what about me? Did it seem like I felt something?"

"Yes."

"Well, thank you. That will be very helpful for tomorrow." And it would be. I hadn't tried the hand thing on Grant. And I'd make sure we were better about maintaining eye contact.

"Did you?" Donavan asked.

"Did I what?"

"Did you feel something?"

Had I? I'd been concentrating so hard on making him feel that I hadn't noticed. "No. But that doesn't matter."

Donavan picked up the packet off the table and handed it to me. "That was interesting. Now let's get to work."

"Can I take off my makeup first?"

"So many excuses."

"Okay, fine. Packet. What's another hour being stifled by makeup?"

There was a knock on my door seconds before it swung open, and Faith came in carrying some pink pages. Faith was young, probably in her early twenties. She wore glasses and always had her hair pulled up into a messy bun. "Revision for tomorrow's scenes."

"Really?" I took the pages and scanned through my lines. They weren't much different, so I would be able to memorize the few changes easily.

"Noah said that you need to get something done to your nails tomorrow too, so you need to be here a little earlier."

"Okay."

"Is there anything I can do for you?" she asked, looking at Donavan like she was offering to kick him out. I had no idea she was so protective of me.

It was tempting. "I'm good."

She left, and I glanced at Donavan. I didn't know him at all, but he didn't hide irritation well. "Hey, Choir Boy, you took the job."

"I'm regretting it already."

I flashed him my stage smile. "You won't regret it for long. I grow on people." Or he'd quit.

Dancing Graves

INT. THE GRAHAM MANSION—DAY
BENJAMIN SCOTT tries to fight off a horde of angry zombies who have broken into the mansion. Several make it past him and find SCARLETT and EVELIN hiding in the library. Scarlett takes the poker from the fireplace and attempts to hold them off, swinging it wildly all around. She connects with several, pushing them back for a while. Eventually she is bitten. Evelin escapes unharmed and finds Benjamin.

EVELIN
Come quick! It might be too late!

BENJAMIN
Where is she? Where is Scarlett?

EVELIN

Come.

Benjamin finds Scarlett unconscious in the library. He rushes to Lord Graham's lab and finds the most recent cure attempt and brings it back to Scarlett. He lifts her head and forces the liquid down her throat, then cradles her to his chest.

BENJAMIN

Don't leave me. Not like this.

FIVE

I placed the packet in my dad's hands. "There. Now you can call off Boy Wonder. Where do you hire these people from anyway? Valedictorians R Us?"

"Is he on track to become a valedictorian?"

"My guess is yes. He takes homework more seriously than any seventeen-year-old should." I wasn't even sure he was seventeen. He'd looked about my age, but he'd acted closer to my dad's.

"Heaven forbid," Dad said. "But, no, like I said before, he goes to the school that sponsors your independent study. The school you'd go to if you actually went to school."

So the school recommended him. That made sense. For some reason I had it in my mind that my dad had scoured the city to find the person who looked most like a tutor.

"If I went to school, I'd be going to the one by mom's house." I didn't realize that would hurt his feelings, but I could tell by the look on his face that it did, which made me immediately regret saying it. I was acting like an ungrateful brat. I knew it was because I was tired and stressed. But I also knew it was because he was treating me like a third grader. My mom would've trusted me more had she been here. But, like that third grader, I didn't admit my mistake. Instead, I mumbled, "Going to bed," and left him standing in the living room.

My phone rang as I was pulling on my pajamas. Mom. "Hello?"

"Hello, my sweet girl. How are you?"

I immediately felt better at the sound of her voice. I didn't realize how much I missed her until that moment. "Good," I said, climbing into bed.

"Just good?" she asked.

"Well . . ." I sat up and adjusted my body against the headboard, settling in to get her advice.

"No," she said. "Don't do that."

"What?"

"Don't pull on the cords, or the television might fall on you."

It took me two seconds to realize she was talking to Colby, my little brother. "Do you need to go save him from a television disaster?"

Back to me she said, "No, it's fine. He's four; he knows better. He was trying to get his blanket and got the cords with it."

"I see."

"Now, what were you saying?"

I started to ask about how to deal with my dad better but stopped myself. That was between me and him. I didn't need to put her in the middle of it. We'd figure things out. So I asked, "Have I ever had a problem with chemistry?" My mom had spent many hours watching me from behind curtains or front row center.

"What do you mean, hon, I— It's in the dryer, Sydney! I moved it over last night! It stinks? It probably sat in the washing machine for three days, then. I'll run them again in a minute."

A lamp on my desk was in the mode where it projected stars onto my ceiling. I mapped a constellation with my eyes while she continued talking to my sister. "Mom, do you need to go?" I asked when she was quiet again.

"What? No. I want to talk to you."

I knew she did, but it sounded like she was on edge. "How is everything? You doing okay? You sound busy."

"You have no idea. Bill just started a new case and it's taking all his time, and I feel like I'm in the car twenty-four seven. It was nice having you around to help. Plus, Colby and Syd miss you."

"I miss them too!"

"What am I saying?" Mom said. "I'm not trying to make you feel guilty. I'm so happy for you. I'm dying up here thinking about how much fun you must be having. This is it. Your big break. And with Grant James. You must be in heaven. Are you? In heaven?"

She didn't need more stress. She didn't need to know what people were saying about me online. She didn't need to know that my chemistry was off. After all, everything else seemed fine. I was a great zombie. And this opportunity felt like my mom's dream as much as mine sometimes and I just wanted her to bask in it. She'd helped me get here. "Yes, Mom, it's amazing. You should come visit the set sometime. You'd love it." She really would. It was amazing.

"I will! That would be great . . . so great. I'll have to see when I can fit— Colby, don't fall asleep right there, sweetie. You need to brush your teeth first."

"Mom, sounds like bedtime routine is in full swing. I'll let you go. Thanks for calling me."

"Okay, Lace. Love you. Good night," she said.

"Love you too. Good night."

I hung up, then reached over and clicked off my light. I lay there staring at the dark ceiling for a while. I was exhausted, but my mind wouldn't let me sleep. I still gripped my phone in my hand, and I swiped across the screen, causing it to light up. I clicked on my contacts and pushed call.

"Hello," Abby said when she answered. "You know most people use chat these days, right?"

"Would you rather me chat you?"

"No. It's good to hear from you."

"Too late," I said. "Now I know how you really feel." Abby was always joking, so in reality, I wasn't worried.

"How are things?" she asked.

"Do you babysit?"

"Um . . . do you have a baby I don't know about?"

"No, my mom could use a night out. I want to hire you."

"You're sweet. Sure, I'll take your siblings out for a night. I won't even charge you."

"You're the best."

"Yes, I am," she said. "How is Operation Making Friends On Set going?"

"Good. I found out one of the actresses is in love with Grant, so I'm helping her out. You know, since I'm a notorious matchmaker."

Abby let out a scoffing sound. "Notorious? You know

you have to actually do something of note before you can be considered notorious."

"Shhh."

"Are you basing this notoriety off me and Cooper? Because if I remember correctly the plan you came up with didn't work at all. It's a miracle we even got together after everything that happened."

"Shhh. Notorious. Anyway, moving on. Thank you for watching my brother and sister. I owe you big-time."

"As in, you can give me a tour of a Hollywood movie set and let me meet some famous people? That kind of big-time? Or like, you'll buy me a milkshake and call it even?"

"Do you want a tour of a movie set?"

"Who wouldn't?"

"Then yes! Come visit me. You will be impressed by my lack of fame and by all of Grant's fans."

"I am always impressed by people who aren't famous. I can't wait."

"I'll look at the schedule and try to find a day where we can actually spend some time together."

"I can't wait."

"And I'll introduce you to Grant, a real-life movie star."

"Yes, please."

Dancing Graves

INT. LORD LUCAS'S LAB—NIGHT
BENJAMIN relates the events that took
place while LORD LUCAS was away, pointing
out where the vial that he had given
to Scarlett was and what it looked
like. Scarlett has been unconscious for
three days and is in her bedroom, where
Benjamin moved her after giving her the
vial. Evelin attends to her.

LORD LUCAS
And how did she react after you
administered it?

BENJAMIN
Her breathing slowed; she seemed to
relax.

LORD LUCAS

That's a good sign. I've never been able
to give a dosage so quickly after a bite.
Maybe it will make all the difference.

BENJAMIN

We can only hope.

SIX

One of my least favorite parts of working on this movie was the hours I had to spend getting my makeup done every day so I could look like a zombie. Which was why I was thrilled when Leah applied it in record time. Not entirely sure what to do with my newfound free time, I wandered over to the set, where Grant and Amanda were finishing up a scene. They were standing under a large oak tree and making a plan about what to do if my change progressed further. I visualized the way I would move later. How I would creep toward them, what thoughts I needed to channel during the scene.

Remy stood just behind the glow of lights, watching with his headphones on.

Amanda was good. It was kind of ironic that her character was in love with Grant's character, seeing as how she liked him in real life too. I wondered if those real feelings helped her act the scene better. I also wondered if the unrequited part of the script was true to real life as well. If it was, we needed to change that.

"Good, very good!" Remy yelled out at the scene break. He turned to me and beckoned me forward. "Okay, zombie girl. Get in there and remind your hunter why he hasn't killed you yet."

I joined Grant on set while the cameras and lights were moved into a new position. Amanda sat in a chair by the monitor, and Noah showed her a playback while Aaron looked over their shoulders. He seemed to be chiming in with suggestions. Noah threw an impatient look over his shoulder, not hiding what he thought of those ideas.

I turned my attention back to Grant. "You haven't killed me yet because my father is on the verge of the real cure, and you really want to inherit his fortune when you marry me," I said for only Grant to hear.

He smiled. He was pacing, going from the tree to the headstone to a cart past the lights with garden tools on it, then back again, mumbling his lines under his breath.

Remy was busy talking to a camera operator, so I

snatched Grant's hand on his second pass and pulled him toward me.

"Do you see my eyes?" I said.

He tilted his head, like I'd said something surprising. "Yes. They're gorgeous."

"Thanks. But more important, makeup-free, right? Don't look anywhere else today. We can do this."

"Do you see *my* eyes?" he asked, bending down to my level. His eyes were even bluer up close.

"Yes. They're gorgeous," I said, mimicking him.

"Most girls actually like to stare into them."

"What?"

"You think it's me," he said. "That trailer visit the other night. This. You think it's me."

"I . . . Maybe." I'd thought it was both of us.

He leaned in even closer, his stare becoming a smolder, showing just how easy he could turn it on. "It's not."

"Oh."

"We good?" he asked.

"Yes. We're good," I said. Only we weren't. He had me flustered now. Second-guessing myself. I had planned to do the things I'd practiced with Donavan the day before, but if I was the one who wasn't projecting chemistry, those things wouldn't help me.

We started in on the scene. "Cut!" Remy yelled in the

middle of a take. "What's that?" He pointed right at me.

"What?" Had I said a line wrong? It wouldn't have surprised me—I felt off.

He stepped forward, his finger still extended until he reached me and his finger met my arm. I looked at where he was pointing, to see a long rip in my blouse. There were a lot of rips in my shirt, but I, too, recognized this as a new one. One that hadn't been there in any other scene, which was a bad thing. It would stand out if two scenes were back-to-back, one with the rip and one without.

"I don't know how that got there," I said. There's no way I wouldn't have heard that long of a fabric rip. Weird.

"Wardrobe!" he bellowed, and I tried not to cringe.

"I'll go get a backup," Faith said.

She took longer than Remy wanted (I could tell by his constant sighing), but when she returned, he said, "Way to be on top of things, Faith."

As she helped me exchange shirts, I said, "Thanks."

She gave me a quick nod, and then we continued.

I left the set for the second day in a row frustrated that nothing had changed. The chemistry was still off. Remy had made sure to let us know. Back in my trailer after yanking off my corset, I pulled out my laptop and googled *Amanda Roth's best kissing scenes.* A whole list came up. I clicked on the first one.

Eight minutes later, I had watched the first three. She was amazing. The chemistry she created crackled through my computer screen. I was so engrossed in figuring out how she was pulling it off that I didn't realize someone had come into my trailer until he cleared his throat.

I pushed pause and looked up to see Donavan standing there.

"I knocked," he said.

"I finished the packet yesterday," I responded.

"You finished one of the three. That's one-third."

"Look at you, using your tutoring skills in everyday conversations."

"It's a talent." He stepped all the way inside and shut the door.

"You should include that in your bio for sure."

"My bio?"

"Right. You probably don't have a bio. I'll write one for you. 'Donavan: Loves homework, haircuts, and harmonizing.'"

"You know I don't actually sing, right?"

"Let's not argue about semantics."

He gestured toward my face. "Is 'can wear zombie makeup twelve hours straight' in your bio?"

I had forgotten I was still wearing it. "I'm trying to become the character." I touched my cheek. "Has it been twelve hours?"

"According to the call sheet your dad sends me every day."

"It's not always accurate," I said. "Just giving you a fair warning."

"Are you already working on your next packet?"

"What?"

He nodded at my laptop.

"Oh, no." I had more important things to work on. I slid down the couch, indicating he should sit. He did. "But I *am* studying." I pushed play on the scene I had paused.

He watched for several minutes in complete silence as Amanda went from a heartfelt monologue to making out with someone.

"Isn't she amazing?" I asked.

"I'm confused."

I pointed to Amanda. "This is an actress in this movie. She's going to teach me how she does this."

"How she does what?"

"I have to convince audiences everywhere that a zombie loves a zombie hunter. So far, it's not happening. So far, the only thing future viewers care about is that I'm not someone else."

"How do you know this?"

"The internet."

"The internet?"

"Well, people on the internet. Mainly Grant's fans."

"You know what a wise philosopher once said?" he responded.

"What?"

"You have to shake it off. Shake, shake, shake it off."

I smiled a little. He *did* know how to tell a joke. "Because the haters are gonna hate?"

He returned my smile, which softened all his seriousness. "Exactly." He looked around, apparently having humored me long enough, his serious face back again. "Do you know where your other two packets are?"

I stared at him for a moment. He wasn't at all enamored by the fact that he was on a movie set or talking to an actress.

"What?" he asked, meeting my stare.

"Nothing." I went to the cabinet, picked up a stack of papers, and plopped them on the table in front of him. Then I went back to watching another one of Amanda's videos.

"These aren't the packets," he said.

"They're in there somewhere."

"What is this?"

I turned my head sideways to look. "Oh. That's my

script." I held out my hand, but he kept flipping pages.

"What does INT and EXT mean?"

"Those are the scene details. Interior and exterior. INT means it's an inside scene and EXT means it's out-side. And then this part is where specifically each scene takes place and then what time of day." I pointed at the different words. "It's mainly notes for the lighting people."

He nodded and continued to read. "Do you really have to say this stuff?"

"No, I just have to read it, then make up whatever I really want to say."

"'My heart aches to be with you, but soon you will only want flesh'?"

"I don't have to say that part. Grant says that."

"Grant James." He said it as a fact, not as a question, so he obviously already knew the answer.

"You want to meet him? I could introduce you," I said. It was obvious I needed to get on my tutor's good side so he'd relax a bit. He may not have cared who I was, because I was nobody yet, but everyone knew Grant.

"I don't want to meet him."

"You don't?" Everyone wanted to meet Grant James.

"He has to say the words: *I wish I could feed your hunger with only my lips.*"

I took the script from him. "You just made that up."

"Close enough," he said.

"No more mocking. Look, I will work out a deal with you. I will do your packet—"

"Your packet."

"If you do something for me."

"What does that mean?" He tapped the top of the computer. "You're not going to try to kiss me again, are you?"

"Ha! I did *not* try to kiss you yesterday. I accomplished exactly what I needed to. No more, no less. If I had wanted to kiss you, I wouldn't have had to try." When I could tell he didn't find that amusing, by the way his face darkened, I added, "But don't worry, I'm not into distractions like that. I don't date."

"And I don't date actresses, so I guess we're clear on our roles here."

I stopped, sidetracked. "You don't date actresses? Did one actress in particular cause this universal ban? If so, tell the story, it must be a good one."

He picked up my packet and held it up, dismissing my question. "What's the deal, then?"

Right, the deal. I didn't need Donavan's dating history anyway. I was trying to spend less time with him, not bond with him. It wasn't Donavan, in particular; it was the interruptions. I wanted to do my homework on my own timetable. When I knew I wasn't working on a scene or studying my performance. I wanted to do it in bits and pieces, not dedicate hours at a time to it. "I will do the packet if you let me check in with you remotely."

"Remotely?"

"Yes, instead of coming in here, I text you a picture of my completed pages. Then when I'm done, I leave the packet at the front gate for you to deliver to school. And what my dad doesn't know won't hurt him."

He studied my face for a moment, and I resisted the urge to start peeling away at the zombie makeup.

"Deal," he said.

I stopped by Amanda's trailer on my way out for the day. She let me inside and then went to the microwave, where she pushed the start button.

"So," I said. "I think I need some help with my chemistry after all."

"Yeah?"

"Yes, I watched some of your soap opera scenes, and you're really good."

"Thanks. Of course I'll give you some tips, but for the record, I don't think it's all you. I was watching your scene today, and Grant's not his normal self."

I took a relieved breath and sank to her couch. "Thank you for saying that. He made me feel like it was all me."

"He has a lot riding on this movie. His last Heath Hall

movie tanked. And the reviews have really gotten in his head. Especially that one that went viral." Heath Hall was the name of the spy that Grant played in a series of action movies. It was a role he had made famous or the role that had made him famous, it was hard to separate the two.

"This is about a bad review?" I asked.

"Not just a bad review," she said. "A scathing, viral one that was retweeted more times than any of his good reviews ever have been. And it won't go away. It keeps resurfacing."

I cringed. I knew which review she was talking about. "Grant James Goes Down in Flames." There had even been a meme made of it—a picture of Grant's handsome face contorted in a scream and engulfed in flames. The meme was now used in completely unrelated conversations. "I thought he had more confidence than that."

"Most of the time he does. Sometimes he doesn't."

I could understand that. "Why did he choose this movie, then, if he feels he needs to redeem his career? Shouldn't he be doing another one of his Heath Hall high-budget films?"

"He's hoping fans will get behind a campy horror movie with heart versus his cold action-driven movies. We need to figure out how to help him get past this bad review, because I can give you all the tips in the world, but if he's not on board too, it's not going to help."

"We should play that Taylor Swift song for him," I said, thinking about what Donavan had told me earlier and smiling despite myself.

"What?"

The microwave beeped and she took out a mug full of water, then dipped a teabag into it and sat down next to me.

"Never mind. Inside joke."

"Okay, so chemistry on camera. My first tip that always leads to loads of chemistry is to imagine your costar, Grant in this case, as the guy you really like."

"The guy I really like? I don't really like anyone."

"Okay, then someone you used to like. Remember and draw on the feelings you had at the height of liking someone."

"Right . . ."

She narrowed her eyes and studied my face. "Wait . . . I know you said you didn't date, but have you *never* dated? You've never been in love before?"

"No?"

"Is that a question?"

"No, it's not. I've kissed a lot of costars in theater, but I've never been in love." I had been focused on this singular goal since the sixth grade. And I'd seen what boys could do to normally rational people—take over their every waking thought. I was too busy making my dreams happen. I had the rest of my life to figure out the love part.

"Wow. Well, I guess you need to work on your personal life. You're seventeen years old and starring in a movie, but you've never been in love? Between you and Grant, this is going to be harder than I thought."

"But I'm really good at pretending. I've acted a lot of ways I've never personally felt before."

"True."

I looked down at my hands and back at her. "Amanda?"

"Yes?"

"Thanks for helping me." I had needed a friend on set. I hadn't realized how much until then. Just sitting there talking with her was making all the difference in the world.

"Of course," she said. "Any time."

Dancing Graves

INT. SCARLETT'S BEDROOM—EARLY EVENING
BENJAMIN SCOTT waits impatiently near
a still-unconscious SCARLETT, hopeful
that the experimental cure might have an
effect even though he begins to lose hope
as each day passes. She starts to stir
and wakes. She takes in her surroundings,
obviously not fully herself but not
fully gone either. He rushes to her side
and takes her hand. EVELIN waits in the
corner, worried and uncertain.

                    BENJAMIN
Scarlett? Talk to me.

SCARLETT tries to speak, but nothing
comes out. Her eyes widen in worry.

BENJAMIN

Don't worry, my love, you will be fine.
Your father will fix everything. I think
we've slowed down the transformation.
Your heart never stopped.

EVELIN

Do you understand us, Scar?

SCARLETT nods.

BENJAMIN

Thank goodness. I can't lose you now.

SEVEN

I opened my eyes, and I knew something was off. The lighting in my room was too bright, and I was hot. I kicked off my covers, then picked up my phone off the nightstand. The time showed it was 7:00 a.m. My phone alarm, the one that had worked every morning for the last week, hadn't gone off. Had I disabled it?

I had five text messages from Leah. I shot out of bed. Call was at eight, but I would barely make it to location by then, let alone be in full makeup. I brushed my teeth and ran for the door, hoping there weren't too many overly observant photographers today.

My dad sat on a barstool in the kitchen, his laptop open, a bowl of cereal next to him.

"Don't you want to eat before you leave?" he asked.

"No, I overslept."

"I noticed."

My hand was on the door, and I stopped and turned. "You knew what time my call was this morning. Why didn't you wake me?"

"Because I figured you could use the extra sleep. You're not getting enough."

My mouth dropped open. "You didn't turn off my alarm, did you?"

"Of course not. I'm sure that was your overly tired subconscious."

I was angry but had zero time to discuss this with him right now. "If that happens again, please wake up both my conscious and my subconscious."

He gave me a wave of agreement, and I ran out the door.

I texted Leah: **Running late. Sorry!**

"I'm so sorry," I said when I arrived breathless to Leah's station.

She checked her watch, which told her we had fifteen minutes until call, and makeup took about ninety. "It's fine."

"Should I go tell Remy or Noah not to wait on me?"

"No. Sometimes they're running late. If they are, they won't even realize that you were too. If they're not, they'll know we're not ready soon enough."

They were not running late. Noah was at our station at five minutes to call. "You don't look ready," he said, wearing his normal scowl.

I went to open my mouth to explain, when Leah said, "Sorry, makeup is giving me issues this morning. Tell Remy it will be another hour."

"He won't be happy."

"Art takes time," she said.

When Noah left, I said, "You didn't have to do that. It was my fault."

She waved something that resembled a small paint-brush at me. "It's fine."

"Thank you," I said.

"Hold still," she directed as she pressed the premade section onto my cheek. "What happened anyway? Why so late?"

"Apparently I slept through my alarm. I was up late doing homework."

"And you finished it?"

"No, actually. I fell asleep. There might be some numbers inked onto my forehead." I rubbed at my forehead as if that was a real possibility.

"But I let a guy into your trailer the other day who said he was your tutor. Donavan? Isn't having a tutor supposed to make homework faster?"

"Well . . . it would if I used him. I kind of made him leave."

"Why would you do that? He seemed really nice. And cute too."

"He is . . . cute, I mean. I'm not sure if he's nice. He acts like a dad number two, so I've been treating him like that."

She laughed. "Your dad's not so bad."

"You've met him. You know how overprotective he is."

She waved her hand through the air like that shouldn't bother me.

"The point is, I don't need *another* dad. The one I have is already doubling up. But I really thought I could do the work on my own. I hardly get any alone time and I needed it yesterday. And I *can* do the work on my own . . . except the math. The math is hard."

"So, thinking about your life choices . . . ?"

"Yeah yeah, send the tutor away *after* I do math next time."

"It's good to learn from our mistakes."

★ ★ ★

An hour later I walked on set, then realized I was holding my phone. I hadn't had time to stop by my trailer in my rush this morning. I panicked but Faith held out her hand with a smile.

"Thank you," I whispered.

She tucked it into her pocket, and I joined Grant.

"Oversleep this morning?" he asked.

My eyes shot to Remy, who was busy inspecting a headstone with the art director. This was our last day at the cemetery. Tonight everything would be packed up and moved to a church. "How did you know I was late?"

"Because Leah did my makeup at a time when she should've been doing yours."

"How much mascara does she use to get your lashes that long?"

He let out a faux gasp. "This is all me, baby."

Despite his jokey tone, he was being honest. He had long eyelashes, which I knew weren't enhanced. He probably only got a dusting of foundation and a bit of eyeliner. And a whole lot of hair gel. "What's your favorite part about this job?" I asked.

"About this particular acting job? Or acting in general?"

"This one." Even though Amanda said he'd taken the job to win back some fans and redeem his reputation,

I wondered if that was the only reason. His salary was probably half the budget, but it still couldn't have been anything close to what he was used to.

"You, of course." He winked.

I rolled my eyes. "You say that to all your costars."

"And I mean it every time."

I laughed, then stopped and lightly touched my face. "Don't make me laugh. You're going to make my chin fall off again."

"That wouldn't be my fault. That would be Leah's. Your chin should be more secure than that."

"My chin is very secure."

Remy raised his voice so everyone could hear, "Who broke the headstone?"

"The headstone?" Grant asked.

"A big chunk of it is missing," he said.

The fake headstone was obviously Styrofoam or something, because the part he was referring to was now white and someone with paints was adding gray to it.

"People," he said, "be careful on set." He looked at me when he said this for some reason. I just smiled, hoping to give him a positive image to associate with me. I realized too late that with my zombie face on, it would be a creepy sight.

Remy walked over the mound of dirt and then stopped in front of us. "You two ready?"

"For over an hour now," Grant said.

"Yes," Remy said. "Sorry about that—makeup mishap."

Grant wiggled his eyebrows at me. I just nodded at Remy.

He picked up my hand and inspected my modified nails. "Very undead, right?" he asked with a smile.

"I like them," I said.

"Good, let's roll, then," Remy said.

Two hours passed, and Remy yelled out, "Cut!" He marched past a camera operator, then came to stand in front of me. He studied my face carefully, then waved his hand in front of it. "I can't see any emotion."

Grant lifted a finger. "May I suggest a little less makeup. For this scene, she is only a partially turned zombie, after all."

Remy waved his hand around my face. "Leah, we can work on that, yes?" he asked as if she'd been following along with the conversation. And maybe she had, because she nodded from behind the monitor and said, "Of course."

"Okay, then work on that. And quickly. We don't have much time left here."

I pressed my phone to my ear as I walked to my trailer. "Tell me something nice about me."

Abby laughed. "You need an ego boost?"

"Yes, a big one."

"You are the world's greatest actress," she said.

"Something sincere."

Her laughter died down. "I'm sorry, I don't mean to make light of this. I can tell your confidence is shot. You really are amazing. I still remember that story you made up inside that empty church last summer. I thought you were speaking about your own life, that's how believable it was."

"You're good at this," I said. "How much would I have to pay you to come and sit in my dressing room and write me compliments all day long?"

"I'd totally do that for free."

"You're hired." I rounded a corner, my trailer in view. "What are you up to tonight?"

"The homecoming game."

"Football? You're going to a football game? I didn't know that was your kind of thing."

"I had to take over your social calendar when you left."

The last homecoming game of my high school career was happening tonight. "I guess school events still go on without me. Huh . . ." A tug of sadness surprised me. Not that things happened without me, but that I was missing them.

"I know, shocking."

I opened my dressing room door and nearly jumped out of my skin when I saw Donavan sitting there, head leaned over a book. "We had a deal."

"What?" Abby asked.

"Nothing. I'll call you later."

He held up his hands. "Leah called."

All my anger was diffused immediately. She was the nicest person ever. "Leah has your number?"

"I had to give it to the security people the first day I checked in."

"Oh, right. What did Leah say?"

"Something about how math nearly ruined your life."

"It's true. Math is a jerk."

He smiled, and I felt guilty. Math wasn't a jerk, but I certainly had been. Donavan was just trying to do his job, and even though he was better than my past tutors at not letting me get away with things, I was still making it very difficult for him with my completely negative attitude.

"I feel like we got off on the wrong foot," I said. "I'm sorry. I've been under a lot of pressure, and homework has been an added stress. Plus, my dad . . ." I trailed off. He didn't need to know that my dad didn't care if I succeeded or failed at this job.

"We can try a new foot today," Donavan said.

I raised a fist in the air. "Yes, to new feet."

"Yes, to finishing this packet so your dad stops texting me for updates."

"I'm sorry." So I wasn't the only one he was bugging. A new wave of frustration hit me. I needed to have a real talk with my dad . . . eventually.

EIGHT

Ninety minutes later packet two was finished, and Donavan was now explaining an equation in packet three.

"And then," he said, "the numbers decided to stop trying to solve each other and just get along."

"Uh-huh," I said, picking at a loose piece of latex on my cheek. I had managed to quickly change out of my costume, not wanting to mess it up, but this was the third day in a row I hadn't taken off my makeup right away.

"Did you hear what I said?"

"What?"

"You are distracted."

"I'm thinking about something my friend Abby said earlier."

"Was it about math?"

"It wasn't. It was about this thing I used to do to help me get out of a rut." It was something I hadn't done at all since I'd been here. And I knew I needed to loosen up, to get out of my own head. It would hopefully help me project chemistry on set. We'd always called them perspective outings. I wished I could call Kara and Abby and beg them to go on one with me. But they were four hours away. I'd have to make do with who I had—Grant and Amanda. I wondered if they'd go along with it. There was only one way to find out.

"Can we take a break?" I asked. "After an hour and a half my brain can't process new info anyway."

He shoved his notebook and pencil in his open backpack. "Sure."

"You don't have to stick around, if you need to go."

"You don't want to finish your last packet after this break?"

"Not really." I offered him my best smile.

He seemed disappointed in my lack of motivation. But I had just done ninety minutes' worth of homework. That had to count for something.

I sighed. "Fine. Maybe. If this plan doesn't work out. Follow me."

Surprisingly, he did. I led him through the large parking lot where the set was being packed away into vans and trailers. The sun was on its way down and had turned the clouds that streaked the sky pink and orange like paints on a canvas.

We stopped by Amanda's trailer first. She answered the door.

"Hey, want to go on a trip with us?" I asked.

"Who is us?" She looked Donavan up and down.

"This is Donavan. Donavan, Amanda," I said.

They exchanged hellos.

"Already working on the assignment I gave you?" she said with a smirk. "You're fast."

"What?" I returned, genuinely confused. Then, all at once, I remembered her telling me that in order to have chemistry on set I needed to imagine someone I liked off set.

"No! Really. No." Even if I had been trying to form a connection with someone (which I wasn't), it wouldn't be with Donavan. He was too uptight and serious and . . . boring.

Amanda just shrugged, then held up some pages. "I can't go anywhere, I have to work on my scene for tomorrow, I'm not ready. Faith gave me some notes."

"Faith gave you notes? Like actual, handwritten notes? She never gives me notes." She only ever brought me dialogue changes.

"Because you're already perfect."

"Ha. Yeah, right."

"You have your phone on you?"

"Um . . . yes, why?" I asked.

She held out her hand. I unlocked it and placed my phone in her upturned palm. She typed something into it, then handed it back. I looked at the screen. She had entered her phone number under the name *Amanda the beautiful one Roth*.

"That's for a report later. You two have fun," she said with a look like this was more than it was. "And you're welcome."

I just sighed as she shut the door.

"What was that all about?" Donavan asked.

"Nothing," I said. "Absolutely nothing." I led him toward Grant's trailer.

Donavan looked out over the cemetery. "Is it scary to sleep here at night?"

"I don't sleep here. I have to go home every night."

"Why?"

"I'm under eighteen. I could sleep here if my dad stayed with me, or signed the waiver, but . . . he won't."

"You actually want to sleep here?" He was still taking

in the expanse of the headstones.

"Absolutely."

In the distance behind a chain-link fence I could see Grant's fans still holding big signs. I wondered if one of those sign holders was the one who had taken my makeup-less picture and labeled me as undead.

"No Lacey Barnes signs today?" Donavan said, noticing them as well.

"You can come be my fanboy tomorrow. Bring a bright-colored sign. Or maybe a big cutout of my head. That seems more productive than this homework stuff," I said.

"Don't tempt me."

A new set of security guards stood at the barricades to Grant's trailer. "Hi," I said, stopping in front of them. "Where are Duncan and Phil?"

"Their shift starts at eight."

"Oh. I . . . we . . . need to see Grant."

"I told you I didn't need to meet him," Donavan mumbled beside me. I lowered my brow. He had been serious about that? He really didn't want to meet Grant? Apparently he wasn't swayed by fame at all. That was new. And interesting.

"He asked not to be disturbed," one of the guards said.

"But he didn't mean me," I said.

"He meant everyone, Ms. Barnes."

"Okay . . . fine. Can you at least give him a message for me?"

"Sure."

"Will you tell him that I need to go on an outing with him to look for my muse."

The guard leveled me with a hard stare as if I had just spoken a foreign language and he was waiting for me to translate.

"That's all," I said. "He'll get it."

"Okay."

"Oh, and tell him I'll be in my trailer." I started to back away. "No, actually, give him my cell number." I patted my pockets and then looked around on the ground as if a piece of paper would magically materialize because I wished for it.

Donavan held one out for me.

"Ah, a true Boy Scout," I said, taking it. "Thanks."

Then he handed me a pen.

I wrote down my cell and gave it to the security guard. "Because I won't be in my dressing room."

"Got it," he said.

"Where will you be?" Donavan asked as we walked away.

"Finding my muse." I met his eyes. I couldn't do this alone. I had to have *someone* with me to play off of. "With you, apparently."

★ ★ ★

"We have to find a place I've never been before," I said, after we walked back through the parking lot, past another set of security guards at the entrance to the cemetery, and to a car parked on the street. Donavan stopped beside it, which I assumed meant it was his. Several long strips of black duct tape were holding the bumper on.

"We'll take my car," I said, pointing to my beautiful cherry-red mustang down the street.

"Have you ever been in a ten-year-old car?" he asked. "That can be the first new place you experience today." He opened the door, raised his eyebrows at me, then climbed inside. He was so frustrating.

I went around the back to the passenger side and slid into the seat. "I have been in a ten-year-old car. Do you think I'm some snob or something?"

He paused for one beat, then said, "Yes."

I smacked his arm, and he laughed. "I'm not," I said. "I live in a small two-bedroom apartment with my dad."

"But that's only because you're down here temporarily. Where do you normally live?"

He had me there. I wasn't sure how he knew this but he did. "In a house," was all I answered. My stepdad was a high-powered attorney on the Central Coast. He had his own firm and everything. So yeah, when I lived with my mom we lived in a nice house on the beach. And yes,

I owned a brand-new car, but I'd bought it myself with television money. So I wasn't *that* snobby.

He didn't ask me to expand on my answer.

"What about you? You live in Southern California, maybe you're the spoiled one."

"Possibly," was all he said.

I couldn't read him well enough yet to know if that was sarcasm or not. He could deliver a line without attaching any emotion to it. It was actually quite impressive . . . and annoying.

He turned the key in the ignition. Loud music with heavy electric guitar sounds blasted from his radio, and he quickly turned it off.

"Really?" I said. "Choir boy likes heavy metal?"

"I'm not as straitlaced as I seem after all," he said.

Maybe he wasn't.

"Where to?" he asked.

That was the million-dollar question. I wasn't from around here, so I wasn't sure. "Do you have any abandoned buildings close by?"

"We're going to trespass?"

"What was that you said about straitlaced?"

He tightened his grip on the wheel and backed out of the parking stall.

★ ★ ★

"What is this?" I asked.

Donavan had stopped the car in the shadow of a three-story building. "It used to be an old folk's home. Now it's nothing . . . obviously."

I opened the car door to get a look that wasn't through dirt-streaked windows. The building was boarded up, but not tightly, so hopefully the windows would let in some of the light from outside. The parking lot was completely empty, cracked and crumbling parking curbs the only other thing besides Donavan's car.

"Let's go see if there's a way inside," I said.

He took a deep breath but didn't argue.

We walked the perimeter of the entire building, over dried weeds, around a dumpster in the back filled with various things people had apparently dropped here so they didn't have to pay or drive to the city dump—a floor lamp, a mattress . . . "Is that a giant dice?"

"Looks like it," he said.

"Why would anyone throw that away?"

He chuckled. "You could take it home."

"Who knows where it's been."

"In a dumpster. Behind an abandoned old folk's home."

I tugged on the brown metal door to the building. It was locked tight. The window next to it had a board across it that was hanging by just one nail. I pulled at the board, and it easily fell to the ground with a clatter. I wiggled my eyebrows at Donavan.

"Is that a good thing?" he asked. "Because there's just a locked window behind it." He knocked on the glass as if to show me it was solid.

I pushed on it and tried to slide it over. Sometimes the windows on old buildings were flexible. And I was right. It was. It popped a little, then slid with the applied pressure.

"Are you sure you're just an actress?" he asked. "And not some cat burglar?"

"Cat burglar? Do people say that? Do people even say burglar *without* adding the cat?"

"What would you call this, then?"

"Not cat burglary." I climbed in the window, first perching on the frame and then jumping down, much like a . . . cat.

He didn't say anything, but it was clear what he was thinking.

"Shut up," I said.

He chuckled, then climbed through behind me. "I still don't understand how this helps you at all."

"Sometimes I need to snap out of my normal way of thinking. So I do something different—see a new place, experience a new emotion—and it helps me have a breakthrough. It opens up something in me that helps me work past whatever block I'm experiencing."

"You're having a hard time relating to the script? That masterpiece back in your dressing room? I can't imagine why."

I ignored him, because it was obvious he thought he was better than a low-budget movie. He apparently would've held out for a script with Oscar potential for his very first feature film. And he thought *I* was a snob. Everyone had to start somewhere, and this was my start. Plus, the movie had somehow scored Grant James. The producers were smart. He'd make it successful. I was smart too—his star power would guarantee people would watch it, would see me.

"Walking through an old abandoned building is going to make you somehow feel something?" He turned toward me, but his face was in the shadows, unreadable.

What Amanda had said came back to me again, that the best way to feel chemistry was to draw on some real chemistry I'd experienced. I didn't want her to be right. I could channel it here somehow. I didn't need to know what falling for someone felt like.

I clicked on my phone's flashlight, lighting up his face and revealing his dark eyes on mine. He squinted, and I quickly turned the light away and searched for the door that would lead us farther into the building. "Let's go."

Dust and spiderwebs coated nearly every surface.

"This seems like the perfect zombie hideout," he said.

Right. My makeup. I was still wearing it. Apparently I *should* add that line in my bio about how long I could endure stage makeup. "Yes, it does."

The first room we came to let in enough light from the streetlights outside that I tucked my phone in my pocket. It had the frame of a bed, still intact but pushed on its end against the wall, its headboard on the floor creating a stable base. I stepped onto the headboard and tugged on the footboard up near the ceiling to see if it would support my weight, then swung on it a couple times.

"Okay, time for some improv," I said.

"Improv?"

"Yes, it's an acting term. We need to make up some stories."

Donavan nodded, then wandered once around the perimeter of the room. He stopped at a small closet and bent down to pick up something. It was a paper of sorts. He wiped it on his jeans, then studied it close.

"What is it?" I asked.

"It's a picture."

"Of what?" I dropped from the bed and inched closer.

He was still for a long, quiet moment before he said, "My grandfather. I thought he died suddenly, from a heart attack. At least that's what my parents said. But they sent him here?"

"What?" I slid next to Donavan, my mouth right at his shoulder level, and looked at the picture. Only it wasn't a picture at all, it was a faded old receipt. "That's not . . ."

"I thought you said we were making up stories. Don't the rules say that you're supposed to go along with mine?"

"Yes . . . actually. I was supposed to. You caught me off guard."

"You literally *just* said we were doing improv."

"I know. I just didn't expect . . ."

"You thought you were the only one who would be able to do it?"

That's exactly what I had thought. "Sorry. That was really good. Have you acted before?"

"No, but it's not rocket science."

"Thanks," I mumbled.

"That's not what I meant."

"Oh, I'm pretty sure you said exactly what you meant." So much for starting on a new foot. Of course that's what he thought. He was Dad Number Two, after all. Why was I letting this hurt my feelings? I didn't care what Choir Boy thought. The only thing that would impress him, I was sure, was if I were genius-level smart. Literally, a rocket scientist. "I'm going to check out the rest of the building."

NINE

Donavan and I had separated (I obviously hadn't talked myself out of being irritated with him), and I was on the third floor, wandering through the dark halls, my phone light shining the way. I ran right into a spiderweb strung across the hall. I blew air through my lips and wiped it off my face. Grime coated my hands so I was sure all I had managed to do was make my face even scarier.

At the end of the corridor, an open door cast a strip of light on the dark ground. I clicked off my phone and tried to get in the mind-set of my character. If I were Scarlett, wandering through this abandoned building, sick with a disease that made me hunt humans, how would I walk, think, feel? I slowed my step, like I was creeping. My body was being ravaged by a disease, I must've been in some sort of pain. I began to limp a little and hold one arm against my chest. I easily fell into character, which didn't surprise me. Channeling Scarlett wasn't hard for me. It was channeling her feelings for Benjamin that was the problem.

I let myself think of Grant's eyes. That's what would keep me going. His eyes for sure.

"You have to come see this room," Donavan said from behind me.

I stopped but didn't turn. I continued my hissing breath. Then I turned slowly, jerkily, until I faced him, looking up from under my lashes with a hungry stare.

He raised his eyebrows. "That's creepy. You obviously have that down well. Come on."

Right, I had this part down. I needed to change something. But how could I show I was still a zombie while also showing I was still in love?

I followed him—still in character—slowly, and dragging one foot. He led me down one flight of stairs, then disappeared behind an open door. When I got inside the room, I didn't look around, I just focused on Donavan. His back was to me. I limped all the way to him. I ran a slow finger up his spine. Then I grabbed him by the head and pretended to snap his neck.

"I honestly don't think you'd be strong enough to snap my neck. You should've found something to knock me out with."

I tried to hide my smile, because he was facing me now. Instead of speaking, I lunged for his neck with an open mouth.

He laughed and backed away, grabbing my arms to hold me at bay. "You're not a vampire!" he said, while struggling to hold me off. He twisted me around so I was facing the opposite direction, then pulled me up against him, wrapping his arms around me and trapping mine in his hold. I let myself relax against him. I was Scarlett; he was Benjamin. His arms were strong, so was his chest, which pressed all along my back.

"If I let you go," he said by my ear, "will you stop trying to bite me?"

The skin on the back of my neck tingled to life. That was new. It was working. Being in this building, away from cameras, interacting with someone as Scarlett was stirring up some feelings that I could draw from.

He tightened his hold slightly. "Deal?"

A shiver went through me. I leaned down and bit his arm. Not hard, but enough to make him feel it.

He released me. "Lacey Barnes, you are so weird. Seriously."

I finally dropped the act and laughed. "Oh, come on, it's fun. You have to admit it." It was surprisingly fun to goof around with Donavan. Maybe because he was usually so serious. I decided it was now my mission to help this boy act like a seventeen-year-old. At least some of the time. "Wait, *are* you seventeen?"

"What? Yes," he said, registering my question.

"And are you opposed to having fun?" I asked. "Does fun mean that you are not learning something new?"

"I am not opposed to having fun."

"Good." I looked around the room we were standing in. It was cleaner than the other rooms. Almost lived in. There was a metal bedframe with an old stained mattress in one corner. A night table with broken drawers sat next to the bed. A picture frame with a real picture inside was on the night table. I walked over to it. A man and woman and three kids smiled at the camera while standing in knee-high yellowing grass.

"Did they forget to clean out this room?" I asked. The rest of the room was cluttered with an array of other things—a hanging rack of clothes like I had in my dressing room (only men's), a stack of dusty books, a lantern.

"I don't know, but check it out. I don't think this old man liked his nurses much." He went to the nightstand and opened the top drawer. It scraped along its track as he did. He shined his phone on the contents.

I peered inside to see a serious knife. "Wow. That knife is not messing around." It was huge, with a serrated edge. It looked like the kind I'd see on the set of a movie about a drug lord. I thought about it for thirty seconds too long. It was like my brain was trying to fit the knife into the nursing home script I'd given when we climbed through the window. But as I slowly assessed the evidence I was coming to a realization.

"And what's in drawer number two?" Donavan tugged open the next drawer and revealed plastic bags full of white powder.

I gasped, then said aloud what I had realized. "Someone is living here now."

He paused, his eyes darting upward like he was thinking, then he cursed. It sounded funny coming out of his mouth, like it was the first time he'd ever done it in his life. He slammed the drawer shut, grabbed a dingy towel off the corner of the bed, and wiped the handles as if he thought his fingerprints would immediately appear in some sort of database.

"We need to go," he said. "Now."

Right as we made it to the top of the stairs to head back down to the first floor, a loud bang sounded somewhere below us.

Donavan cursed again. I remembered a hall closet behind us and took him by the hand and dragged him there. We both stepped inside, and I pulled the door closed.

"Whoever that is saw my car," Donavan whispered. "They had to have. It's the only car in the parking lot. We are going to get caught. Either by the cops or by whoever owns that knife. This is going to go on my record."

"Or you'll be dead," I whispered back.

"Exactly." He was quiet for a moment. "Do you think this is funny? How do you think this is funny?"

"I don't . . . well, it is a little. I feel like I'm in a Heath Hall movie." I was scared too. My heart was racing, and my nerves were heightened. But it was also kind of exciting.

"A Heath Hall movie?"

"That's the character Grant normally plays in movies."

"I know who Heath Hall is," he snapped.

"Oh." I reached out and my hand met with some part of Donavan. His back? His chest? It felt like a shoulder blade maybe. "Don't stress so much."

"When should we start stressing, then?" He paused for a minute. "Wait, is this some kind of joke? Did you set this up?"

"You're the one who brought me here. How would I set this up?"

"True."

We both went quiet as a set of footsteps sounded outside the door. They didn't slow down, just walked right by. I could feel the tension release from Donavan. We stayed in the closet until I could no longer hear any noise at all.

"Thanks for coming with me tonight," I whispered.

"Is this the new experience you were going for?"

I was shut inside a small, dark closet with a guy, tension and heightened awareness thick in the air. It kind of was. "It's actually helped a lot."

"I'm glad something came out of it."

"Should we sleep in here tonight or make a run for it?" I asked.

"Those are our only two choices?"

"Yes."

"I guess we're running." As if he'd been waiting for the suggestion all along, he swung open the door and ran for the stairs. When we got to the window where we'd entered, he practically threw me out, then flung himself out, rolling to the ground with his momentum before he stood and stumbled to his car.

I caught up with him, not able to control my laughter.

"It's not funny," he said when we were safely inside his car, the doors locked.

"It is funny. Like one hundred percent. Not even one percentage point less than completely funny."

He turned over the ignition and drove out of the parking lot, then finally said, "I'll give you seventy-five percent. No more."

I laughed again.

After a few quiet minutes, Donavan said, "What would you have done?"

"What?"

"If whoever was in there had opened the door and discovered us. What would you have done?"

"Turned on my zombie mode. The hissing, the limping, the works. It would've confused them just enough for us to get away."

"You really would have done that," he said as a statement, not a question.

"Yes," I answered anyway.

"You're crazy."

"Don't forget it." I studied his profile as he looked out the window. His jaw was tight, his lips set in a thin line. "What would you have done if we'd been discovered?"

"I have no idea. I think I might be a flight kind of guy in the fight-or-flight scenario. My only instinct was to run."

"You sound sad about this."

"I am. I always knew I hated conflict but this . . . I'm extremely disappointed in myself."

"You wish you would've what? Went charging after

him in a blind rage? Asked him if you could join him for his recreational pastime?"

"No . . . I don't know."

I grabbed hold of his shoulder and shook it. "Lighten up, dude. You totally pushed me through the window first. You can hang on to your man card for another day."

"Did you just call me dude?"

"I did. Better or worse than Choir Boy?"

"Equally bad."

"I think you mean equally charming."

"You do think you're pretty charming, don't you?"

"Yes, I do. And you do too, so don't try to deny it."

He shook his head, but the smile on his face proved I was right.

Something caught my eye out of the side window. I pointed. "All those new experiences made me hungry. Let's go eat."

"With you looking like that?"

"Will this embarrass you?"

He gave me a sideways glance, then shrugged. "Probably not."

"Let's do the drive-through." It was better that way. I didn't think anyone would recognize me off set, but just in case, I didn't need more bad pictures on the internet.

Dancing Graves

INT. THE MANSION LIBRARY—DAY
SCARLETT is getting worse by the day. She
has not transitioned but feels like she
is dying a slow death. She wants to leave
to spare her family and BENJAMIN pain,
but he is worried for her safety.

                    BENJAMIN
Where will you go?

                    SCARLETT
The cemetery, I think, with that old
abandoned church nearby. You can leave me
supplies there.

                    BENJAMIN
I cannot bear it. You must stay. For just
a little longer.

SCARLETT

Promise me something. If I start to
worsen, if I begin to require what the
others eat, you must stop me. By any
means necessary.

TEN

What I'd told Donavan was true. Getting out of my daily rut was important when I was feeling uninspired. And our experience the day before had definitely fired me up. I felt ready to work. Or I *would* be ready if I could find my kneepads. I had to crawl over benches today, and wardrobe had given me a pair just for this purpose.

I got down on my hands and knees again and looked under the rack of clothes. I couldn't find them. I took every hanging piece and moved it to the couch. The only thing on the floor was a pair of Converse I'd forgotten I'd brought to the trailer.

"Faith!" I called out my trailer door as if she stood waiting for me at all times. She wasn't there. I glanced at the time on my phone; I had two minutes to be in the church building. I wasn't going to be late again.

I hopped down the steps and halfway there noticed my favorite helper across the way. "Aaron!"

He was talking to someone from the crew and looked up when I called his name.

"Have you seen my kneepads?"

He put his hand to his ear as if he couldn't hear me. I waved him off and kept walking. Faith stood at the doors to the church.

"Faith. Are there any extra kneepads?"

"You lost yours?"

"I thought they were in my trailer, but I couldn't find them."

"I'll bring you another pair. Hurry in, they're waiting for you."

"Thanks."

Grant nodded his head as I joined him by the pews at the front of the chapel. It was a gorgeous room, with dark wooden benches and steps leading up to the pulpit, which was backlit by the most amazing stained glass I'd ever seen. A large tapestry hung on the wall displaying the words: *Matthew 5:44 Love your enemies, and pray for those who persecute you.*

"Hey," I said, noticing all the people lining the walls to watch. My eyes caught on a familiar face, someone I'd seen Grant talking to before. "Who's that guy in the flip-flops?"

"That's my agent."

"Wow. He's very involved."

He rolled his eyes. "He's the one who talked me into this job. He thinks it's going to redeem my reputation."

"Does it really need that much redeeming? I see fans lining up at every location for you. And you probably get a million online mentions a day." Like Amanda had said, we needed to get Grant out of his head. I needed to help him stop thinking he was somehow a failure.

"I used to get more, and they used to be mostly good. But it's not just the fans we're worried about. It's the producers and casting directors. They need to see I have range, that I can act."

"Right."

Grant went from looking at his agent to turning back to me. "You ready to climb over benches?"

My knees felt bare as I said, "So ready. Are you ready to run?"

He smiled. "Yes. I got your message yesterday and tried to text you, but it was after ten. Does your dad take your phone away after ten?"

It bothered me that my dad had made a reputation for

himself—one that made it seem like I was a child. I was not a child. "No, he does not. I was already sleeping. I was exhausted after the adventure I had. My tutor and I went to this abandoned old folk's home and found a drug dealer."

"What? Not sure that's the answer for our chemistry issue."

I smiled. "Yes, that sounded bad. That's not what I meant. I don't do drugs. What I should've said was that we found a drug dealer's lair and had to escape."

"This was the muse thing the security guard was telling me about?"

"Yes."

"You have a tutor helping you find a muse?"

"I do now," I said.

He smiled his hundred-watt smile and took a step closer, into my space. "You don't need a tutor. I'm not hard to fall for if you let yourself."

"I'm not trying to fall for you."

"Exactly."

We were talking about the characters, weren't we? "Well, Scarlett has fallen for you . . . I mean Benjamin . . . obviously."

"You need to let yourself be her." He took my hand in his and tugged me a little closer.

I knew what he was saying. I needed to relax into the character on set. I needed to become Scarlett. At least for the next eight weeks.

Out of the corner of my eye I saw Amanda watching us. She gave me a small wave. "Don't you think Amanda is great?" I asked.

"Yes, I do. I gave Amanda the same speech yesterday about letting herself fall for me. She's doing a better job of it."

A light flashed on, blinding me for a moment. I squinted.

"Is that okay?" Remy asked. "Or have you become an actual zombie, afraid of the light?" He smiled.

"It's fine," I said. I had just been surprised. I was used to the spotlight. I turned back toward Grant and tugged my hand from his grip. "Good thing I don't need to fall for you today, just try to kill you."

"You ready?" Remy asked.

I looked around for Faith with my kneepads but couldn't see her anywhere. "Let's do it."

"Nice zombie work," Remy said as I passed the monitor, limping slightly. Now I understood the need for padding.

"You were channeling some serious death," he said.

"Thanks," I said. I'd felt that way too. He nodded, his attention already back on the footage playing on the screen in front of him.

Faith joined me with a pair of kneepads in her hands. "Sorry, I know these are a little late. It took me forever to find an extra pair."

I took them from her. "It's fine."

"You can keep them for next time."

"Okay."

"You'll see on your call sheet that everyone has tomorrow off. And then Tuesday we'll be filming only Grant and Fredrick." Fredrick was the actor who played my father, Lord Lucas, in the movie.

"Oh, okay. See you Wednesday, then."

Amanda grabbed hold of my hand as I reached her. "You did awesome today!"

"Thanks." I saw my dad standing against the far wall. "How old were you when you got your first steady soap opera job?"

"Fifteen," she said.

"And how old are you now?"

"Twenty," she said.

"And your life isn't ruined?"

"What?"

I nodded toward my dad, who had almost reached us. "Think you can talk to my dad so he doesn't worry about me so much?" I knew he did. I knew that's why he dropped by so often and felt the need to be so strict with my schedule.

He reached us just as I finished the sentence.

Amanda stuck her hand out. "Hi, Mr. Barnes. I'm Amanda. I'm twenty and I'm not screwed up yet."

"Thanks, Amanda," I said. "Very helpful."

She laughed. "It's so nice of you to visit the set so often. The bigger the audience, the better."

"It's fun to watch," Dad said.

"You're a brat," I said to her.

"I'm being serious!"

"I know you are," I said, then gave her shoulder a shove. "Go talk to Grant before he gets away."

She looked over to where Grant was heading toward the exit.

"Yes, coach," she said, and hurried off.

"She's interesting," my dad said.

"She's really great. I like her a lot."

"I'm glad you're making friends."

"Me too." I put my arms out to my sides. "So what do you think about the new location?"

"It's beautiful."

"I agree." My knees ached. I shifted my weight and tried not to grimace. Dad did not need to know about my hurting knees. He wouldn't like that. "I didn't know you were coming today."

"I had a client on this side of town, so I thought I'd drop by on my way home and check out the new location." There was a set piece to his right, one that wasn't used today but would probably be added the day after tomorrow— a big wooden table. Red candles, with wax melting all the way down to the brass candleholders, sat on top. One candle lay on its side with a crumpled piece of paper near it. My dad righted the candle and picked up the paper. Then he looked around as if searching for a trash can.

"Dad," I said. "That's a hot set. Don't mess with it."

"What's a hot set?"

"It means that an art director put that table together, and even things that look like trash are part of the scene. So slowly put everything back exactly the way you found it."

"Oops." He put the paper down carefully and returned the candle to its side.

I smiled. "Rookie mistake."

"Mom would've known about this."

"Maybe."

He draped his arm over my shoulder, and we headed toward my trailer. "How are things going?"

"Good. . . . Things went well today."

"And how about your new tutor? Is he working out okay?"

"He's very helpful." I thought about how he'd gone

on the adventure with me the day before. That's probably not what my dad was referring to, but he'd been helpful with my homework too, so what I said was true.

We stopped outside my trailer door. "Are you coming in?" I asked.

"I actually need to go home and get some work done."

"Okay, I'm going to do homework here."

"And you'll be home by curfew."

"I will be home by curfew."

Dad left, and I gave a little nod. That wasn't so bad. He hadn't made any comment about going over hours on set or felt the need to tell me how much homework I should finish tonight. Maybe he was realizing that I could handle this.

I opened my trailer door, fully expecting to see Donavan despite the deal we made, but he wasn't there. I made quick work of removing my makeup, thinking he'd show up at any second and I would have to stay a zombie for the fourth day in a row. But he didn't come.

Good. He'd rescued me with math when Leah called, but now he was honoring our deal from before about my wanting space. I'd have to text him some pics of completed pages.

I kicked my shoes off into the corner, then inspected my knees. They were red, sure to be bruised tomorrow. I needed some ice.

I found Aaron sitting in a camping chair outside his dad's trailer, staring intently at a notebook. "Psst. How can a girl get some ice around here?" I wasn't even sure there was ice anywhere.

He jumped a little but then smiled and climbed to his feet. "I can get it for you. Do you want it in a cup?"

"A plastic bag would be best."

"Okay, I'll be right back."

"I'll come with you."

"Okay."

As we walked he asked, "You have social media accounts, right?"

"Yes. Why? Does your dad want me to publicize the movie more?" I tried to think about how I might do that. I didn't have tons of followers, nowhere near as many as Grant had, but I'd been avoiding posting altogether. I could change that.

Aaron looked down as if embarrassed. "No, I was just wondering if I could follow you."

"Oh! Yes, of course."

He pulled out his phone, and I told him my online handles. He typed into his phone for a while, then tucked it back into his pocket.

"I don't have my phone on me, but I'll follow you back when I get to the trailer."

"Thank you!"

We rounded the church building to the back side, where craft services was set up, and I saw Grant's agent picking at the food on the table. Aaron let out a sigh.

"What?" I asked.

"Peter is so annoying, always hanging around and making demands."

"What kind of demands?" I asked.

As if he realized he had said more than he should've, he shook his head and said, "No, it's not a big deal. Things most agents ask for."

I wondered if my agent had made any demands for me aside from all the things my dad had wanted added into the contract, like extra breaks and no working after 10:00 p.m.

We made it all the way to the food table, where Peter looked up with our arrival. He nodded at Aaron, then gave me the once-over like he didn't realize who I was without the zombie makeup on. I just smiled.

"I'll be right back," Aaron said, then walked over to a metal box on wheels. He opened a hatch at the front of it but then looked around, probably realizing he had nothing to put the ice in. He held up his finger to me and then ran off.

Feeling a bit awkward standing there next to Grant's

agent in silence, I began surveying the food table. And even though I wasn't hungry, I picked up a yogurt cup and took a spoonful.

"Do you have a publicist?" Peter asked me. Of course he knew who I was.

"Um . . ." I actually wasn't sure. My agent may have mentioned one before.

"You need a publicist," he said. "To work on your image." He grabbed a chocolate-drizzled strawberry off the table, and then he and his tan legs and flip-flops walked away.

Aaron came back a few minutes later holding a gallon-size ziplock bag full of ice that I hadn't heard him get. "You okay?" he asked.

"Yes."

"What's this for, then?" He shook the bag.

I took it from him. "My knees are sore. Benches are hard." I pointed over my shoulder. "I better get to homework. Thanks for your help."

Back in my trailer, ice on my knees, I worked on my homework for a while before I became distracted with a thought. I tapped my pencil over and over again on the paper. My phone sat beside me on the couch. Why had Peter asked me about a publicist? Was there more than the original horrible picture and caption that I had seen the other day? I picked up my phone and googled my name. I held my breath as my phone worked. Nothing new came up, and the original post I had seen had fizzled out, not turning into anything viral. I let out my breath in relief and sent a text to my dad: Do I have a publicist?

He responded back almost immediately: No. Too expensive for how little money you make.

That was probably true. But I sent off an email to my agent anyway. *Do I need a publicist?*

No matter how much I stared at my inbox, she didn't answer back. I'd survive without a publicist for now. I'd done it up to this point.

ELEVEN

"This is all you got done last night?" Dad said when I walked into the kitchen the next morning. I had tried to sleep in, but my body was used to waking up early now.

"What?" I asked, rubbing at my eyes, then searching the pantry for something to eat. I pulled a granola bar from the box and unwrapped it.

"Your schoolwork. You answered like two problems."

"Oh, right. I'll finish—that's why I brought it home. I have the next two days off," I said through granola.

He set my work on the table. "Yes, you will finish.

Right now. And then you will take this to the school today and turn it into your mentor teacher. It's about time you met her."

"Dad, this is my first day off since we started."

"If you did your work when you were supposed to, you could actually have a day off. But you don't. So have a seat. It shouldn't take you very long."

I groaned. Why were we always having the same argument over and over? "Dad, do you hear that?"

He went still and listened for a moment. "Hear what?"

"The sound of your blades whirling above me as you hover."

"Are you saying I'm one of those helicopter parents?"

"So you *do* hear it?"

"It is my job to make sure you don't get behind in school. So get to work."

"Fine." I sat down hard in the chair, biting back the *ouch*. Maybe it was because I was mad, or maybe it was because I really wanted to leave the house, but I finished the rest of my independent study homework faster than any I had before. Half the answers were probably wrong, but that wasn't the point. The point was I was free from my prison guard.

School had been in session for over four weeks. But I, personally, hadn't been on a high school campus since before summer break. And I had never been on this high school campus. It felt different than my old school. Bigger, for one. But in some ways it felt exactly the same.

I stopped in the middle of the walkway and took a deep breath. High school. I couldn't decide if I missed it.

One day I'd walk around a place like this and people would recognize me. That thought made me smile. Today wasn't that day. The late bell had just rung, so there were only a few students walking the halls, but nobody gave me a second glance. I wondered if even Donavan would recognize me today without my zombie makeup on. I'd washed my hair the night before too, something I hadn't done in a while per instructions and I couldn't help pulling on the silky ends.

I'd parked in a visitor spot and was now trying to find the office. Shouldn't it be clearly marked? There were four buildings surrounding me, each multiple stories, none with the words *This is the office* on them.

"Excuse me," I said, quickening my pace and catching up to a long-haired guy walking in front of me. "Can you tell me where the office is?"

He started to point when he caught my eye. "Do I know you?"

"No." Was it possible he'd seen the negative posts online?

"I've seen you somewhere before," he said.

"Probably here. Office?"

He snapped his finger, and his eyes lit up. "Zits."

Oh. I was almost relieved. When people *did* recognize me it was for one reason and one reason only—the zit-cream commercial I'd done. Why had my agent let me do that commercial? It was decent money, but it was always on. Even still, two years later, I could turn on the television and that commercial would be playing.

"Yes. You caught me."

"Don't worry, I'd say half this campus has been in embarrassing commercials."

"Half?"

"Okay, that's an exaggeration, but sometimes it feels like half the people here are aspiring actors."

"Oh." I wanted to say I wasn't aspiring. I was in an actual movie. With Grant James. But I had a feeling he wouldn't believe me. "Office?" I tried once more.

"Right." He pointed. "Follow this path between these two buildings. It will be on your left."

"Thank you." I took the path he indicated down a flower-lined walkway and past a big hand-painted *Homecoming Dance* sign and found the office. When I stepped inside, a blast of cold air hit me in the face. It felt nice after the heat from outside. I walked up to the counter.

"Hi, I guess I need a visitor's pass. I'm here to see Mrs. Case. She's my mentor teacher for independent study." My dad had told me this was her free hour, and I hoped he was right, because I didn't want to disrupt her teaching.

A girl sat behind the counter. A white sticker on her shirt read: *My name is* with *Taylor* written in green beneath it. She looked like a student. "Sign in there, take a badge from the basket. Mrs. Case is in the C building, room 303."

I signed my name on the sign-in sheet and took a badge. "Which one is the C building?"

"The big one on the right."

"On the right of what?" Every building was big. "Can I get a guide?"

"A guide?"

"Someone to show me around?" We did that with new students at my school back home. I'd given at least a dozen people a tour of the campus, which usually started with an extensive list of where to find the best food.

"Do you need to see the whole campus?" Taylor asked. "Or just the one teacher?"

I only needed to see the one teacher, but apparently this wasn't a good enough excuse for Taylor, so I put on my best persuasive smile and said, "This might be my future school. Can I request a tour guide? I actually know a student who goes here who would probably do it."

"Why not," she said, obviously bored with me. She picked up the headset of a corded phone on the counter. "What's the student's name?"

"Donavan." I had given myself a mission: bring a little fun into his life. I imagined school was where he was most serious, if I could loosen him up here, I'd consider myself a miracle worker.

"Donavan . . ." Taylor trailed off, waiting for me to fill in the blank.

I pursed my lips. "I don't know his last name. Is there more than one Donavan?"

"I personally know three Donavans."

I stared at her for a long moment, trying to decide if she was kidding. If she was, it didn't show. Maybe she was an aspiring actress, the star in a million embarrassing commercials. "Really?" I finally asked.

She hung up the phone. "Donavan Lake, Donovan O'Neil, and Donavan Ritter."

"Wow. You really do. I'm not sure which one of those he is. I wouldn't be opposed to an all-the-Donavans tour. I can assess which one should be used again for future tours." When she didn't laugh I said, "No?"

"Does he play football?"

I couldn't imagine my tutor playing football. He seemed too . . . cynical for that, but I had no idea. "I don't know."

"Does he have a younger sister? Or play the guitar?"

"Maybe?" He was listening to rock music in the car,

so that was possible. "He's a tutor."

She shook her head as if that detail didn't help. "Does he write?"

"*Does* he?" I asked, surprised.

She continued to stare at me blankly.

"He has dark hair and is about this tall." I held my hand up and then moved it higher and then lower again when I realized I wasn't exactly sure how tall he was.

"So when you said you knew him . . ." She trailed off.

"Yes, apparently I don't. Where did you say Mrs. Case's room was again?" I asked, giving up.

She gave me directions, and I left the building. "I can't believe there are three Donavans who go here," I mumbled to myself. How big *was* this school?

Mrs. Case was writing on a whiteboard when I walked into her very empty classroom. She was a tall, athletic woman, and I wondered if she coached the volleyball team here. I almost asked her but decided that was rude. Heightist . . . or something. Did tall people get asked if they played sports all the time? Tall people didn't have to play sports.

"Hi," I said instead. "I'm Lacey Barnes." I presented her with my finished packet.

"Lacey, we finally meet. Come in, come in. Have a seat." She pointed to the chair on the opposite side of her desk, then she sat down across from me. She started flipping through my packet. "How have you been faring? Too hard? Too easy?"

"Just right," I said.

"Does that mean too easy? You answered that very quickly."

"No. In fact the math has challenged me quite a bit."

"Challenging is good." She shut the packet and placed both hands on top of it. "Well, I'm not going to grade this right here, but I'll email you. You *have* been getting my emails, yes?"

"Yes."

"There's a little button called 'reply' that you push, and then you can write back. I know it's probably an outdated media for you kids, but I have faith that you can learn."

I smiled. "Sorry. I'm really busy. I'll work on that though. I *could* just deliver you my packets that way too—by email."

"I know. I told your father that, but he said this was part of your compromise."

"Of course he did." One I hadn't realized we'd made.

"I was wondering if you'd actually ever make it in here. I've seen a lot of your delivery boy."

"Yes, Donavan. He . . . plays guitar." I took a guess

because that was the only one I could imagine him doing.

"He does?" she asked.

Maybe I was wrong. "And writes?"

"Yes, he does," she said this time. "For the school paper."

Again, I was surprised. But then I remembered how quickly he'd pulled out that improv the other day. He obviously had some creativity in there somewhere.

She pointed to the corner of her desk where a folded paper sat.

"The school still has an actual paper?" I was thinking she was referring to an online issue.

"We do, in fact, as archaic as that seems to most. I think it's because about thirty years ago, we got our own small printing press. It's still in our journalism department, humming along happily. We're too proud to let print die now."

"I still like holding words in my hands." I craned my neck and tried to find Donavan's name on the front page. I couldn't make out much at this angle.

She nodded. "Me too."

"Do you have an extra school paper lying around?"

"Oh! Yes, they'll have extra ones in the journalism building. I would give you mine, but apparently I'm quoted in here somewhere. I haven't read it yet. Plus, you can check out the printing press while you're over there."

I'd never seen one before. I tried to take advantage of opportunities where I got to see or experience new things. I never knew when I'd need knowledge like that for a character. "For sure."

"It's two buildings down, room 114."

I stood. "It was great to meet you. I think I'm all caught up for now."

"You are caught up until tomorrow, when you will have a whole new packet to start."

I wondered if my dad knew that. Who was I kidding? Of course he did. "Right. Thank you."

"If I had known you were coming, I would've had the next one ready for you."

"Sorry, I thought my dad told you I was coming. Donavan will bring it for me."

She nodded, slid my packet into her top drawer, and walked me out of the room.

I headed toward the building she'd said housed the journalism department. Room 114. That would be on the first floor. It would be easy to just walk by and look inside, see the printing press, maybe pick up a newspaper. What were the odds that Donavan had journalism this period? The odds were low.

When I got to the room and peered through the window, I couldn't see this machine or the newspapers. I saw only rows of desks and computers and students typing

away as if they couldn't keep up on all the news happening at that very moment. I backed up to look at the
number beside the door: 114. So where did they keep the
press? In some back room? Had Mrs. Case been joking
about the school owning one?

I moved to leave when I saw a big bulletin board that
filled an entire wall inside the classroom. Pinned to it
were newspaper clippings. I wouldn't disrupt anyone if
I walked inside to look closer, see what kind of articles
this school put out. Okay, fine, I didn't care about the
articles so much as I was curious about what Donavan
wrote. Finding out he was a writer was surprising, and I
wondered if his writing would give any insight into his
personality. If I was to succeed in loosening him up, this
could help. I opened the door.

I was wrong. I disrupted pretty much everyone. They
all looked my way, their fingers pausing for a moment
on the keys to watch me skirt around the outside of
the classroom. Now I needed to act like I was there for
some official reason. I stopped in front of the teacher and
flashed my visitor badge. "Hi, sorry to interrupt. I'm
new here and just on a tour of the campus."

"And you're interested in journalism? You write?"

I gave him my best sincere, studious look. "Of course."
Now maybe he could point out where the printing press
was hiding and let me look for Donavan in the sea of

newspaper clippings.

"Donavan," the teacher said, as if reading my mind.

I opened my mouth to respond when a deep voice to my right said, "Yes?"

"Why don't you show this young lady the department?"

I swallowed hard and followed the teacher's gaze to a side office that I hadn't seen from the door. Donavan sat at a desk, flipping through some printed-out pages.

"She's a writer," the teacher continued.

I could tell Donavan didn't recognize me yet. He was kind of far away and . . . I wasn't a zombie. I wasn't one to get embarrassed easily, but I could feel that my cheeks were pink. Why was I blushing?

"That's okay," I quietly said to the teacher and took one step back. "I see that he's busy."

Donavan had put the pages on the desk and stood. I suddenly understood the flight instinct he'd had the other night. But I couldn't run. What if he recognized me? Instead, I channeled all my acting abilities and willed my face to normal.

"Hey there, Choir Boy," I said when he was in front of me.

TWELVE

"Lacey?" His eyes danced over my face.

"Hey, I finished the packet, so I dropped it off to Mrs. Case."

"Oh. Great. That will save me a trip."

"Yes, exactly."

The journalism teacher stood. He was shorter than he'd looked sitting down. "Sounds like you two know each other. Can you show her the department, Donavan? She's a writer."

"Sure."

I hoped he'd show me some of his work, but he walked

toward the hall door, preventing me from studying the board.

When we were out in the hall and the door shut behind us, he said, "You're not a writer."

"Maybe I am. Maybe I'm an aspiring journalist."

"Are you?"

"No. But I'd make a good investigative reporter. For example, today I found out at least three Donavans go to your school. Three! How is that possible?"

"It's a big school."

"With a lot of Irish heritage?"

"One of the Donavans is black."

"The guitar player or the football player?"

"What?"

"Or the one with the little sister?"

"Are you stalking Donavans?"

"That would make a good movie title."

His eyes sparkled as if he really did find me amusing and was trying his hardest to pretend he didn't. I'd never had to win anyone over like this and I had to admit, it made the small victories more satisfying.

I glanced around the empty hall. "So does the tour end here? Your teacher told me you would show me the department. I feel like this isn't happening. I'm going to make a report to Taylor that you are a horrible tour guide. I'm moving on to the next Donavan."

He looked at the palm of his hand and picked at a streak of black ink there. "Did your dad tell you I was a writer?"

"No. Why? Was it on your tutoring résumé?"

"No. I just . . . never mind." He took a deep breath and straightened his shoulders. "Do you really want to see the rest of the department?"

"Absolutely. I've been told all about this thing called a printing press. Where does it live?"

He pointed at a door across the hall, then led the way. "You're in a good mood today."

"It's because you're not holding an empty homework packet in your hand and expecting me to get it done in an inhuman amount of time."

"Three hours is hardly inhuman. I think my little sister can get it done faster than you."

"So you do have a little sister. How old is she?"

"Freshman."

I rolled my eyes. "You made it seem like she was five. I am no longer offended at you telling me she can finish homework faster than me."

He stopped outside a door. "Are you ready?"

"Is something shocking going to happen when we go inside?"

He smirked and opened the door. The press was bigger than I expected, with lots of metal bars and handles.

"I totally chose the wrong electives when I was in school. If I went here next semester, I would take whatever the class is that gets to operate this beauty. Do you run this?"

"Sometimes. So you're saying you wouldn't take drama?"

"Of course I would. I wouldn't take math."

He laughed. "Not sure you can trade math for journalism."

"I'll be Lacey Barnes. Famous. They'll let me do what I want, right?"

"Pretty sure most people already let you do what you want."

"If that were true, you'd be doing my homework packets for me." I turned and gave him my best pleading eyes. "It's not too late for that to happen."

"Funny." He watched me walk around the machine twice. "*Are* you going to go here next semester? When you're done filming?"

"No, I'm going to finish out my senior year at home." I wondered if he cared. Why did I care if he cared? I ran my finger along a black knob. "We should print something. A paper that says, *Lacey Barnes is the next big thing.* That's some hard-hitting news."

"I would get in serious trouble for that."

"Would you, though? With those cute boy-next-door

looks of yours, I'm pretty sure people let you do what you want, too."

"No, they don't, actually. Never." He opened the door for me, and we stepped back into the hall.

"Never? Here, let's test it. Ask me for something." I turned toward him and put my hands behind my back as though patiently waiting for a request.

"Can I go back to class now?"

"No." I smiled. "Huh. You were right, you don't have a face that people want to give things to after all. You have to smile." That's what tempted me, at least—his smile. No, not tempted me. I wasn't tempted.

"Ha. Ha."

I pointed across the hall. "And what's behind door number three?"

"Graphic design. They help with the layout of the paper."

"Nice. My dad's a graphic designer."

"He is?"

"Yes, he'd love it if I took that class instead."

"Instead of what?"

"Instead of starring in a movie."

Donavan's brow crinkled. "Really?"

I shrugged. "It's no big deal." I turned a circle and changed the subject. "So this is your world? What articles do you write for the pap? Is that what you call it, because it felt right."

"No."

"You should start calling it that. Any school who still has a physical paper, printed from a printing press, has to call it a pap."

"Isn't that a British nickname for paper?"

"Is it? You need to research that. I bet you could write a whole article about it."

"I bet I couldn't."

"Because you write the . . ." I squinted my eyes and studied him. "Current events section?"

"No."

"What, then?"

The bell rang, and suddenly the halls were full of students. Donavan lifted up his arms as if that would make the crowded hallway easier to navigate and then headed back toward the first classroom we'd been in. I followed closely behind him, hanging on to the back of his shirt.

We made it into the room, and he went to a far station and picked up his backpack. I waved to the teacher. "Thanks for letting me borrow your prize writer. He did a good job selling the journalism department to me."

The teacher waved in return. "You're welcome."

I waited for Donavan, and we exited the class together.

He didn't say a word until we were outside, then he said, "Well, I better—"

"You're not going to say you better get to class, right? You have to finish my tour."

"That was pretty much the whole department."

"I want to see it all, baby. The whole campus."

"I'll be late to class."

I gave an exaggerated eye roll. "Please. You are a hard-hitting journalist. You don't care about rules. You sneak into abandoned buildings and bust drug dealers."

"Or run away from them," he said.

"Besides, Taylor in the front office gave me permission to have you as my tour guide." I held up my visitor's badge. "I'm an official guest here. Now, show me your favorite place."

"I don't really have a favorite place . . . and if I did, it would probably be the room we just left."

"Okay, then show me what *my* favorite place would be if I went here."

I thought he was going to say no, but he stood there for a moment, looking at me. I wondered if he was still trying to process my face without makeup. Then he said, "Okay." He turned in the opposite direction from where we had been headed, and I took several quick steps to catch up. I wondered which building housed the theater department. That's where he was going to take me, I was sure of it.

He marched me inside the largest building and, sure enough, at the end of the hall were two sets of double doors. Above the doors were the words *Edwards Theater*. As predictable as this choice was, I was actually excited to go stand on a big stage. It had been a while. But instead of heading for those double doors, he peeled off to the right and up a set of stairs and then another. We climbed four flights without exchanging a word, until we got to a single door at the top.

"That was my cardio for the day," I said.

He took a card out of his pocket, waved it in front of a black square on the door, and when it lit green, he opened it.

"Okay, who are you and where are you taking me?"

"This is the student gardens."

I stepped through the door and onto the rooftop. Bordering the entire edge of the roof were pot after colorful pot of plants. In the center were several groupings of lounge-like areas with couches and coffee tables and more plants. Several students sat around reading or doing homework. The view over the campus from up here was incredible.

I waved my hand at Donavan's pocket, where he'd

stored the key to the door. "Why? What?"

"You have to earn access."

"How?"

"Grades and a teacher recommendation and extracurriculars and seniors only."

"Wow. This is amazing." I slowly walked around, taking in the different plants and what I now saw was art displayed around as well. "But this wouldn't be my favorite place if I went here."

"No?" he asked, surprised he had guessed wrong.

"No, because I wouldn't be allowed in here."

"Drama counts."

"I barely maintained a 3.0."

"It's not only 4.0 people up here, though probably most are."

I walked to the far end of the roof, where a group of chairs sat empty, and I collapsed into one. He was absolutely right. I loved it up here and I'd been here less than five minutes.

"I'm sure you'd figure out a way to score a key to this place if you went here. Didn't we already establish that you get what you want?"

"Did we? Because I thought we established that you aren't doing my homework for me."

"You don't want that."

"I do, I really do."

He lifted a corner of his mouth into a half smile. Yes, that was very satisfying to have earned.

"How did you know?" I asked.

"How did I know what?"

"That I'd like this?"

He took in the rooftop, his eyes scanning slowly over the path we just walked. He opened his mouth like he was going to say something but stopped. Then he shrugged one shoulder and said, "Who wouldn't like this?"

I looked up at the clear blue sky and let out a sigh. "I've decided I do miss it a little."

"Um . . . what?"

"High school."

"Why?" he asked as though he didn't understand that thought.

"Mainly because it's senior year and I've missed things like this." I gestured around us.

"You had a student garden at your high school?"

I sat up and met his eyes. "No, but there are certain perks that come from seniorhood and I'm missing them." I fell back in the seat again. My dad would probably have gloated if he heard me repeat this realization. "But then, I remember what I actually get to do right now and know it's all worth it."

Donavan nodded, then his attention was drawn to the door, where a group of students came in and sat on the other side of the roof.

"So you still haven't answered my question about what you write for the pap," I said.

"Stop using that word."

"But it's bugging you so much. I can't stop now."

"I write . . ." He toed at the edge of a blue-and-green-striped rug that sat under the coffee table. "Entertainment."

"Entertainment? Like book reviews and such?"

"Yes. And plays and television and . . . movies." With that last word he looked back at me.

"Oh. So you'll be reviewing *Dancing Graves* for the paper when it comes out?"

"Not necessarily. We vote on which movies we're going to see and which will make the section."

"And my movie won't be good enough for the section?" I already knew he thought it was second-rate.

"I'll vote for it."

"You better." I twisted a bracelet I wore around my wrist. "Do you review your school plays or just professional theater?"

"School ones too."

"I want to read something you've written."

He was back to picking at his palm again before he

said, "You probably already have."

"What? No I haven't."

"One of my reviews went viral."

"I thought your school only has a physical paper."

"I have a personal review site online as well."

"Oh." I slowly started piecing a few clues together. I gasped. "Wait. 'Grant James Goes Down in Flames'? Was that you?"

He bit his lip and shrugged. "I stand by it."

"You're not a Grant James fan?"

"He has enough fans without me."

"You'd be surprised at how much the review bothered him."

"He's *read* it?"

"Of course. It's all over social media."

"I wasn't the only one who reviewed it badly. There were a lot of big-time reviewers who did as well."

"I know, but yours got passed around more. It was witty and clever and funny and very, very shareable."

He ran his hand over his hair a few times. "Thanks."

I was right. Reading something he had written did give me more insight into who he was. It wasn't that I didn't think he was witty or clever or funny, I'd seen bits of all of those things, but how much they popped on page surprised me. In real life, he seemed more reserved. Maybe he was just private. Pretty much the exact opposite of me. "So is that why you didn't want to meet Grant? Because of the review?"

"No, because I'm not a fan."

I chuckled. "Yeah right. If I had written that review I wouldn't have wanted to face him either."

"I'll face him."

If I were talking to anyone else, I might not think that were true. But this was my tutor. This was the guy who was on the set of Grant James's movie all the time. He probably would have to face him. I wondered how that would go down.

"So is that what you want to do with your life? Become a professional reviewer?"

"Yes, actually."

"Wait," I said, a realization coming to me. "Is this why you don't date actresses? So you don't have to worry about trashing their performances?"

He laughed, but then the smile slid from his face. "Pretty much. I like to stay objective."

"I'll do you a favor and warn all my costars away from you."

"No need. I've never been tempted."

Ouch. Well, the feeling was mutual. I wasn't tempted at all.

Dancing Graves

INT. ABANDONED CHURCH—NIGHT.
SCARLETT's appearance has changed. She looks more zombie than human now even though her logic hasn't left her. BENJAMIN brings supplies to the church, fearful that any day he'll find her mind fully changed. She hides in the shadows when he arrives.

BENJAMIN
Scarlett? Are you here? It's me.

SCARLETT
I can't stay here much longer. What if the other hunters find me?
Look at what I have become. They won't spare me.

BENJAMIN

You must come home. We can protect you there.

SCARLETT

But who will protect you from me?

THIRTEEN

As soon as I was back in my car in the parking lot, I picked up the phone and called my mom.

"Hello, Lace," she answered. "How are you?"

Between the fight with my dad, being back at high school again, and discovering my tutor was a critic who might one day trash my movie, I was feeling very low. "I'm okay."

"Thanks for sending Abby and Cooper over the other day. That was so nice. I got to run some much-needed errands."

"I'm glad it worked out." I had forgotten I'd asked

Abby to do that. I had the best friends ever. "So I have the rest of the day and tomorrow off. I was thinking about driving up to see you and the littles tonight." It was only noon. I'd be there by four and could have twenty-four hours with my family. It sounded like exactly what I needed—my mom.

"Yes, you should come!"

"Okay, I will. See you in a little bit." I sent my dad a text and didn't wait for an answer. I didn't need permission to see my mom. The fact that I didn't go home to pack had nothing to do with not believing that.

I was so excited that the four hours it took to drive home felt like four hundred hours. The Central Coast was cooler than LA, and as I finally reached my neighborhood, I rolled down the windows and took a breath of fresh coastal air. I was surprised at the lump rising in my throat as I parked the car and hopped out.

My mom was waiting for me on the porch, and she came running down the walk when I stepped out of the car. She looked as beautiful as ever with her dark hair and even darker eyes. We collided into a hug. I held on longer than normal.

"I've missed you," she said.

"You too." I stepped back and moved toward the door.

"Didn't you bring anything?" she asked, gesturing toward the car.

I cleared my throat and waved my hand through the air like it wasn't a big deal. "No, I left a lot of my stuff here because it doesn't fit at dad's."

"I know. It's just . . ."

I was worried my dad had called and tattled on me, so I rushed on, not wanting another fight. "Where are Colby and Syd? I'm dying to see them."

"They've made you a special treat."

"Oh yeah?"

"Try to choke down a little, at least. We'll throw the rest away when they aren't looking."

"I'm scared," I said.

"You should be."

The house felt the same but different when I walked inside. The same paintings hung on the wall. The same bench and kids' shoes scattered the entryway. But it felt bigger. Much bigger than I remembered. I assumed this was the result of a month in a small apartment.

My mom kicked a stuffed animal out of the way and said, "Guess who's home!"

My brother and sister came tearing out of whatever corner they'd been hiding in, and each grabbed an arm. "Lace! Lace!" they yelled.

"Hi, guys. I missed you. Have you each grown a foot since I was gone?" This was why adults said this. I now understood.

"We made you a salad!" Sydney said.

"A salad?" I raised an eyebrow at my mom.

"I told them you'd given up sweets for a couple of months."

"How thoughtful," I said.

They dragged me into the kitchen, where a bowl full of what looked like everything they could find in the fridge sat on the counter. "Am I going to get salmonella if I eat this?" I asked my mom under my breath.

"I think it's mostly fresh," she answered back.

"So comforting."

"I'll put the ranch on it for you," Sydney said, retrieving it from the fridge.

As she poured it on my salad, coating each and every item in the bowl, Colby said, "We got a cat! It lives in your room!"

"Colby," my mom said sharply. "That was going to be a surprise."

My head whipped over to my mom. "What?"

"I know, I know, you're not a fan of animals. But you weren't here, and it's good for the kids to learn responsibility, and it's really cute."

"So you got a kitten?"

"It's not a kitten," Mom said. "It's a rescue cat."

My sister pushed the salad across the island to where I stood. My stomach flipped. I wasn't sure if it was from the smell of ranch that now overpowered me or the thought of a cat living in my room.

"Does it sleep on my bed?" I asked.

"We put a cat bed in the corner," Mom said, which didn't answer my question. She pulled a fork out of the drawer and handed it to me. "Eat up."

Three very ranchy bites later I crept my way down the hall. So what? A cat lived in my room. It couldn't be that bad. People liked cats for a reason. It couldn't be their constant shedding or sharp skin-piercing claws, so something else.

I opened the door, and the smell hit me first. Some sort of urine mixed with Lysol. People absolutely couldn't like animals for their smell.

"I haven't had a chance to clean the litter box in a couple of days. It's Syd's job, but I usually double-check," Mom said, following behind me. "But I did vacuum when you called. Pepper hates the vacuum."

"Who?"

"The cat."

"The cat's name is Pepper?"

"Yes, she came with that name. Come here, kitty, kitty," Mom said, walking around me and into the room.

"She takes a while to warm up to a new person. Also she likes to jump out at legs when you walk by."

My mom continued to talk, but I was busy looking at my room that wasn't my room anymore. It was a cat haven. There was some sort of tower in the corner, rope was tied around each of the legs of my bed, creating scratching posts, a plastic mat with a litter box on top was tucked beside my dresser, and cat toys were scattered all over my bed. In my closet, my beautiful closet, all my clothes and shoes were gone, replaced by stacks of boxes. I couldn't decide if I was more angry or sad.

My mom must've noticed my gaze because she said, "Pepper was batting at your hanging clothes and she peed on a pair of shoes, so I decided to pack away everything in your closet."

"Why do people like animals again?" I mumbled.

She bit her lip. "I'm sorry. We were just getting the cat used to the house. She has trust issues, and they said it would be good to keep her in one room for a while and slowly introduce her to the rest of the house, and your room, seeing as how it was empty, seemed like the best option. She doesn't really like people."

"You adopted a cat that doesn't like people?"

"She has the potential to like people. She wasn't treated very well in her last house. Are you mad? You're mad."

My mom looked so stressed, and my siblings had

seemed genuinely excited about this, so I said, "No, of course not. I'm only here for one night."

"Thank you, honey. I promise by the time you get back, your room will be cat-free."

"Sounds good." I pointed to the boxes in the closet. "Do you remember which one might hold my sweats and tees?"

She gave me her sad eyes again. "I have no idea. You'll just have to go through all of them."

"Okay. I will."

I went to the closet and pulled down the first box. My mom left the room and closed the door behind her, presumably so the cat wouldn't get out.

"Is now the time you're going to jump on me?" I asked the air around me. The cat didn't respond. I snapped a pic of the litter box in the corner and sent it in a text to Amanda with the words: **I've been replaced by a cat.**

Your dad got a cat? Maybe it will divert some of his attention.

I smiled. **I wish. No, my mom got a cat.**

She needs to play the card game with you so she knows the important details about your personality.

Right? What are you doing with your day off?

I have escaped my trailer and am going to crash at a friend's place.

Have fun!

I sat down and opened the first box from my closet. It

was everything that had been on my dresser and taped onto my mirror—mainly pictures and jewelry. My mom hadn't mentioned packing away the top of my dresser but when I looked over there now, sure enough, it was bare except for a weird-looking ball. The cat must've gotten into my things up there as well. It was fine. This was fine.

I turned my attention back to the pics and flipped through them. Most were from a musical I had directed over the summer—*The Music Man*. I had been a good director; I encouraged the actors and gave positive feedback. At least most of the time.

I dropped the pics in the box. No, I wasn't going to let myself obsess on my day off. I needed a distraction.

FOURTEEN

After digging through five boxes to find clothes, reading my brother and sister a book before bed, and filling my mom in on the exciting world of moviemaking, I asked, "Do you mind if I hang out with some friends tomorrow, Mom?"

My mom sat next to me on the couch with a big glass of ice water. "No, of course not. You should."

"Thank you." The clock on the wall said it was close to ten. "Where is Bill? I thought he'd be home by now."

"It's that case I was telling you about. It keeps him late almost every night."

FAME, FATE, AND THE FIRST KISS

"Tell him I said hi, then. I'm going to bed."

She squeezed my arm. "I will. I'm glad to have you home, Lace."

"I'm happy to be home."

The cat hadn't shown her face the whole time I'd been in my room—her room?—earlier. Mom had said she hid under the bed a lot. "Don't jump out at me," I said as I walked in the room this time. It didn't smell anymore because my sister had cleaned the litter. "We'll just have a mutual understanding, yes? You leave me alone. I leave you alone. It will be for the best." I tiptoed to my bed, then hopped into it quickly.

It didn't take long for me to fall asleep.

It had been a while since I'd been to a milkshake or burger place, but Abby had suggested the place in town that served both in equal quantities.

Abby jumped up and gave me a hug. "I'm so happy you're here."

"Just for a couple more hours."

Cooper offered a wave and a smile. I didn't know Cooper as well as Abby. I'd gotten to know her mainly in the time where she was trying to get over him because she loved him fiercely and he didn't know he loved her back yet. He'd obviously come to his senses. He was cute. His look screamed surfer boy—blond hair, tan, athletic build.

"Do you surf, Cooper?" was the first thing I asked when I joined them at the table.

"No, I do not."

"Huh." I sat down and put on my smile. "Hi."

"What's with the surfing question?" Abby asked. She had her hand in Cooper's, and their chairs were close.

"He just looks like a surfer boy. Don't you think?"

"Is that an insult?" Cooper asked. "It felt like an insult."

I laughed. "Do you have a problem with surfers?"

"No, but it feels like you do."

"It does? I don't. Surfers are cute."

"She thinks you're cute, babe," Abby said.

"I do," I said.

Cooper winked at Abby. "Are you going to let her flirt with me like this?"

"I will defend you with my life if I need to," Abby said. "But not until after I have a milk shake."

I picked up a plastic-covered menu from the table. "No lives need to be sacrificed. I was just pointing out beauty. I also think Abby is cute, and I'm not trying to steal her either."

"Speaking of beauty," Abby said. "How is Grant James?"

"You find Grant James attractive?" Cooper asked Abby.

"You *don't*?" she said back, as though this was the most shocking thing he'd ever said.

He shrugged his shoulders. "I've seen hotter."

As they proceeded to get into a debate about Grant James, I realized the last time I talked about Grant was with Donavan. That conversation came back to me—his admitting he'd been the writer of the viral review. The review that was messing with Grant's head and in turn messing with our chemistry on camera. Even if Grant didn't think it was him too, Amanda thought it was and so did I.

"For the record," I said out loud, maybe too loud, "I liked his last movie. I thought he was great. He's a good actor."

They both paused in their discussion and looked at me, confusion on their faces. "We didn't say he wasn't," Abby said.

"Oh, I thought that's what you were talking about."

Abby tilted her head. "No, we were being much more shallow. Are you okay? Is everything okay?"

"It's fine." Apparently I was letting Donavan get in *my* head now.

"Has the infamous kissing scene happened yet?" Abby wiggled her eyebrows.

"Soon." I remembered when I first read in the script that I had to kiss Grant James I thought it would be fun. Now it sounded like a test I wasn't prepared for. Something I needed to study for. Something I'd *been* studying for. Well, except in the way Amanda had suggested—by finding someone in my real life to have real feelings for. I wondered if I kissed someone for real, someone I wanted to kiss, if that would help. No. I shook my head. I didn't need to do that. I was an actress. "I just have to become Scarlett," I said.

"Who's Scarlett?" Cooper asked.

"My character. I need to channel her and it will be fine."

"Order number seventy-two!" the worker behind the counter said, and Abby jumped up.

"Oh, you already ordered. I better go place my order or you'll be staring at me while I eat," I said.

I ordered grilled chicken and a water, even though the guy behind the counter looked at me funny, then I sat back down. Cooper's fries looked so good I almost stole one, but I kept my hands to myself.

"So talk to me," Abby said. "You seem stressed about things. Normally when you talk about a project, you're overflowing with excitement."

"Overflowing? Really?"

"Is it that chemistry thing you mentioned?"

"I hate chemistry," Cooper said.

Abby laughed. "The other kind of chemistry."

"Oh, I take back my statement, then." Cooper squeezed Abby's hand, and she made the slightest movement toward him, their shoulders brushing.

Speaking of chemistry, they'd had more in the last ten minutes than I'd had with Grant in two weeks.

"Is there someone else you'd rather be kissing? Is that the problem?" Abby asked.

"What? No!" I knew my mistake the second I'd spoken it. I'd been too quick and adamant in my response. I should've just rolled my eyes or waved it off. After all, there wasn't someone I'd rather be kissing, but I'd just made it seem like that wasn't the case.

"Spill," Abby said.

"There's nothing to tell. I live, eat, and breathe my script and zombies. Who would I kiss?"

"For an actress, you aren't a very good liar," Cooper said.

"I take offense to that statement."

"You want to be a good liar?" Abby asked.

"Absolutely. But I wasn't lying, so that means I wasn't acting, so your statement was false anyway." I waved my hand. "Enough about me. Tell me everything about you."

"Everything?" Abby said. "That would take forever."

"At least tell her about the float at homecoming."

Abby laughed, and Cooper followed suit. "It's a long story," she said after a minute.

"I like long stories," I said.

"Abby jumped on the float and lip-synched."

"You what?" I said, surprised.

"That was a very condensed version of the real story, but basically the girl who was supposed to lip-synch vomited in the end field and—"

"That's a condensed version too," Cooper interrupted with a laugh.

"True, but it was an important detail." They went back and forth sharing other details that made zero sense. Details that I wished I could've seen, been part of. It sounded like my kind of night.

Abby finally turned back to me and said, "So I had no other choice but to jump on the float."

"No other choice," I said, and I could hear the hollowness in my voice.

Cooper and Abby met eyes and laughed again.

I repacked the clothes I had taken out back into their boxes and pushed them into my closet. Then I got down on all fours and looked under my bed. It was too dark under there to see much, but no glowing pair of eyes shone back at me. I pointed my phone flashlight all around. Nothing. "Mom!"

She came to my open doorway. "Yes?"

"Are you sure you actually still own a cat? Maybe it escaped."

"I'm sure." She looked around. "Wait, are you leaving?"

I sat back on my heels. "Yes, I want to be back before it gets dark. I have an early call tomorrow." Plus, I hoped getting home early would make up for the fact that I hadn't responded to my dad's texts. Technically, I didn't think they'd required a response. The first one had read, Long-distance trips are something we should discuss before they happen in the future. The second had read, I talked to your teacher, she said your last packet wasn't your best work. Statements did not require answers.

I climbed to my feet, picked up my bag, and gave my mom a hug. "You should come with me, see the set, meet Grant and Amanda and my director. It would be fun."

She nodded slowly. "It would be fun. But . . ." Her eyes looked around my room as if searching for the invisible cat.

"You can't," I finished for her.

"I'll find the time. Just not this week."

"Okay. Soon though."

"Soon."

I hugged her, then found my siblings in the kitchen. They sat at barstools eating frosting on graham crackers. I squished them each into a hug and assaulted their cheeks with multiple kisses. "Try not to have too much of a life without me."

I made it all the way to the door before I realized I'd forgotten my charger on my nightstand. I turned to tell my mom as much but she hadn't followed me to the door like she always used to do when I left the house. I backtracked to where she had joined my siblings at a barstool of her own and was spreading pink frosting onto a cracker.

"Tonight, we should have a movie night in your room," Sydney said to Mom.

"Absolutely," Mom responded.

"Can I pick the movie?" Colby asked.

"We'll do the hat trick," Mom said, and they both laughed. The hat trick? I had no idea what that was. I swallowed a lump that wanted to form in my throat and quickly retrieved my charger before leaving.

I walked through the door after my four-hour drive, not feeling at all how I'd hoped I would after my visit home. I hadn't anticipated feeling like such an outsider in my own house. Like life worked perfectly fine, if not better, without me. Dad stood at the counter, and we locked eyes. I was too emotionally drained for a fight tonight.

"Next time I'll tell you before I go to mom's," I said, defeated.

He pulled a plate out of the fridge that was covered in plastic wrap. "You hungry?"

I nodded, and he removed the plastic and put it in the microwave.

I plopped onto a barstool at the counter. "Thanks."

"I'm not trying to hover, Lacey. I want what's best for you."

"Have you ever thought that maybe this *is* what's best for me?"

The microwave beeped, and he placed the plate of pasta in front of me. I took a few bites.

He sighed. "I'm worried about you."

"Why? I'm fine."

"I'm worried something is going to happen that will shatter your spirit. Call it a gut instinct or a—"

"Overprotective father."

"Sure, you can call it that. I just want to make sure you have a life to go back to if this experience ends badly for you."

"This experience? Meaning, starring in a movie?"

"Yes."

"What's the worst that can happen, Dad? Bad reviews?"

I asked, thinking about Donavan and his viral smack-
down on Grant.

"I don't know."

"Even if the worst happened, I wouldn't give this up.
I'd try again. I'm tough."

"I know you are."

"This is what I'm supposed to be doing." Now I just
had to prove that was true. Maybe when this was all
over, when my dad saw the results, he'd finally realize I
could do this.

He shook his head, indicating that I was searching in
the wrong place for the support I needed. It was never
going to come from him.

Dancing Graves

EXT. FOREST BEYOND THE MANSION—NIGHT.
SCARLETT leads a group of zombies to a cave near the mountains, where she is hoping to gather them all and barricade them to keep them and the humans safe while her father works on a cure. She feels like she belongs with the zombies but still understands that she shouldn't feel that way. She has moments where she is more aware than others and this is one of those moments. BENJAMIN follows her and waits until he can speak with her alone.

                    BENJAMIN
Scarlett. Is it safe?

                    SCARLETT
Never fully safe with me.

BENJAMIN

I know you would never hurt me. Why have
you led them here?

SCARLETT

Buying time until my father can work a
miracle.

BENJAMIN

This might not be a good idea to have
them all together like this in the same
place. If the wrong hunter finds out it
could be disastrous.

SCARLETT

Then don't tell anyone.

FIFTEEN

Those two days off were not good for me. I felt more out of character now than ever, having been only myself for the last two days.

The morning started off bad and didn't get any better. Each scene required more takes than usual—Grant and I were not in sync. Remy got grumpier and grumpier as the day wore on. Especially when my advocate said I'd hit my hours limit for the day. I left the set probably as frustrated as Remy.

I was tough, I told myself. I needed to forget about

the real world, my real life, for a while and put on my character off camera. I went out to the parking lot, fully costumed, to retrieve my *Dancing Graves* book from the trunk of the car. Grant's fans were there, lining the barricades as always, holding their handmade signs. I thought about going up and saying hi. Showing them that I was nice and hoping they'd post something good about me. But in response to my publicist email, my agent had said, *Just keep your head down and work. If we need a publicist, we'll worry about that after filming, during movie promotion, when it will matter.* I wondered if that was her nice way of saying I couldn't afford one for a long period of time so I needed to time it right.

I focused on my car, trying to keep a neutral expression on my zombified face as I walked. I popped my trunk and retrieved the book. I took a deep breath and tried to channel Scarlett. Maybe I needed to start calling Grant *Benjamin* on and off set. I flipped to page one as I walked back to my trailer. It had been a while since I read the book. Unlike the script, it fully immersed me in the character and world that surrounded her with detailed descriptions and back stories.

I opened the door to my trailer, put the book facedown on the table, and went into the bathroom. The curtain was drawn around the small shower, which wasn't how

I'd left it. I reached toward it, ready to throw it open, when it was ripped to the side from within followed by a loud scream.

I picked up my hairbrush from the counter and swung it with a scream of my own before I registered that the person standing in my shower was Amanda.

"Were you going to kill me with a hairbrush?" she said through her laughter.

"You are evil. Pure evil," I said.

She bowed, then stepped out of my shower.

"The devil herself is what you are. You almost made me pee my pants."

She blew me a kiss and skipped out of my bathroom.

"How did you even get over here before me? I just saw you on set," I said as she laid herself on my couch.

"I'm a fast runner."

"This is why Grant has security guards outside his trailer." Apparently mine was Grand Central station, anyone and everyone was allowed in. Despite my still-racing heart, I found myself smiling.

"Grant has security guards outside his trailer because he's a *big* star." She said the word *big* in a sarcastic voice, like it wasn't true.

"Uh-oh. What happened?"

"Nothing. Absolutely nothing. That's the problem."

"You just gotta let yourself fall for me," I said in a

deep-voiced impersonation of him. "Are you sure you still *want* something to happen?"

"He gave you the speech too?"

"Yes."

She nodded slowly. "He's just doing what he always does, what works for him. Once he realizes that he likes me, he won't flirt with everyone else."

"If you say so."

"Have you thought of a brilliant plan yet?"

I hadn't, but that didn't mean I couldn't. "Too bad it's not you who's kissing him on camera next week. I watched your videos. That would totally sway him." I straightened up. "That's it."

"What's it?" she asked.

"You're going to kiss him under the pretense of giving me some pointers."

She sat up. "That's a brilliant idea."

"I know!"

"You'll suggest this practice session at some point? If I do, it will be obvious."

"Yes, I will."

"You're the best." She put her feet up on my coffee table. "How are things going with *your* boy?"

"He's not my boy."

There was a knock at the door. Speaking of Grand Central. "Come in!"

Donavan walked into the trailer, and my heart stuttered. Why did it do that? I scowled at the reaction.

"I see you're so happy to see me," he said.

"She's so happy to see you," Amanda said. "We were just talking about you and I was just leaving." She turned toward me and wiggled her eyebrows. I shook my head with a laugh, and she left.

"I just came to bring you a fresh new homework packet," Donavan said when the door was shut.

"Scarlett doesn't do homework."

"Lacey doesn't either."

"Funny."

"Who is Scarlett?" He obviously didn't remember my character's name.

I held up the book in my hand.

"Oh, right." He put the new packet on my table and turned to go. "So you'll just text me a pic when you get some done, then?"

He was leaving? "You're not going to do the math with me?"

He wrinkled his brow in confusion. "I thought . . ."

He needs to leave, Lacey. You need to work on being Scarlett. He is a distraction. "Will you do it in character with me?" I asked, ignoring my better judgment.

"I have no idea what that means."

"You tutor me while in character. I do my assignments as Scarlett. It's called method acting."

"And who am I supposed to be?"

"His name is Benjamin. He's a zombie hunter."

"Is that who Grant James plays?"

I smirked. "Is that a problem?"

"I am probably equally as good an actor as Grant James."

"So you *have* done some acting," I said.

"No. I'll be horrible."

"Ouch, Mr. Reviewer. Pretty sure you're already on Grant's bad side. You don't need to be walking around the studio bad-talking him."

He looked repentant. "I'm sorry. That was in poor taste."

I smiled. "I was teasing you." I looked over my shoulder to make sure my trailer door was closed. "Sort of."

"So you want me to sit here and pretend to kill you for the next hour?"

"No, he's not trying to kill me, remember? He's in love with me. Just basically say whatever you're going to say, but in a British accent. I'll figure out the rest."

"You really do always try to get out of schoolwork." He sat down on the couch.

I grabbed my packet and my book from the table and

sat down next to him. "This is the opposite of that. This is a creative way of doing schoolwork. How is your British accent?"

"Horrible. Very, very horrible."

"Hold on, before you start, let me . . ." I reached over and messed up his perfectly styled hair. He was cute—big brown eyes, nice lips, defined jaw. "There. Better. Oh wait. Can I just?" I pointed to his shirt.

"What?"

"Just the top button. Isn't this choking you?" I unbuttoned the top one, then assessed the new look. Just those two changes made him look more relaxed, which was more him, I was learning. As much of a taskmaster as he was, he actually did have a pretty mellow personality. One that radiated calm. "This is what you choose to wear on a Wednesday?"

"I came straight from work."

I cleared my throat. "Isn't this work?"

"I am also a waiter."

"Really?" I leaned over and smelled him. "You don't even smell like food."

"You are so weird."

"Where do you work?"

"It's this little family-owned restaurant by my house called Bella's."

"So wait, you're a waiter and a tutor *and* you write

reviews? When do you find the time to do your own homework?"

"I'm not really a tutor."

I squinted my eyes. "Um . . . what do you call what we're doing, then?"

"Well, I mean, I tutor you. But you're the only one."

"Oh." I was even more confused now. "That's why Taylor in the front office at your school had no idea what I was talking about when I said you tutored."

"Probably."

"Then how did you . . . ?"

"Your dad seemed really desperate."

I nodded. "He often does." Knowing my dad, he'd probably had the school give him the names of the three students who had the highest GPAs and he personally called them.

Donavan patted the packet in my hand. "Are we going to do this or what?"

"Yes, method acting. Let's hear it. We are now in eighteenth-century England."

He gave me the world's biggest sigh. "Here is you always getting what you want."

"You're right. I do always get what I want. My father owns this mansion, this town, and you in it," I said as Scarlett.

He gestured for me to hand him the packet, and I did.

He began reading the first page of instructions in what I assumed was his attempt at a British accent. "Don't look at me like that. This was your idea."

I laughed. He was being a good sport. "Please, carry on."

"Are you going to stay in your makeup again today?" he asked.

I'd forgotten I had it on. "Makeup? What makeup?"

"Okay, you weren't kidding," he said. "I guess we're doing this."

"While I'm reading these word problems, you read this chapter." I handed him *Dancing Graves* and turned to a Benjamin-heavy chapter.

"Why?"

"It'll help you."

"You mean it will help you."

"In this room, that is the same thing."

He took the book from me and handed me my homework.

He was a focused reader. He concentrated on each page—his eyebrows drawn together, the tip of his right thumb clamped lightly between his teeth, fully immersed.

I skimmed the first word problem and then skimmed it again. Easy enough. But of course doing this immediately took me out of character. How would Scarlett have completed this?

"I'll be right back," I whispered. I wasn't sure if he heard me, because he didn't look up.

I left my trailer and walked with purpose to the mansion. It wasn't a real mansion, obviously. They had shot some B-roll film of a real mansion somewhere in a forested countryside. But here in the studio each of the three rooms they'd built only had three walls. In the room that represented the library, I remembered seeing a quill and inkpot. I wasn't sure if it actually worked. So many things were fake. But so many things weren't. Amanda had to write something at some point, so I hoped this was one of those set pieces that actually functioned. I riffled through the items on the desktop. When I didn't see it, I opened a side drawer. I started to shut it again when something caught my eye—my flesh-colored kneepads. I pulled them out, confused. How did these end up here? Maybe I'd left them on set one day and they got shoved in the drawer when things were getting packed away.

"What are you doing?" a voice from behind me asked.

I whirled around, tense, then immediately relaxed. "Oh, it's just you."

Grant stood there between two stacks of coiled extension cords, holding an apple.

I tucked the kneepads under my arm and said in a British accent, "I'm after a writing apparatus." He was the one who told me to be Scarlett; I was going to be Scarlett.

"Oh, are you now?" he said, easily slipping into a perfect British accent. Much better than Donavan's.

I smiled at him. "My father has sent a tutor to help me in my studies."

He hopped up into the mansion library with me. "You and your tutors. A woman shouldn't take on more than she can handle," he said. It's what Benjamin would've said, and he knew that.

"But alas, I do what I'm told."

"I have a sneaking suspicion that assertion couldn't be further from the truth." He plucked the quill and ink I hadn't seen off the corner of the desk and handed them to me, then took another bite of his apple, his blue eyes sparkling with humor.

"Thank you, kind sir."

"My pleasure." He took my hand in his and kissed my knuckles.

I started to walk toward the exit, our hands still linked. He didn't move, and eventually our hands pulled apart. We maintained eye contact while I took several more steps, then I turned, flipped my greasy hair, and walked away. This method acting could actually work. That was more chemistry than I'd had with him since auditioning.

I smiled as I walked down the hall, my kneepads still tucked under my arm, quill and ink in my hand. I came to the corner and was about to turn it when I heard voices. One I recognized immediately as Remy's. The other I couldn't place because it was a bit muffled, but it was low and intense. I didn't want to interrupt them, so I stopped a moment, trying to figure out if I should turn back or wait it out. That's when I heard, "She's too new, and not very good. Nobody knows who she is. And those who do, don't even like her. You should read the posts on social media about her."

I couldn't even tell if it was a guy or a girl, because the voice was spoken in a loud whisper.

"It would cost the studio a lot of money if we replaced her now."

"It might cost them a lot of money if you don't."

I backed up slowly, careful not to scuff my feet on the floor. When I got far enough away, I turned and took another exit, for the long way around to my trailer. I got inside and leaned against the door, out of breath.

SIXTEEN

Donavan hadn't moved from his position on the couch; he was reading my book. But when I continued to stand there, he looked up. "What's wrong?"

I put the ink and quill on the table and tossed my kneepads into the corner. "I heard someone talking in the hall to my director about how they think I suck. I kind of do right now."

"Someone said that? Who?"

"I have no idea. What if my director listens to them? What if they're someone who has a lot of influence?"

Donavan stood and walked over to where I was

standing by the window of my trailer. He took my hand and led me to the couch. "Sit down."

I did.

"How do you take this off?" He pointed to my face. "Is there a special method?"

I nodded toward the vanity. "There's some Q-tips and a bottle of solution. And there are some makeup wipes up there."

He gathered the things I'd mentioned and brought them back to the couch. Then he handed them to me and sat down.

I turned toward him, pulled my legs up onto the couch and crossed them. I dipped a Q-tip in the solution and held it out for him. "You use this when it doesn't come off easily."

He hesitated as he stared at me, and I realized he hadn't meant that he was going to take it off. He'd brought it over for me to do. My mind was a mess. I started to say as much when he took the Q-tip from me and asked, "I . . . does it hurt?"

"No, it's fine."

He reached for a section and gently tugged. After freeing that piece, I held out an upturned hand and he dropped the latex onto my palm. Then he turned more fully to face me, matching my cross-legged position. He leaned in, his eyes as intent on my face now as they'd been on that book moments before, while he carefully removed more sections. My heartbeat picked up.

I shifted, hugging my knees to my chest.

"I'm surprised you don't have a makeup-remover person," he said.

"I know, what kind of second-rate joint is this?" Our position made it so I couldn't look anywhere but at him. He was close, his brown eyes studying each section he removed as if this was the most important thing he'd done all day. His hair that I had messed up earlier flopped forward. I pushed it back for him, out of his eyes.

"Thanks," he said. Then he brushed a finger over a bare section on my cheek. "Why are you always missing this big part? Have you not fully transformed yet?"

"It's the only section that's premade, and Leah, my makeup person, takes it off before I leave the set for the day. She doesn't trust me with it."

He nodded like this made perfect sense. Like he wouldn't trust me with anything valuable either.

He was quiet for a moment and then said softly, "You don't suck. You deserve to be here."

I shrugged. I hadn't been feeling like that at all lately.

"You landed a movie with *the* Grant James," he said.

I smiled a little.

"Not to mention, every episode of *The Cafeteria* was near perfection."

My breath caught in my throat. "You're a fan of *The Cafeteria*?"

"I am."

"So you saw my episodes?"

"You were brilliant."

I was used to getting compliments, but from Donavan—the critic, the guy who seemed to disapprove of half the things I did—it felt bigger somehow. It made my cheeks go pink. I wondered if I still had enough makeup on to mask it. My eyes dropped to the collar of his shirt. "You're just saying that to make me feel better."

"No . . . well, yes, I am. But I don't say things I don't mean."

"What happened to being objective?" I asked.

"I *am* being objective. I don't think you need to worry about people gossiping in the hallways. You were hired because you're good."

I bit my lip. "I didn't realize you knew me before . . ."

"I didn't know you before."

"I mean, I thought this was how you saw me for the first time." I held up the handful of latex in my palm.

"No." His eyes slid to mine. "I'd seen you. But I didn't want you to think that's the only reason I took the job."

"So it was *one* of the reasons?"

"What? No."

I raised my eyebrows.

"Fine, it didn't hurt."

I smiled. "So what was the main reason you took this job?"

He hesitated, like he didn't want to tell me but then finally said, "I took it because your dad had submitted an ad to the paper, and I read it but didn't want to print it because that seemed . . ."

"Super embarrassing?" I finished for him. My dad was going to put an ad in the school paper? Anger surged through my chest. "Does the paper have other ads?"

"Yes, it has a classified section. People sell instruments and cars and promote yard sales, so don't be too mad at him. Like I said, he seemed desperate."

I sighed, trying to take his advice but failing. "What did it say? 'Come help my daughter, who's a bad actress and even worse student'?"

"No. I don't really remember what it said, but not that. And we already established you're a brilliant actress."

I narrowed my eyes. "I like how you didn't refute the bad-student part."

"You're a horrible student. But only because you have zero desire to do schoolwork."

I tried to hold back a laugh. "I wouldn't say zero."

"Zero."

I rolled my eyes. "So does everyone see all the ads? Or are you the editor of the paper or something?" Actually, he probably was. That's why he sat in that little office in the journalism room.

He shrugged one shoulder like it was no big deal.

"So you could probably assign yourself any section to write. Why entertainment?" I asked. "Why do you like to write reviews?"

"I love stories. I love watching them play out and trying to guess the endings. I love being surprised and learning new things about people or about myself."

"And then you love saying how it could've been done so much better?"

He laughed, a soft, deep laugh that made my stomach flutter. "Or how it was done well. Don't forget I do write good reviews too."

"So no hard-hitting, investigative journalism for you?"

"I have the flight personality, remember? I like to avoid conflict when I can."

"Says the guy whose movie review became a meme."

"Not by choice. I have no desire to pick a fight with Grant James."

My hand was full of latex, and I could tell he was done when he did a final scan of my face. I pulled out a makeup wipe and finished the job. "Thank you," I said. "For talking me through that."

"Any time."

"You should ask my dad for a raise." I don't know why I said that. Maybe to remind myself that Donavan was here because he was paid to be here.

"Should I add *listening* to my bio? What was it? Haircuts, harmonizing, and . . ."

"Homework," I said with a smile.

"Oh, right. How could I forget homework? The only one that is actually true."

"But you can't add listening. That doesn't fit the *H* theme we have going on."

"Hearing? Helping?

"Better." I took a piece of latex from my hand and stuck it to his cheek. "You'd make a cute zombie." The piece fell off his cheek and onto his leg.

He picked it up with one hand and used his other hand to steady mine while placing the latex onto the top of the pile. When he didn't let go, I met his eyes. He averted his gaze, dropped his hand, and then stood. "I'm sorry. I have to go. I promised my mom I'd be home earlier tonight."

I threw my whole handful of scraps into the garbage. "Oh, that's okay. I wasted all our time."

"Text me if you get stuck on any of the math."

"For sure. Thanks."

I moved in to hug him as he was turning toward the door.

"Oh," he said, and patted my back awkwardly. "See you."

"Bye."

He closed the door behind him, and I sank down to the couch. Why had I turned that weird? What was I doing? I did not like Donavan Lake. He was just a very helpful friend who I felt comfortable around, which was great, because that's what I needed right now. That's all I needed.

What I didn't need was people talking about me to Remy. I took a deep breath, but Donavan was right, it was just on-set gossip. People talked about other people all the time. Remy was probably used to it too. It wouldn't influence him . . . I hoped.

Dancing Graves

INT. LORD LUCAS'S LAB—LATE NIGHT
LORD LUCAS mixes chemicals and herbs in
a glass beaker, measuring each carefully.
His large wooden table is a mess of dirty
beakers, spilled formula, and scattered
ingredients. His eyes are bloodshot. His
hair is disheveled and his nerves are on
edge. Every noise outside makes him jump.
He spills a chemical and it splashes onto
his wrist, burning him. He curses and
throws the glass beaker across the room,
where it shatters against the far wall.
BENJAMIN rushes in.

                    BENJAMIN
Was there a break-in?

                    LORD LUCAS
No, but I think somebody is tainting my
ingredients.

BENJAMIN

Who? Why?

LORD LUCAS

There are some who believe we shouldn't
help the infected. They believe we should
eradicate them to stop the spread.

BENJAMIN

Don't let them influence you. Don't give
up on her.

LORD LUCAS

Death is the only thing that can stop me.

SEVENTEEN

The next morning, after hair and makeup, I had some extra time, so I walked to Amanda's trailer. "Come in!" she said after a single knock, and I stepped just inside her doorway. She was flipping through some papers, and when she looked up her hand flew to her chest. "You really shouldn't do stuff like that when you're in full zombie makeup. You're going to give a girl a heart attack."

"Says the girl who hid in my shower yesterday."

"You're right. I deserve much more than a casual scaring." She studied my face for a moment. "Everything okay?"

"Ugh." I leaned my head back against her door. "Someone here doesn't like me and shared their feelings with Remy yesterday."

"And Remy told you this?"

"No, I overheard them talking to him."

"You seem to attract drama: lights falling, ripped wardrobe, missing kneepads, and now on-set gossip." She laughed.

I started to laugh too but then stopped and walked farther into her trailer. "Wait, do you think . . . ?"

She waved her hand through the air. "I was kidding. Accidents happen. And people, don't get me started on people. They talk trash on set all the time. They complain and whine. It's part of being in a cast. I once worked with a girl who complained about every single person in every single one of her scenes to anyone who would listen. She thought she was the absolute best actress in the universe, and any time there was a mistake it was someone else's fault. So take this for what it is: someone venting."

"You're right." It's the conclusion I had come to the day before too, but it felt better to hear her say it.

She held up a remote and pointed it at the television that was behind my head.

I turned to look and saw on the screen a frozen Amanda. "What are you watching?"

"I'm watching my audition. In some of Faith's notes she mentioned how I performed in the audition, so I wanted to see what she was talking about because I didn't remember."

"Ooh, fun. Push play. I want to see your audition." I sat down on the couch.

She pushed play, and we watched her standing in the room I remembered so well, delivering lines to a table full of people taking notes. It had been an intimidating process.

"What do you think about tomorrow being the day?" Amanda asked while the television version of herself was talking.

"The day for what?"

"Kissing. I'll swing by your trailer after filming with Grant, you suggest a practice kissing session. I step in to show you how it's done."

"Oh yeah. Tomorrow is really the only day, considering we're filming that scene the day after that."

"Exactly."

"Then yes, I think your plan will work."

"It's really your plan."

"True. It's a good one." I pointed at the screen. "Does this have everybody's audition on it or just yours?"

"I think it's all of them. Want me to find yours?" She started fast-forwarding, her body on the television jerking and moving in fast unnatural movements. After her was a guy I didn't recognize, obviously someone who didn't end up making the movie.

"Ooh, look who we could've been acting with," Amanda said, pushing play so we could listen. He had a deep, velvety voice. "He's cute."

"He's okay," I said. "Kind of old."

"Not too old for me," she said. "But speaking of cute guys, if Donavan isn't your boy, why is he always hanging around?"

"Oh, I didn't tell you he's my tutor?"

"Really?" she said. "I would've done every last bit of my homework if I had a tutor like that. Dark hair, intense eyes, I don't see why he can't help you find your chemistry."

"Stop."

"What? He's cute. It shouldn't be that hard."

"I'm not going to use him to help with my chemistry."

"I didn't say anything about using him. I'm talking about real feelings here, not fake ones."

Maybe I didn't know the difference, I'd been acting too long. "I can't even conjure up feelings for a cat, maybe I'm not built to form attachments to living things."

She rolled her entire head along with her eyes.

A familiar voice came onto the television, and I looked over to see that a new person was reading lines. A very familiar person. Before I could say anything, Amanda said, "Hey, that's Faith."

"Faith auditioned for this movie?" I asked.

"Apparently. Who knew." She pushed fast-forward again. "Here, let me find yours. Are you one of those people who can watch yourself on television, or do you freak out?"

"I had a great drama teacher in high school who made us record monologues, watch them, and analyze our performances in front of the whole class." I'd gotten used to seeing myself on a screen as well as using the opportunity of watching myself as a way to improve.

"Nice, because here you are." She pushed play. As I watched, I noticed something: I had been more confident that day performing, more sure of myself, than I had been since actually landing the job.

"What's wrong?" Amanda asked after a minute. "You were great."

I must've sighed out loud while watching. I stood. "I better get to set before I'm late. Thanks for that. It was actually very helpful."

Watching that audition had reminded me that I had earned this role. And I took that feeling and used it. The lights, the people, energized me today.

"You're feeling it today," Grant said during a break to move lights.

"I am. It's like I remembered what I was doing."

"You're kind of hard on yourself, I've noticed." He put his hands on my shoulders and squeezed. "Never doubt that you're exactly where you should be." And as if he didn't have the ability to be nice without ruining it, he added, "Right next to me."

I shook my head with a smile, knowing he was at least partially kidding. "You were *almost* supportive."

"I'm the most supportive person I know."

"Can I ask you a question?"

"Sure."

Even if I was trying to forget about the person talking about me in the hall, there was one thing they said that was absolutely true. "You've been in the public eye pretty much your whole life now. How do you recommend I change the online narrative of me?"

"Is it bad?"

"You haven't seen all the things people say about me? That is, if they're talking about me at all."

"No, I haven't. I only ever look up my own stuff, which hasn't been great lately. I don't know if I have an answer for you. Hire a publicist?"

The same thing his agent had suggested. "And if I

can't afford that? What do you think about me going to talk to that group of fans that always lines the fence holding their devotion to you on poster boards? Would that be good for me or bad?"

He shrugged. "Couldn't hurt."

"Do you talk to them?"

"Sometimes."

"Would you go out there with me sometime? Maybe say something nice about me. Sign some autographs or something? Maybe they'll post about it. Or maybe *you* could post something online."

"I'd have to ask my publicist if that's a good idea for me. I'll let you know."

"Right. Okay." Did I really expect that we were good enough friends now that he would do something as a favor to me? Whatever. It didn't matter. I'd gotten here with my own group of people supporting me; I'd keep going forward the same way. I didn't let this affect me. I finished out my day as strong as I started it and left the set with determination to make things work.

EIGHTEEN

The next morning, as I climbed out of my car at the studio, a car pulled to a stop next to mine, revved its engine, and then idled. I looked over to see Aaron sitting behind the wheel of his dad's black convertible. I only knew it was his dad's because I'd seen Remy driving it before.

I smiled. "Excuse me, sir, but aren't you too young to be driving that?"

"My dad lets me drive it around the studio."

"Your dad is very brave."

"Do you want to go for a ride?"

"Your dad is much braver than me."

"You can at least sit in it."

"Fine." It was a nice car. I didn't know makes or models of cars very well but it had a tan leather interior that looked brand-new. I opened the door and sat down.

"What do you think? When I turn sixteen, he's giving it to me. Does it seem like an old-man car?"

"It seems like a rich old-man car. But if my dad had given me a really expensive convertible when I turned sixteen, I wouldn't have complained."

He shrugged. "It's a guilt gift."

"Guilt gift?"

"Yeah, we were supposed to go on a big trip this year, but then my dad got this job."

"Where were you going to go?"

"Lots of places, but I was looking forward to Thailand the most."

"Maybe you can still go, when filming is over?"

"Well, then there's editing and then there's promoting and then they start talking about sequels. You know how it is," he said.

"Actually, I don't."

He smiled. "You will."

"Sorry about your trip."

"No worries, I'm getting a guilt gift." He patted the

steering wheel. "By the way, I meant to tell you that you did great yesterday."

"Thanks, it felt pretty good."

"I'm just going to drive you to the entrance." He pointed to the opening in the gate fifty feet in front of us.

My eyes went wide.

"Really?" he said. "I'm that scary?"

"I can just see the headlines now. 'Lacey Barnes in Accident with Underage Driver.'"

"There are literally zero cars between me and that gate."

"Fine. But drive really, really slow."

"Maybe my dad should give *you* this old-lady car."

Seriously. Had Donavan been rubbing off on me? When had I turned into an old lady? When had I started worrying so much? Aaron lifted his foot off the brake and the car moved slowly. It felt like he didn't even apply the gas at all before he came to a stop in front of the gate. "There you are, madam. Have a good day."

"Thanks for the ride, and be careful."

For the second day in a row, Remy smiled when we finished filming. Then he added a thumbs-up and "Nice job, Lacey." Sure, we were working on zombie scenes and not love scenes, but it still felt good.

In my trailer, I changed into some street clothes and made short work of my makeup. We'd finished a little early today because it had gone so well, and for a second I thought about going home, but then I remembered I'd promised Amanda I would help her with Grant. Why she liked Grant was becoming less and less apparent by the day. Didn't she talk to the same Grant I talked to? Whatever, maybe he was different with her. Maybe he thought she was a bigger star than me. I hadn't seen anything bad about Amanda online when I'd googled her kissing scenes.

Revisions sat on my table next to my very much untouched packet Donavan had left the other day. I looked at both and picked up my packet. I'd have time to look over revisions later.

I settled in and had only completed three problems when there was a knock on my door. "Come in!" I called, fully expecting Amanda and Grant.

It was Donavan. "Hey," he said. "You're not a zombie today."

My cheeks went hot, the memory of our last, awkward interaction still fresh. I refused to be awkward today. We were friends. "So observant. What gave me away?" I moved some papers I had spread out on the couch so he could sit. "I didn't think you were coming today."

He slung his backpack onto the table. "We got zero

done last time, so I figured I could come help you power through the math."

"Thanks, dude," I said with a smirk.

"Ha. Still not loving that."

"Do you have a nickname? Donnie, maybe?"

"In grade school people called me that. But now, surprisingly, everyone says my entire three syllables all the time."

"It's a good name."

"I'm glad you approve."

"Sit your butt down already."

He sat down next to me. "How did everything go today? Did you ever find out who was talking about you?"

"No, but it's fine. Just on-set drama. Thanks for listening, by the way, and for . . . taking off my makeup." So much for not being awkward.

"No problem," he responded with perfect poise. He seemed perfectly normal to my weird and embarrassed.

Focus. I could be normal too. "I actually felt good in front of the camera the last two days."

"Good."

"Yes, all is right in the world."

"I'm not sure all *is* right in the world."

A jolt of panic went through me. "Why? Is everything okay?"

He cracked a smile and nodded toward my packet. "You actually started homework without someone forcing you to."

I let out a breath. "I know. I was just thinking earlier that you were rubbing off on me. The world must be ending."

He laughed. "Oh, Mrs. Case asked me to give you this test." He pulled some stapled pages from his bag. "She said you couldn't use the computer, but she didn't think that would be a problem, since she wasn't sure you knew how to anyway."

"Ah, Mrs. Case. Who knew she was a comedian."

"Comedian slash volleyball coach."

"So she is a volleyball coach? I thought she might be."

"My sister plays on the team."

"Nice. I don't know that I've ever actually watched a volleyball game."

"They're fun to watch."

"My sister does dance and my brother does T-ball. But they're both so young that most of the time it's just kids chasing each other around. It's also fun to watch, but in a different way, I'm assuming."

"Probably." He picked up my packet and looked over the few questions I'd done. "Looks like you don't need my help after all."

"No, I totally need your help," I said too fast.

Donavan looked up from the packet and was about to say something when my trailer door flew open and Grant stepped in. His eyes went back and forth between Donavan and me.

"Geez, Grant, you scared me. Don't you know how to knock?" I said.

"Knocking? What's that?" He gave me his schoolboy smile. "Do you really want me to knock? I can knock." He stepped out of the room, deliberately shut the door, and gave three slow knocks.

"Who is it?" I called.

He cracked open the door. "It's your biggest fan, here to have you sign my forehead."

"I didn't bring my Sharpie today. Maybe you can borrow one from your fan club outside. Tell them how awesome I am while you're at it."

He came into the room, and this time Amanda followed. I hadn't realized she was with him before.

"Hi," Amanda said. "Oh, hi, Donavan."

"Hey."

"We wanted to see if you wanted to hang out." She gave me the eyes that said now was the time for our plan.

"Oh, um . . ." My eyes went to Donavan, who was looking at his palms—his nervous habit, I was learning. "I'm doing homework. This is Donavan, my tutor. Donavan, this is Grant, and you already met Amanda."

Donavan nodded.

Grant turned his wide smile on Donavan. "Ah. The infamous tutor. Nice to meet you." *Dancing Graves* sat on the coffee table in front of Donavan, and Grant picked it up. "If you have a writing instrument, I can give you an autograph. I love my fans."

I held in a laugh at the irony of that statement. "That's my book, dork. And I don't want your autograph."

"Well, I want yours," Grant said.

I rolled my eyes because I knew he was trying to be funny.

"So you're busy, then?" Amanda asked, her mind apparently on only one thing.

"Just for a little while longer. I was thinking, Grant . . ." When Amanda and I had talked about me suggesting this, Donavan wasn't supposed to be present. I don't know why it made a difference, but it made me uncomfortable. I forced it out anyway. "Maybe we can practice our kissing scene after I'm done with home-work?" I knew Grant wouldn't find this suggestion odd. He'd understand why I was giving it. We had been told repeatedly we needed to work on our chemistry and that was without adding kissing to the mix.

Grant flipped the book in his hand and set it back down on the coffee table. "Sure thing."

"Amanda? Maybe you can give us feedback?" I said.

"Of course. We'll meet you in Grant's trailer in a little bit?" she said.

I nodded.

They headed for the door. "Nice to meet you, Jonathan," Grant said, then just like that his bigger-than-life presence was gone.

Amanda leaned back through the door. "Thank you," she mouthed, and pulled the door shut behind her.

Everything was perfectly still for three beats, then I said, "About that. It's just . . ."

Donavan reached forward and picked up the packet. "I'm just here to tutor. You don't have to explain anything to me."

"Okay." I was going to tell him I'd done that for Amanda, but, apparently, he didn't care. Which was good. I didn't need him to care. I didn't need anything from him except homework help.

"I can come back tomorrow if you need to go," he said.

"No, stay. I have a little time."

"Thanks for not outing me," he said, placing the packet in my hand.

"Why would I do that?"

"You were right," he said. "I didn't want to tell Grant who I was."

"He was acting overly confident anyway. He didn't

deserve to know who you are. Maybe he needed those bad reviews. People need to hear hard things sometimes to push them to be better."

"You think so?" he asked.

I met his eyes. "I think so."

Dancing Graves

EXT. FOREST SURROUNDING MANSION—NIGHT.
BENJAMIN clutches a vial of bright green
liquid, hoping it's finally the cure
they've all prayed for, and searches
desperately for SCARLETT. A noise in the
trees makes him whirl around. He sees
a zombie, but it's not her. The zombie
advances on him quickly. He pulls his
sword. The zombie is undeterred. After
a scuffle, Benjamin kills him. Scarlett
appears from the left, surprising
Benjamin. He turns and swings his sword
at her, narrowly missing. When he sees who
it is, he drops his sword to the ground
immediately and rushes toward her.

                    BENJAMIN
Scarlett! Did I hurt you?

SCARLETT

(eyes on the dead zombie)

What have you done?

BENJAMIN

Forgive me. I had no choice.

SCARLETT

Soon you will have no choice with me
either.

BENJAMIN

That's not true. I have the cure. Drink
this.

NINETEEN

I knocked on Grant's trailer door after Donavan left. Amanda answered, pushing it open farther for me and stepping back to let me in. "Hey."

Grant was sitting on his couch. "Is it time to make out?" he asked.

Amanda's hopeful face deflated a bit. Grant was so clueless.

"I've been studying your videos, Amanda. I need some serious advice."

"What videos?" Grant said. "Do you have kissing tutorials online?"

"She should," I responded. "But, no, I mean her actual scenes with fellow actors."

"Oh, cool," he said.

"Kissing on camera is different than just making out with a boyfriend," Amanda said. "Come here, Grant. Stand right here." She pointed to the spot right in front of me.

He stood, pulled down the leg on his sweatpants that had ridden up, and moved until he was in front of me.

"I'll keep this professional," he said.

I laughed. "Because sticking your tongue in someone else's mouth is very professional."

"You know what I mean," he said.

"Yes, I do."

"There will be very little tongue," Amanda said. She was so calm. Probably because she knew that in seconds she'd be standing where I was.

He took my hand in his and looked into my eyes. Then he paused and looked up. "What's my line right here? Before we kiss?"

"'I don't want to have to live without you,'" I said.

"I'm so passionate," he responded with a smile.

"I know. You're really invested in this."

"Money, huh? You think I'm doing it for the money?"

At first I thought he was talking about himself, and I said, "No, I never thought that, I didn't think you were getting as much as . . ." I realized quite suddenly that he was talking about Benjamin, his character, and what I'd said the other day on set about him being after my father's money. "I mean, yes, I do. You'd know that if you'd actually read the book."

"So you don't think I love you, then? Truly love you? True love requires sacrifice sometimes."

"I think maybe you're trying to make yourself believe that so you don't feel guilty. You are a kind-hearted man. But if my father doesn't come up with an actual cure, it will be hard for you to stomach my looks and not fall for my best friend. She's already helped you through a lot."

"Yes, I have," Amanda said. "Including this. Now say your line."

Despite what Donavan thought of Grant's acting, I was always amazed at how easily he could fall into character. Like now, he stopped the questions, held my gaze with soft eyes, and said, "I don't want to have to live without you."

"I don't want to make you live with what I will become," I said back.

He moved toward me ever so slowly, and just before his lips reached mine, I said, "Wait. This feels awkward."

"It does?" he asked.

"Amanda. Can you play me for a minute so I can watch?

Maybe if I see what you do, then I can replicate it."

Grant looked between the two of us, and for a second I thought he was going to call us out, say he knew what we were up to. But he didn't. He just released me and let Amanda step into my place.

"So remember the first tip I gave you the other day?" Amanda said. "To imagine Grant as someone you actually like."

"Hey," he said.

She patted his cheek. "Don't worry, babe, *I'm* imagining you." The way she said it made it sound like a joke, even though I knew it was true. "But maybe you can imagine that cute tutor of yours," Amanda said to me.

I smiled. She was relentless.

She shrugged. "It's obvious."

"What cute tutor?" Grant asked.

"The one we just saw," Amanda said.

"Really? I didn't think he was that good-looking."

"He's good-looking," I said.

Amanda raised her eyebrows at me as though I'd just proved her point.

"It means nothing," I said. "I was just stating a fact."

"Whatever. Imagine *someone* you're attracted to."

"Are you implying she's not attracted to me?" Grant held his hands out to the sides, putting himself on full display. "I'm good-looking too."

"Life lesson, Grant," I said. "Just because someone says another person is attractive doesn't mean they're saying you're not. And just because you're good-looking doesn't mean everyone is attracted to you."

"This is a great life lesson," Amanda said. "Now put your arms down." She put one hand on Grant's shoulder and the other she ran along his jawline. "Next, do something intimate before actually locking lips. Something that will clue the viewer into the fact that you are about to kiss so that they can prepare themselves. If you rush into a lip-lock, it can seem too sudden, which can lead to discomfort for the viewer. I'm not saying a kiss can't be fast or look desperate. But something, even if only a beat of something, needs to precede it—connecting eyes, a sip of a breath, a touch."

He wrapped one arm around her waist and pulled her up against his chest. "Just kissing has always worked for me."

"Then you haven't been kissed by an expert." She reached up and pushed his hair back, then she pressed her lips against his. And then they were kissing. I wasn't sure if both of them were still acting or if neither of them were. But what I saw was a very convincing kiss. Maybe Amanda was right, maybe it helped to know what it felt like to kiss someone you actually cared about. If I'd never done that, could I really convince an audience I was in love?

The kiss continued, and I now felt like I was intruding on a private moment. Was I supposed to leave now? Wouldn't that make it even more obvious that this was a setup? "Um . . . I thought you said there would be very little tongue."

They pulled away from each other, and Grant laughed. "Sorry," he said, though I wasn't sure to who.

"That was good," Amanda said, her breath quick and shallow.

"Should *we* try now?" he asked, holding out his hand to me.

That wasn't exactly how this was supposed to go. I wasn't sure how I imagined this playing out, but it wasn't with Grant James scoring a kiss from both of us in one sitting.

"Actually, I think I got it," I said. "That was really good info. Kissing for the first time on camera might give us an edge."

"But, Scarlett," Grant said, slipping into his accent. "I love you so deeply. I'm not after your father's money."

I plopped into a chair at his kitchen table.

Grant sat across from me, and I watched as he processed

something. "Wait. You thought I was talking about me a minute ago."

"What?" I was lost.

"When I asked if you thought I was doing this for money? You don't think I'm getting paid well?"

"I didn't think you were getting paid as well as you normally do."

"I'm getting paid enough," he said.

"But you're really doing this for a reputation boost," I said.

"Do you actually think this movie is going to help with that?" Amanda asked.

"People like horror. I've gotten out of touch with the average fan while playing Heath Hall and pumping out my multimillion-dollar movies. I'm trying to regain my core audience with an indie film. Plus, there is less running and shooting and more . . ."

"Eating brains?" I suggested.

"Cutting off heads?" Amanda offered.

He rolled his eyes. "There's more chances for me to show heart."

I held up a fake glass. "Here's to hoping it works."

Amanda joined me. "Here's to hoping you don't get any more bad reviews that go viral." Her tone was light, but it immediately altered the mood.

I cringed. "I don't think the review swayed anyone," I said. "They either felt that way on their own or they didn't." I felt a need to try to save Donavan from Grant and Amanda.

It didn't work. "You're kidding, right?" Grant said. "If that review didn't exist I'd be in a much better position now."

"You'll bounce back."

"I wouldn't have had to."

I sighed.

"So really," Grant said. "We should kiss."

"Not happening." I stood. "Amanda can be my stand-in tonight if you need more practice though." I made my way to the door.

"Bye, lover," Grant said.

Amanda walked me outside. "Thank you."

"How was it?" I asked.

"Amazing, and I'm going to go pretend he needs more work now." She winked at me. "See you tomorrow."

"You're not going to kill me when I have to kiss him tomorrow, right?"

"Of course not, because I'll make sure he's imagining me."

TWENTY

It was only eight, but I decided to head home. I was so used to staying at the studio as long as possible, but I hadn't talked to my dad since Donavan told me about the classified ad he'd almost taken out. I had been avoiding him, but we needed to talk.

Our apartment complex was quiet when I parked and walked through the courtyard to our front door. Rather than dig through my bag for the key, I knocked on the door. "Dad, it's me," I called, my mouth close to the line where the door met the frame. He didn't answer. Was he already asleep? It wasn't even nine o'clock.

I swung my bag off my shoulder and to the porch, where I squatted and dug through the contents in search of the keys. There were mints and pens and hair clips and old receipts, but no house keys. I searched a second and third time, only to come up empty. I didn't have them.

I took my cell phone out of my pocket and called my dad. He picked up on the third ring. "Hello?"

"Hey, I'm on the porch. Come rescue me."

"I would, but I'm not home. You'll have to use your key."

"You aren't? Where are you?"

"I'm at Anchor."

"The restaurant?" I paused for a moment. The *fancy* restaurant? "Wait. Are you on a date?"

"Perhaps. I'll see you later, okay?"

"But wait, I don't have my keys. I think I left them on my dresser. Yes, I'm replaying this morning step-by-step, and I see myself walking by my keys and out the door, which has led me to this terrifying moment of being stranded on the porch alone in a strange town in the dark."

"So dramatic, Lacey."

"Thank you."

I could hear the smile in his voice when he said, "It wasn't supposed to be a compliment."

"It's the very best compliment I can receive. So are

you going to save me? Bring your date so I can meet her."

"Do you see that potted plant by the front door?"

"Yes."

"On the back side, just below the soil, there is a key hidden in a fake rock."

I held my phone against my ear with my shoulder and rooted past leaves and soil until I found a rock that twisted open, dropping out a key. "You hid a key to our house right by our front door? It's like you're asking strangers to come and rob us or abduct me. You want me to get abducted?"

"I think you meant thank you. I'll see you later."

"Bye, Dad."

The phone line went dead.

I let myself in the front door and tugged my bag in behind me. I locked the door, then put the now-empty rock and key on the counter in the kitchen. The only light came from a small bulb above the stovetop. I flipped on a few more lights, then turned a full circle, which revealed nothing new in the apartment world.

I pursed my lips to the side, scratched my forehead, and slowly made my way back to my room.

Why had I left my homework in my trailer? I'd finished the math portion with Donavan earlier but that was it. I could've finished history or English right now because I wasn't tired at all. Maybe it was the nerves I was feeling about the kissing scene that was finally happening the next day. As funny as it was, I wished Amanda didn't like Grant, because I actually could've used the practice. I lay back on my bed and clicked on my constellation lamp. I stayed like that for several minutes before I pulled out my phone and sent off a text to Donavan.: **Can you send me a pic of my packet pages? I left them in my trailer.**

My phone rang five seconds later.

"Wow, you're so personable," I said when I answered. "A written response would've been fine."

"Sometimes typing it out takes twice as long as just saying it."

I remembered what Abby had said to me about how I called more than I texted. "I feel the same way."

"I don't have your packet. I just had the one that I gave to you, which I didn't think to document with pictures."

"Will you do that next time?" I teased. "For moments like this."

"Of course. I live to serve you," he teased back.

"I've long suspected that might be the case." I put my feet up on the wall beside my bed. "I've been told people give me anything I want."

"Whoever told you that should've kept it to themselves."

"He really should've, because now I'm impossible to deal with." I tapped my foot on the wall, knowing I should probably hang up but not ready to. "So . . . how's life?"

He chuckled a little. "Are you bored, Lacey?"

"Yes, tell me more about you. I know you have a younger sister. Any other siblings?"

"No, just me and her."

"And what do your parents do?"

"My mom is a nurse, and my dad is a camera operator."

"Like for movies?"

"For a news station right now."

"That's cool. I've always thought that would be a fun job."

"It's not as glamorous as it seems." Was that bitterness in his voice?

"You're right. Fun and glamour are two totally different things. Do you not get along with your dad?"

"Not usually."

That sounded like my life lately. "Why?"

"Has anyone ever told you that you're nosy?"

"Yes, actually. But then they answer me anyway."

"You really are impossible," he said.

"And yet . . ."

"My dad? You want to know about my dad."

"Yes."

"My dad is the type of person who says he's going to be there, show up for things, and only does about ten percent of the time." Considering how private Donavan was, I suspected that was hard for him to say.

"I'm sorry."

"I've long stopped expecting him to, but my sister still holds out hope, and that's what makes me angry."

"Is it because he's busy? I mean, what's his excuse?"

"Work. Always work. He's always trying to get ahead. He takes on all sorts of side projects—short films and indie features—thinking that one day some big production company is going to pick him up, but the odds of that happening are so low."

"It's easy to start thinking that something is going to launch a career. I mean that's what I'm doing: taking on this campy horror in hopes it will send me to the next level." The now familiar anxiety that accompanied that thought expanded in my chest.

"It's not the same," Donavan said. "You're seventeen. He's been running in circles at the expense of his family for decades."

"I'm sorry," I said again.

I should've hung up now, let him go to bed or do whatever it was that he was doing before he called. I sensed he didn't want to be on the phone with me talking about this. But I couldn't end our conversation on that note. "What are you doing?"

"What am I doing?" he asked.

"It was a pretty straightforward question."

"I'm talking to you."

"You know what I mean."

"Before this I was writing a review of *Sail in the Wind*."

"Oh yeah? Was it good?"

"It was actually." Two breaths went by, then he said, "What about you? What were you doing before this?"

"I was not getting abducted."

"That's a good thing."

"I know. I got locked out and my dad's on a date and he leaves keys lying around by the front door. I'm lucky to be alive."

"Does your dad go out a lot?"

I rolled over onto my stomach and propped my head up with one hand. "That's a good question. I didn't know he went out at all, so this is news to me."

"And you don't like his date?"

Had I sounded like I didn't like her? "I don't know who she is. So, yes, I probably hate her."

He laughed a little. "I suppose it's good that everyone starts on an even playing field with you. Even if it means you don't like anyone in the beginning."

"So true." That really was true. How had I not realized

that about myself until now? Probably because I was really good at faking it until said people eventually grew on me. But Donavan had obviously seen through that. I took a deep breath. "It's just I'm . . ." What was I? Was I upset about the date? I didn't think so. "I actually have the opposite problem as you in the dad department."

"How so?"

"My dad is always around, always there. And you'd think that would be a good thing, that I would feel supported, but it's actually the opposite. I don't think he's there to see me or hear me. I feel like he's there waiting for something to go wrong, waiting for my dreams to blow up in my face. And I'm sure he'll be there to support me then, but somehow he can't bring himself to actually support me now." I'd just said all that out loud to my tutor. Why? I was usually pretty open, but only because I didn't ever share anything important. I wanted to take it all back, I felt exposed. Like I'd let him see some of my insecurities. The one that said: I need my dad to be proud of me in order to feel accomplished. "Anyway," I said, when he didn't say anything. "Poor me, right? I get to star in a movie."

"You're allowed to feel upset."

"I'm not, I'm just annoyed more than anything. And I'm happy that my dad is on a date tonight. Maybe it will give him something else to focus on."

"Maybe," Donavan said.

"I better go. I'll let you know when I finish the rest of my packet."

"Okay."

"Bye," I said, and hung up quickly. I buried my face in my comforter. My face felt warm. Why did I care that I'd shared so much with him? We were friends. He told a story. I told a story. We were even. I was just tired. I needed a shower and sleep and then I'd feel normal again.

Dancing Graves

EXT. FOREST—NIGHT.

SCARLETT, who drank the formula but still seems to be deteriorating, stalks an unsuspecting TOWNSPERSON as he and his dog are following a trail through the woods home. Because she has maintained some of her human traits, she is smarter and more deadly than the other zombies, who only operate by instinct. She knows how to hide, sneak, reason, and predict reactions.

> TOWNSPERSON
>
> Did you hear something, Pepper? We better walk faster. It's not safe out here.

It's too late. SCARLETT has him cornered, and he doesn't even know it yet.

TWENTY-ONE

"Did you miss me?" Grant asked on set the next day. We still had one more day in the library before we moved on to the lab. And today, for the first time since we started filming, we were shooting my prezombie scenes, so for today, I was human.

"Since yesterday?" I asked.

"Yes."

"Surprisingly, very little."

He laughed like it was a joke.

"My mom's cat is named Pepper," I said.

"What?"

"I was just thinking of that scene where Scarlett kills her first human. The scene we're filming at the end of the week in the mountains. The dog's name is Pepper. I just remembered that. It's crazy that her cat is named Pepper too. It's a rescue cat and came with that name." I was rambling because I was nervous, I realized. Today was the day. Today I had to (got to?) kiss Grant James.

"So crazy."

"You don't think it's crazy." I glanced over at him and realized he was right next to me.

"You know," Grant said. "If you were a human all the time on set, chemistry would be no problem whatsoever." He rested his hands on my shoulders.

I pushed against his chest and rolled my eyes. "And if you were this shallow all the time, you'd have to fight off the girls with a stick," I said drily.

"Already do." He leaned close. "Get ready to have your world changed forever." He said it like he was kidding, but I got the sneaking suspicion that he really believed it.

Remy was going over blocking with the camera operator. Half the time on set was waiting around for something to happen, the other half was repeating the same scenes over and over while the camera shot different angles. It was nothing like theater, where there was only one chance to pull off a perfect performance.

"So hey," I said, changing the subject because,

seriously, Grant really wasn't helping me at all in the pretending-to-be-in-love-with-him department. "What did you and Amanda do after I left yesterday?"

"Not much. She thought I needed kissing tips. You'll have to tell me today if I do."

If I rolled my eyes anymore they might roll onto the floor.

Remy stepped over to the desk behind us. "Did someone mess with the hot set?" The art director scurried forward and rearranged a few items on the desk.

"This has to look exactly the same every time for continuity," Remy announced.

"We're missing the ink and quill," the art director said.

Oh crap. "Sorry, I borrowed it. I'll go get it."

I didn't wait to see Remy's reaction to that statement, just left quickly. I got to my trailer, found the items, and then leaned against the counter by a mirror on the wall. "Okay, Lacey, you can do this. You may not like Grant James romantically, but Scarlett loves Benjamin. You are Scarlett." My stomach churned uncomfortably when I realized that wasn't going to work. "How about this, then?" I said to my mirror self. "Pretend he's Donavan."

A small smile touched my lips, and I watched as color came into my cheeks. "Are you happy, self? You finally admitted it. Amanda was right. You like Donavan. Too bad there's nothing you can do about it." Aside from my self-imposed ban on boys, Donavan didn't date actresses. It was just my luck that the first guy I ever liked wasn't interested.

Back on set, I gave the ink and quill to the obviously irritated art director.

"Sorry," I said.

She didn't respond but took them to the desk, where she placed them carefully onto their spot.

"You're in trouble," Grant whispered.

"I know. I should've told them that you were the one who gave them to me. Nobody gets mad at Grant James."

"This is true."

Remy stepped out of the library and behind the monitor. "You two ready?"

I nodded.

Grant said, "So ready."

This was the scene that took place two days after I was bitten and it was obvious I was slowly turning, just like the others Scarlett's father had tried the cure on. I closed my eyes and put myself in that situation. How would I feel if I knew that unless my father produced a miracle, I was going to slowly forget the person I liked? How would I feel if I never got to see Donavan again? A surprising weight of sadness settled on my chest. I hung on to that feeling.

"Quiet on set," Noah called. "Slate in, sound rolling, camera rolling."

"Scene nine, take one."

"And action," Remy called.

"Come here," Grant said. He took my hand. "Everything is going to be okay."

I pulled my hand away and turned my back to him. "It's not. It will never be okay again. I should leave, me staying here, you watching this, will only make it harder."

Grant wrapped his arms around me from behind and put his face in the place where my shoulder met my neck. "I don't want to have to live without you."

"I don't want to make you live with what I will become."

He put his hands on my hips and turned me to face him. My arms were trapped between his chest and mine. I let my eyes flutter closed so I could imagine Donavan there, his brown eyes, his lips about to meet mine. His lips on mine. My breath caught and I rose slightly on my toes, pushing my lips more firmly against his. His hands traveled to my back, steadying me. My hands inched up his chest and then gently followed the line of his collarbones.

"And cut!" Remy yelled, startling me. My eyes flew

open and our lips separated, but Grant kept hold of me.

He leaned his forehead against mine and whispered, "Wow."

"That was perfect," Remy said. "Let's reset for a wide shot."

Eighteen times. Between the establishing shot and the mid-shot and the close-ups from each side, that's how many times I had to kiss Grant James. And as nice and "perfect" as that first kiss had been, we had to replicate it eighteen times. Eighteen.

I walked off set opening and closing my mouth to stretch it out.

"Lacey," Grant called, catching up with me. "Guess we didn't need practice after all. We're kind of naturals at that."

Was he fishing for a compliment?

"Yeah, it went well." A smile played on my face. It went well because of Donavan.

He continued to follow me. Where was Amanda? I thought she'd have been watching the kissing scene but I hadn't seen her anywhere.

"Don't you have a scene with Lord Lucas right now?" I asked. I was done for a couple of hours.

"After lunch."

"Okay. Well, I'll see you later. I have some home-work I need to finish." In my completely hopeful and very optimistic heart, Donavan would be waiting in my trailer. He would've read my mind, realized I liked him, ditched school, and come to see me. Then I would . . . I would what? Tell him I liked him but couldn't date him because I was in the middle of making my dreams come true? Ask him if he'd wait a couple of years for that to happen?

Even if I found a way to make this work . . . some-how . . . I knew Donavan. Not only would he not ditch school and be in my trailer, but he would also never date me. He had a future career to think about too.

I went to my very empty trailer.

My phone was sitting on the table where I left it dur-ing filming. I picked it up to see if Donavan had texted. It went straight to the home screen without making me enter my passcode. Which meant it had been on recently. I checked my morning alarm. It was set for 6:00 a.m. like always. I checked my calendar. It didn't look like anything was missing. I clicked off my screen, then clicked it on again. The prompt for a passcode came up. I entered it and was admitted to the home screen. My head snapped up, and I looked around my small trailer. I went still, listening. I couldn't hear anything. I walked slowly to the bathroom and checked the shower. Nobody was there. I shook out my hands. Who did I think would be here? A zombie hunter?

I laughed a little, then exited the trailer and walked down the row to knock on Amanda's door. I stood there for several minutes. There was no answer. I moved to walk away, when I heard Amanda call out from behind me, "Are you looking for me?"

"Where were you today?" I asked as she let us both into her trailer. "I thought you'd want to be there for the big kiss."

"You really thought I'd want to be there for that?"

"No. I don't know." I sat on her couch and leaned my head back against the cushions.

"Grant and I had our own really good kissing session yesterday. I didn't want a new image in my head. How did it go?"

"Good, actually." I sat up.

Her eyes went down to the floor.

"Because I did that thing you told me to."

"What thing?" she asked.

"I imagined someone I really liked."

"Oh yeah?" A slow smirk came onto her face. "Who?"

"You know who," I said grudgingly.

"Tutor boy?"

I smiled. "I don't think he'd like that nickname."

"So you finally realized you like him."

"Yeeees," I groaned.

"Why is this a bad thing?"

"Because I need to stay focused. I have a career to develop."

"And kissing a boy you like is going to somehow ruin this?"

"It's the *liking* part I'm worried about. That's just going to distract me, get in my head. I've never really had the need to like anyone before. Freshman year, I was kissing Hayden in *Guys and Dolls*. He was a great kisser. Need satisfied. Sophomore year it was Ryan in *The King and I*. Junior year there was Brady in *Some Like It Hot*."

"Okay, I get it. So what you're saying is that your pattern of kissing costars has gotten you to where you are and you're worried to disrupt the pattern?"

"Something like that."

"So it needs to be: senior year, kissing Grant James in *Dancing Graves*? Need satisfied?"

"That sounds pathetic."

"It does," she agreed. "And I just realized something."

"What?"

"You've never really been kissed. That's so sad."

"Yes, I have, I just told you about all of them."

"You just told me your only kisses have been scripted. Lacey, you have no idea how much different it is off script. You need a real kiss. Your first real kiss. Seriously, it's so much better. You will never want to stop."

"You do realize you're not helping. That's exactly what I'm worried about. That this will completely derail me. Do you know my mom quit college for my dad? They had to move for his grad school, and she didn't want to be left behind. And she never finished."

"And she regrets this every day of her life?"

"They got divorced. She quit something important for a love that failed. I'm sure she regrets it."

Amanda put her hand on my arm. "You can't think of love like that. You have to think about everything you gain while it lasts. I'm not saying to quit acting. I'm just saying, you think it will dilute your abilities, distract you. What I'm telling you is having those feelings that come with a relationship—love, anger, heartache, longing—will only heighten your abilities. I promise."

I opened my mouth to disagree with her when I realized that I had already proved her right. Just today on set, I had imagined Donavan and how I felt about him, and it had made for the best scene ever. "He doesn't like me back though," is what I ended up saying.

"I doubt that."

"He doesn't date actresses."

"What? Why?"

"He reviews movies and wants to be able to stay objective."

"Oh, please. That's a ridiculous excuse. One you can easily talk your way past, especially because he likes you. He wants to be talked into this. Believe me. You have to convince him that actresses are just like everyone else. So? Will you give this a chance?"

"Maybe . . ." I wanted to scream yes but had at least a little bit of self-control left.

She stood with determination. "Then let's go talk him into it. Where is he right now?"

A nervous volcano erupted in my stomach as she headed to the door without waiting for an answer.

TWENTY-TWO

"Do you two really think I can go out somewhere in this town without causing a scene?" Grant stood at his open trailer door, where Amanda was trying to convince him to come with us to the restaurant where Donavan worked.

"He's right. His fan club will find him," I said. I was nervous enough showing up to Donavan's restaurant *without* Grant in tow, but Amanda had insisted that it would look more casual if all of us went together, just some coworkers out for a quick bite to eat.

Amanda wasn't taking no for an answer. "What about

Lacey's car, a small restaurant, a waiter we know, and a hat and sunglasses?"

"That sounded like you just solved the murder in a game of Clue," I said.

Grant stretched. "Why not?" He must not have really cared about causing a scene, because I didn't think this plan would actually work. But I didn't care if people recognized Grant. My whole body was terrified with the thought of seeing Donavan, with the plan of telling him how I felt.

"I thought you had the sunglasses and hat," Grant said when we pulled up outside the restaurant. He was in the back seat, where he had been lying down almost the entire time.

"I was just making a suggestion. I thought you'd bring them." Amanda pointed to the seat next to him. "Put on Lacey's hoodie."

"And I have some sunglasses," I said, picking them up from the center console.

"Nice," he said, putting them both on. My hoodie was too small on him, and the sleeves rode up his arms. I sucked in my lips to keep from laughing. Amanda and I walked on either side of him up the sidewalk to the restaurant.

My phone buzzed in my pocket, and I ignored it at

first. Then it buzzed three more times. I pulled it out to see a string of notifications down the screen. Amanda reached for the door of the restaurant, but I stopped.

"What is it?" she asked.

"Some article. I've been tagged in some online article, I guess."

"Let's read it inside."

I nodded and followed her and Grant in. It was a Saturday but still pretty early, so it wasn't too busy. Plus it was a pretty small restaurant.

Amanda approached the hostess station. "Can we be seated in Donavan's section?"

The girl nodded. "He's the only one waiting right now."

"Great."

He was here. We were here. This was happening.

"Follow me, please." She led us to a corner booth in the back of the restaurant. The lighting was dim, and a candle sat on the middle of the table. "Can I get you anything to drink?" she asked.

"Diet whatever," Amanda said.

"Just water for me," I said.

"Do you have carne asada fries here?" Grant asked.

"First of all," Amanda said, "she's getting our drinks. Second of all, pretty sure this is an Italian restaurant."

"It is," the girl said.

Grant still hadn't taken off the sunglasses or hoodie. "I'll take water, too."

She left, and Grant said, "I thought you said we'd know the waiter."

Before I could answer, Donavan walked up with a small pad of paper and a pencil. Amanda hummed a happy hum next to me. It was the first time I'd seen Donavan since admitting to myself that I liked him, and my heart tried to escape my chest. He looked so proper in his tightly buttoned shirt and black pants, and he was so cute. When he saw me, his eyes went wide. I couldn't decide if that was a good thing or a bad thing.

"You should never tell a girl where you work," I said, offering him my best smile.

He returned it, which made my heart beat even faster, and then he seemed to notice Grant and Amanda. "Hi. Um . . . welcome. Did Ash already take your drink orders?"

"She did."

"Have you had a chance to look at the menu?"

"No, we'll need some time," Grant said, taking off his sunglasses. Apparently he recognized Donavan or realized we were basically the only people in the restaurant. We'd passed one other couple, but they were across the room. "What's good here?"

Donavan opened the menu in front of me and pointed

to a few dishes. "These are the most popular."

Ash returned with the drinks, and Donavan helped her pass them out.

"I'll give you a couple of minutes," he said, then left.

My phone buzzed again, reminding me that something was happening online. I brought my phone back out and clicked on one of the links. It directed me to a big entertainment site. Dread took over my chest. The title of the article read: "Zombies Are Chewing Up Grant James's Career." My eyes skimmed past the title to the words written beneath. *Reports out of filming for Grant James's latest movie say that it is off to a rocky start. While most leading ladies would risk being infected by zombies to have a chance to act opposite Hollywood's hottest hunter, Lacey Barnes, a no-name actress, has reportedly said she is having trouble connecting to Grant. That might not be Grant's fault though. An undisclosed source says she's a mess on set: misplacing items, knocking over set pieces, and showing up late. Perhaps she's too green to star alongside a well-seasoned actor like Grant James. Time will tell.*

Amanda was saying something beside me, and I looked over, my eyes stinging.

She took my phone from me and read through the article. "What the . . . ?"

"What's going on?" Grant asked.

Amanda passed the phone to him and turned to me.

"It's just talk," she said, but I could tell that this time even she didn't believe that.

I shook my head. "Someone called and reported that. Someone who's obviously been on set and knows what's been going on. Who would do that?"

"You think someone is purposely messing with you?" Amanda asked.

Grant handed me back my phone. "It would be a pretty poor attempt."

"You think?" I asked.

"It's just a stupid article," he said.

"But it's not just an article, is it?" I said, realization coming to me. "Someone has been trying to sabotage me on set too. Knocking over lights, ripping my wardrobe, stealing things." I paused. "Someone was on my phone too. I think they changed my alarm that day I was late."

"Who would do that?" Amanda asked.

"I have no idea."

Grant didn't seem to think this was a big deal. "Even if any of that was purposeful, what would be the point? You're overthinking this."

It was hard not to worry about it. Just because I finally realized what was going on didn't mean that the sabotage—if that's what it was—would stop. I held up my phone. "Will you call them for me, Grant? Tell them we have all sorts of chemistry? Maybe they'll write another article about it."

"I think we should just let it die. If I call, it will just draw attention to it."

"Grant," Amanda said.

"It's true," he said defensively.

Donavan came back to the table, a notepad in hand. "You ready to order?"

"Yes," Grant said, like nothing at all had just happened.

He put in his order, followed by Amanda. I managed to swallow down my feelings over the article and point.

"You want the sampler?" Donavan asked. "It's three different entrees. It's pretty big."

"Oh, then whatever is good."

He slowly nodded, wrote something down, and walked away.

Grant said, "That's your tutor, right?"

"Yes," Amanda said. "And her future boyfriend."

"Shh," I hissed. I watched Donavan stop at the other table and talk to them for a moment, then I said, "I'll be right back."

"You going after him?" Amanda asked with a smile.

I didn't answer, just slid out of the booth and walked down a long hall where I saw Donavan disappear through a set of double doors. When I reached them, I pushed my way through as well, finding myself in the kitchen.

Donavan picked up a plate of salad off a metal counter, then turned around. He jolted to a halt when he saw me.

"Hi," I said. "Is this okay?"

He looked at a guy who stood behind the stove, stirring a big pot of sauce. "Is what okay?"

"Us being here."

"Customers aren't typically allowed in the kitchen."

I smiled at the cook, who gave me a nod.

Donavan smirked. "Of course the rules wouldn't apply to you."

"I meant us being at your restaurant."

"Yes, it's fine, Lacey." He held up the salad in his hand. "But I do have to work."

He started to brush by me when I said, "Wait."

He stopped, inches from me. Now was the time where I told him the realization I had today about him, but my crushed spirit was making everything feel all wrong.

I caught my breath and tried to concentrate. I met his eyes, thinking that would help, but his seemed guarded, and I found myself saying, "There was an article written about me today. It talked about all these things that have been happening on set. Things nobody off set would know about."

He seemed to calculate what that meant, just like I had. "You think the person who was talking to your director the other day tipped off a reporter?"

"You tell me," I said. He was a journalist, after all. He had to know something about tips and sources.

"I'd guess yes."

I quickly filled him in on the other things that the article had said. "Do you think it's all related?"

"One too many accidents begin to look a lot like evidence," he said. He wasn't acting like this was all in my head, like Grant and Amanda had.

"Will you help me try to figure out who's doing this?" Because whether it was a case of absentminded crew members or someone with ill intent, I didn't want to be caught off guard if someone really was trying to sabotage me for some reason.

"Absolutely," he said, then left the kitchen in a hurry.

When the door swung shut behind him I whispered, "And I really like you."

TWENTY-THREE

"Lacey," a voice called from behind me as we were walking out of the restaurant. I turned to see Donavan, so I slowed down to wait.

"Thanks for being our waiter tonight," I said. "You were awesome."

He had three twenties in his hand and held them out to me. "Tell Grant that a hundred-dollar tip is excessive."

I hadn't realized Grant left that much. "Just take it. Grant can afford it."

"It feels weird."

Grant must've overheard what we were talking about,

because he joined us, putting one arm around my shoulder. "I don't need people calling me cheap online."

"I wouldn't do that," Donavan said.

"Well, maybe now you can brag about how three actors sat at your table tonight and tipped you well."

"I wouldn't do that either," Donavan said.

"Why not?" Grant pulled me close. "You know who this is, right? It's Lacey Barnes. She's going to be really big one day. If you post about it now, you can say you knew her back when. Do you want a selfie? We'll take one with you."

"Grant, stop," I said.

"Seriously," Amanda said, taking Grant by the arm and trying to pull him away.

Donavan took my hand and put the sixty dollars in it. "I'll see you later." With that, he turned around and left.

"You're kind of a punk," I told Grant.

"A really handsome one." He put his other arm around Amanda and led us toward the door. "Come on, let's go."

I looked over my shoulder to where Donavan was helping another table. Now wasn't the time to talk to him.

"That did not help your 'actresses are just people' argument at all," Amanda said.

"I just screwed that all up," I said.

"Don't worry. You can make it better," Amanda said.

"Maybe I don't deserve to. You know what I did in the kitchen when I chased after him? I panicked about my career. Instead of needing to tell him how I felt, I asked for his help. It's obvious that I will always put my career first; he doesn't need someone else like that in his life."

Amanda squeezed my hand. "It's just a habit. Bad habits are meant to be exchanged for good ones."

"Donavan is a good habit?"

"I'm sure he can be," Amanda said.

"Are you guys ready to make a run for the car?" Grant said. "It looks like your friend called the press."

I saw a person with a camera waiting across the street.

"Donavan didn't do that," I said.

Grant didn't look like he believed me. He just put the sunglasses back on. "Keep your head down."

At home my dad was sitting watching television. It felt like I hadn't seen him in forever. He turned off the TV but didn't stand. I sat next to him. I was tempted to tell him about the article but I knew how he'd react and I didn't need that tonight. Plus, there was still something I needed to get off my chest.

Instead of jumping right into my complaints though, I started with "How was your date the other night? I didn't know you were dating anyone."

"I'm not, really. Just someone I met . . ." He trailed off like he didn't want to finish that sentence.

"I assumed it was someone you had met."

He didn't smile like I expected him to, just patted the arm of the couch. "I met her on set."

"On set?" At first the words didn't make sense to me out of context like that. "Wait, do you mean on *my* set?"

"Yes."

"Who?"

"Leah."

"The makeup artist? *That* Leah?"

He nodded. "Does that bother you?"

I thought about it. I already had enough drama on set, I didn't need my dad creating more complications. "I don't know, Dad. Sort of. It sort of bothered me when I heard you were going to put an ad in my school newspaper for a tutor too."

"Donavan told you?"

"I wish you would have told me."

"I'm sorry, but I had run out of options. I'd called all the students from the tutoring list. I'd gone to a tutoring center, but they didn't have anyone willing to travel, not for the amount of money I could pay. It was my Hail Mary."

I laid my head back on the couch, feeling more tired than I realized. "I wish you would've just listened to me and let me do the work on my own." I didn't really wish that, because then I wouldn't have met Donavan. But right now, it's what I felt.

"I'm sorry, but, Lacey, you weren't doing the work on your own. Let's not rewrite history here."

"You're right."

He coughed a little as though surprised.

"I know. I don't say that very much. It's not my fault you're rarely right."

He laughed, and I smiled. Then we both sat there in silence until he said, "So you want me to stop seeing Leah?"

"You like her?"

"I do."

It would be so selfish of me not to let my dad have a relationship because it was someone I worked with. I was seventeen. Almost grown up. My dad needed a life even if it might make things even more complicated at work. "I like her too. She's always been nice to me. You should see where it leads."

My dad ran a hand over my hair. "Thanks, I was hoping you'd say that."

I stood up. "Just no more surprises."

He held his right arm up as though making a vow. "No more surprises."

I walked back toward my room. I hadn't even come

close to saying everything to my dad that I'd wanted to, everything I'd realized I felt when I was talking on the phone to Donavan the other night. But I was tired, and he seemed happy, and it was hard.

Dancing Graves

EXT. CAVE ENTRANCE—NIGHT
SCARLETT, getting worse each day, carries
a bag of supplies toward the cave where
she has gathered the zombies. The first
sign of trouble is bloody footprints in
the dirt leading away from the cave. She
drops her armful of things and goes to
investigate. Nobody is left. All she finds
is carnage. There was only one person who
knew about this location. He had betrayed
her.

                    SCARLETT
                  (whispers)
Benjamin.

All the rage she'd been suppressing lights
a fire in her chest. She is unleashed.

TWENTY-FOUR

arrived at makeup early the next day and wondered if it would be weird to see Leah. Had my dad told her that he told me? I didn't have a chance to analyze what was or wasn't said because Leah was frantic when I reached her station. She was picking up things on the table and moving them a couple of inches only to pick them up again. She moved to the couch in the room and started looking under the cushions. When she saw me she let out a big sigh. "Please tell me you have it."

"Have what?" I couldn't help but stare at Leah with my new knowledge that she was dating my dad. I had

256

never noticed before how edgy she was, or at least never thought about it. Way edgier than my dad. She had several tattoos down her arms, a nose ring, and cute choppy purple hair.

"Your premade cheek section," she said, bringing me back to the moment.

"Why would I have that? You always take it."

She cursed under her breath, then went back to the couch cushions.

"Is it missing?"

"Yes."

Crap. Crap, crap, crap! So I wasn't being paranoid at all. Someone was messing with things on set. Did this have to do with the conversation I'd heard in the hall? Did someone not want me here? Was someone trying to make me look bad? But this newest sabotage would be more of a reflection on Leah than me. Maybe the person didn't realize that I wasn't in charge of that zombie piece.

I immediately started helping Leah look. I began at one end of the room and thoroughly inspected everything. It wasn't until I was to the other end of the room that I said, "I'll be right back. I'm going to check a few places."

"Do you have any ideas?"

"Maybe."

She shooed her hand in my direction. "Go. Hurry."

The only place I could think to look was where I'd found my kneepads. Maybe the thief had put the zombie cheek in the same place. But when I got to the dark set and opened every single desk drawer, it wasn't there.

It was early, but I decided to head to the row of trailers anyway. Grant's security guards let me through, and soon I was pounding on Grant's door. He answered, pulling a shirt on, then running a hand through his hair.

"What is it? Did you want to practice our kissing scene again? Just let me brush my teeth."

"Have you seen my zombie face?" I pointed to my cheek.

"Yeah."

I took a breath of relief. "You have?"

"Of course. I see it all the time."

"No, I mean off my face."

He shook his head. "No. Why?"

"It's missing."

"That's weird."

"You still think it's nothing?" I asked. "That someone is not purposely messing with things?"

"I think there are a lot of hands moving things around and yes, things happen. Accidents."

"Whatever. I'll see you later." I ran toward Amanda's trailer and pounded on her door.

She opened it. "Where's the fire?"

"Did you take my zombie face?" Maybe she'd been pranking me like she had that day in the shower.

"What? No."

"That's too bad."

"You wished I had?"

"Yes, actually. Then I'd have it now. It's been taken."

"By who?"

"I don't know."

"I'll come help you look for it. It probably just got misplaced." She stepped out in what she was wearing—shorts and a tank top without shoes. It was pretty similar to my outfit, except I wore flip-flops. We rushed back to makeup together.

"Tell me you found it," Leah said when we arrived.

"No, we didn't."

She released a slow breath. "I guess I need to go tell Remy the bad news."

She left, and Amanda and I looked at each other, then began searching the room again.

"What will happen if we can't find it?" I asked.

"They'll have to make another one, which could take a day or two. Did you finish all your human scenes yesterday?"

"The ones that take place here in the studio."

"Then I guess you get an unexpected day or two off. Yay?"

I closed my eyes. I was thinking this would be worse for Leah than me, but had this been the end game—to make sure I wasn't on set for a couple of days?

"It will be okay," Amanda said.

"I'm going to go look in my trailer," I said. "Maybe someone stashed it there to frame me."

"I'll come with you."

We searched the trailer for quite some time. "Do you honestly think this is just a series of accidents?" I asked.

"I don't know. I've seen enough weird things on set to think that maybe it is."

"But that article wasn't an accident."

"That's true."

There was a knock on the door. "Come in," I said.

Noah poked his head in and said, "Remy's called a meeting you both need to be at."

"When?" Amanda asked.

"Now," he said, and shut the door.

"Well, let's go face the music," Amanda said.

I stayed where I was on the floor by my wardrobe. Amanda walked over and held her hand out for me. "Are you seriously worried?"

"Yes. I don't know why someone would do this."

"I think this will all blow over."

I took her hand and let her help me to my feet. "I hope you're right."

Remy was beyond angry as we joined the rest of the cast and crew in the studio. He was pacing the floor, and if this were a movie, I would imagine the director would add steam coming off his head.

"Where is Grant?" I whispered.

"He's the big star. They probably won't make him come out here for this," Amanda answered.

I didn't respond because Remy started. "The big section that Lacey wears on her cheek while playing the zombie is missing. This is obviously unacceptable. Has anyone seen it?"

An eruption of chatter followed, people obviously surprised by the announcement. I looked around to see if there was anyone who didn't look surprised. Noah, who stood off to the side alone was the only one. But that's probably because he found out when Remy did, when Leah told him. Where was Leah, anyway?

"Lacey obviously can't film today, so we'll be changing up the call sheet to some scenes without her. Check your emails in thirty minutes to see if those scenes involve you. You may go."

People scattered as though they were grateful they didn't get sprayed with fire.

"I better go to makeup," Amanda said, "because I'm sure those scenes will involve me."

"Yes, go. I guess I'm going home." I turned to go

collect my things from my trailer when Remy stopped me with, "Lacey. A word."

I swallowed hard and joined him by a large light. I noted the sandbags on its base that kept it from falling over.

"Are you sure you have no idea as to what might have happened to it?"

"I'm positive. Leah usually takes it."

"Leah has been let go."

"What?" I asked in shock.

"Her assistant, Simone, will be taking over the rest of filming. Luckily we have the original mold, we should be able to get a rush on it and have a new one in hand by tomorrow. Keep your eye on your inbox." With that, he left.

In my trailer I put on some actual clothes for the day and sat on the couch. Leah was fired. The woman my dad was dating. I wasn't sure how he would react, but I wasn't going to find out over the phone. As much as I didn't want to, I headed home.

TWENTY-FIVE

What was my dad going to say when he found out the woman he liked was fired because of me? Well, maybe not exactly because of me, but it felt like it.

The sun was bright as I pulled up to the apartment building. The paint on the outside was a fading yellow, and the stucco had long cracks extending all the way to the eaves. I'd never noticed that before. I usually came home after dark.

I unlocked and opened the door with a creak. "Hello!" I called out because I wasn't sure who was here.

"Lace?" My dad stood in the small kitchen, a pan of

scrambled eggs on the stove. "You're home really early."

"I am."

He pulled another plate from the cupboard and spooned some eggs onto it. He set it down at the bar for me.

"Thanks." I plopped onto a barstool. His laptop was open on the counter, and just as I was about to ask him if Leah had told him what happened, I saw what he was reading—the online article about me.

"Were you ever going to tell me about that?" he asked.

"About what? Some online gossip?" Like I needed my dad to find out someone on set might be targeting me. I wasn't sure what he'd do if he knew, but I was sure it would involve talking to Remy. And considering Remy just fired Leah, I didn't need any more attention on me.

"If it's not true, then I'm going to call them and demand that they print a retraction."

"Dad, my name is already all over the internet. My picture too. You can't run around demanding people take down something that I'm purposely putting there."

He jammed his finger at the screen of his computer. "You purposely put this out there?"

"Not that specifically, but myself. I'm going to be famous one day, and there's nothing you can do to stop that." I was standing now.

"Until you're eighteen, I can try my hardest."

"Why don't you just support me?" If he supported me, I could tell him that the article really did hurt me. That I hated reading that stuff about myself. If he had made it easy to talk to him, I could ask for his advice.

"Because you're too young, odds are all this attention is going to change you. And not for the better."

"And if I was older, I'd be fine?" I asked, anger tightening my throat.

"Yes, actually. If you were older, you would be more grounded in who you are."

"It's nice that my own father has no faith in me!"

"It not that; Leah has told me all sorts of stories about—"

"About me?" I asked.

"No, but about other young stars."

"Well, then I guess it's a good thing she won't be around to spy on me anymore. She got fired today!" I spit out the words and immediately wanted to take them back, deliver that differently, because I could tell it was the first time he was hearing this. She hadn't told him yet. But I couldn't, and no matter how I'd delivered it, he needed to know. That announcement stunned my dad silent, and I took the opportunity to flee to my bedroom.

I lay on my bed staring at the empty text box on my phone. For the last hour I'd been trying to compose a text to Donavan. I had typed and erased several variations of: *Sorry about showing up at your work last night with a narcissist actor, a demanding one, and a clueless one. You figure out which one was which. We're actually probably interchangeable.* But I couldn't send it. I always did better face-to-face. Except with him, it seemed. With him I'd been a mess from day one. So maybe I needed to just let him go. I didn't want to, because it felt like I needed his help now more than ever. Yes, we were definitely interchangeable. Or maybe I was all three qualities by myself.

I sighed, put my phone on the nightstand, and pulled the blankets over my head.

Amanda crushed me into a hug the next morning as I was exiting my trailer, heading toward makeup. "I missed you yesterday."

"How was yesterday? Did anyone seem super happy that I was gone?"

"Not that I saw, and I was looking."

"I need to get to makeup with . . . Quick, remind me what the makeup person's name is. I feel bad; I should remember." What I really felt bad about was that Leah was fired. And about the fight I'd had with my dad the day before. Not just how I delivered the news but about everything he'd said leading up to that.

"Her name is Simone."

"Simone. That's right."

"I still don't believe Leah was fired," Amanda said.

"Me neither."

"Although maybe I should've expected it with her history with Remy."

"She has a history with Remy?" I asked, surprised. "As in . . ."

"Yes, they used to date." Amanda looked over my shoulder. "I have to run. I'm happy you're back." She gave me another hug, then took off quick.

Leah had a history with Remy and now my dad was dating her . . . could that be some sort of clue?

TWENTY-SIX

"Lacey Barnes," Grant said as he joined me in the room representing Scarlett's bedroom. I was sitting on the edge of the bed, and he sat down beside me.

"Grant James."

"You look like you've been through death."

"Haven't you heard? I'm a zombie," I said.

He smiled. Grant was charming, I had to admit. But I also had to admit that he was a suspect on the list I had started in my head of people who might want me gone. He was trying to redeem himself, and like the article stated, I wasn't up to that task. Was it possible that whoever was sabotaging me was trying to get me fired like Leah?

"Why are you looking at me like that?" he asked.

"Like what?"

"Like you want to eat my brains."

"Just getting into character."

The lights were bright on set, we were filming a day-time scene, but I looked out over the crowd in the studio who were regulars. They all moved through and around props and lights and monitors like an ant colony, hard at work. Remy was talking to the camera operator as he often did before takes. My eyes caught on one of the bod-ies that wasn't moving. He wore flip-flops and long shorts, his gray hair was slicked back, and he was on the phone.

"Your agent is here again."

Grant lifted his hand to block some of the light and squinted. "Oh yeah." He waved, and his agent waved back.

"Why is he here again?"

"He likes me. Plus, I'm his biggest client. He wants to make sure things are going smoothly."

"And does he feel like they are?"

"Yes, Lacey. Speaking of random people hanging around the set," Grant said. "Isn't that your tutor guy?"

My heart leaped into my throat, and I immediately scanned the studio. Sure enough, Donavan was toward the back, some sort of notebook in his hand, talking to someone.

"What's he doing?" Grant asked.

"Not sure," I said. What *was* he doing? "Maybe he wants to be an actor when he grows up and is taking notes."

Grant nodded a little. Then said like he was presenting a huge gift, "Tell him that if he wants, he can interview me."

"I'll let him know. I'm sure he'll be very grateful."

Grant smiled. "You're welcome."

Even though I knew he'd been at the studio today, I was still surprised at how happy I was to see Donavan sitting in my trailer when I walked in. "I wasn't sure if you were coming today," I said, walking to the mirror and immediately getting to work removing my makeup.

"I thought I could help."

"With what?"

"With trying to figure out who's behind all the sabotage."

A feeling of gratitude warmed my chest. He was the first person who wasn't trying to downplay my feelings. "Thank you." I cleared my throat and nodded toward his notebook. "So what did you learn?"

"Did you know that Simone, your new makeup

person, is married to Noah?"

"The assistant director?"

"Yes."

"I didn't. So what does that mean in all this?"

"I don't know. I'm just making notes on people. We'll figure out motives later."

I was so happy he was helping me that I couldn't hide the smile that had taken over my face. "Okay." I dropped the last piece of latex onto the counter, grabbed a makeup wipe, and joined him on the couch. "Speaking of makeup people, my old one, Leah, had something going on with my director, Remy."

He scribbled that down in his book.

And I added quietly, "And now she's dating my dad."

"She is?"

I nodded.

"Does that bother you?"

"A little, but I was just thinking it might be a clue."

"You think Remy is sabotaging his own movie?"

I groaned. "No. I don't. I don't know; I'm grasping here."

"I get it."

I scooted closer to Donavan, putting my elbow on the back of the couch, so I could read over his shoulder. I saw the name Peter right below Simone's. "Grant's agent? You talked to him?"

"Yes."

I waved my makeup wipe several times over his name. "He's evil. Doesn't he just give off an evil, self-righteous vibe?"

Donavan moved his hand in the "so-so" way.

"Really? Just meh about him?" I finished wiping off the rest of my face and threw the wipe toward the trash in the corner. It missed. "Why don't you have any notes next to him?"

"Because he didn't say much."

"What's your spiel anyway?"

"My spiel?"

"You're walking around with a notebook, saying, what? 'Hey, I'm Donavan, tell me your life story and how that might relate to screwing over my friend.'"

"You know, that was my backup line. I decided to go with the more boring, 'Hi, I'm doing a class project about moviemaking.'"

"Probably a good call. So they don't find it weird when you then ask personal questions, like their marital status?"

"I don't ask personal questions. They usually end up divulging personal stuff when I ask work-related questions. Like if I ask, are the long hours hard on family life? They either say, oh, I'm not married or no, not really, my wife works here too, so it's not a strain."

"That's what Noah said?"

"Exactly."

"I'm surprised he talked to you at all. Not sure if this is motive or helpful, but I think Noah hates me. I've always felt an impatient negative vibe from him."

"I felt like he hated me too, so maybe it's just his default." He glanced over at me, and I realized how close we were, his face inches from mine. I didn't move away, just met his eyes. He didn't move away either. It would be wrong of me to close the space. To kiss him right now. So wrong. I was giving him up because I cared more about my career. I was selfish.

"You're good at this," I said before I talked myself into doing what I wanted to do.

"At what?"

"At investigative reporting. Maybe it's in your future, after all."

He laughed a little and shook his head. "No, I dread doing it."

And yet, here he was doing it . . . for me.

"Who else?" I asked.

"Who else?" he asked.

"Who else made the notebook?"

He looked back down. "Oh, right. Did you know that Faith tried out for the movie?"

My mind went back to that video I'd watched in

Amanda's dressing room. "I did know that. I'd forgotten." Could that be something? Was Faith jealous?
"What else did you find out? Have you talked to Grant
yet?"

"I haven't talked to him yet."

"When I saw you walking around the set he asked
what you were doing. I told him you were interested in
acting. Then he said that you could interview him."

"How big of him."

"It actually is kind of big of him. He's a big deal,
Donavan. It's nice that he'd be willing to give you an
interview."

"Me? As in a nobody?"

"That's not what I said."

He pressed his lips into a thin line.

"I know you don't think he's a great actor and didn't
like his movies, but he doesn't know you're the viral-
review guy, so if you're scared that—"

"I'm not scared."

"What is it, then?"

"I just don't think it's him. It would be a waste of time."

"Really? What happened to everyone is a suspect?"

"I think he's too prideful to think that you could
screw up his career."

"He's not. In fact, one day he told me he didn't want
me to screw up his career."

"Wow. Nice. Then I don't think he has enough foresight to plan out something like this. To string together a bunch of mistakes that he hoped would be enough to get results."

"You don't think he's smart enough? Is that what you're saying?"

"Maybe."

I shook my head. "Even if he's not, he has his agent, who could easily be helping him."

He nodded but didn't look convinced.

A knock sounded at my door, and I backed up, putting some space between Donavan and me. "Come in!"

Aaron opened the door. "Hey," he said. "Do you need anything?"

"I'm good."

"I'm glad you're back. Sorry for all the drama with the missing zombie face. I wish there was something I could've done." It was so cute when he acted like a mini adult. Like he was somehow in charge of anything on set.

"There wasn't anything you could have done. Thanks though."

"Let me know if you need anything."

"I will. Thanks, Aaron."

He smiled and left.

"Who was that?" Donavan asked.

"That is the director's son and my biggest fan."

Donavan raised his eyebrows. "Who has a huge crush on you?"

"No. He's just nice."

"What did he mean by missing zombie face?"

I lowered my brow and pointed at my cheek. "That section Leah always took off my face went missing sometime in the last two days— Wait, you didn't know that?"

"How would I know that?"

"I guess I thought you heard somehow. . . . So you are helping me because of what I said at the restaurant about the article?" I felt my cheeks go pink but tried to pretend they weren't.

He met my eyes. "Yes."

"Thank you."

He smiled. "You already said that."

"It's just I've felt so alone in this. Like nobody truly thinks it's a big deal."

He held up his notebook. "So what about that kid? Aaron. Does he have a reason to sabotage you?"

I thought about it. "This is really sad that it's come to this."

"I know."

"I can't think of any reason he would. He really does like me. But maybe? I don't know. What would be his motive?"

"I don't know." Donavan nodded once. "I'll talk to him."

"I guess everyone needs to be on the suspect list," I said.

"Well, everyone but me."

I let out a burst of laughter. "No, you are at the top of the list. Remember, you used to think I was a spoiled, entitled snob."

"Used to?"

I scrunched my nose at him. "So mean."

His eyes dropped to the cushion of space I'd put between us when Aaron had knocked. "Who did you think was at the door?" he asked.

"My dad."

He wrote two more names in the notebook: Aaron and Donavan. Next to his own name he added, *revenge for all the math Lacey makes him explain.*

I smirked. "I'd want revenge for that, too. I don't blame you."

He shut the book. "I have to go. I have to work tonight."

I looked down at my hands. "Sorry about that, by the way."

"About what?"

"About showing up at your work and acting . . . I don't know, however I acted."

He smiled a little. "You were fine. Just a little demanding."

I gave a half-hearted laugh. "That's the quality I would've assigned to myself too."

He stood and lingered for a moment.

I stood too. "Fine, you can go. But let me look at our list one more time. I'm going to hang around and try to talk to a few more people."

"So demanding."

I pushed his arm.

He flipped open the book, and I scanned over the names of the suspects we had added. "I'm going to try Phil and Duncan."

"Who are they?"

"Some of Grant's security guards. Maybe they've seen something."

"Good idea."

"Will I see you tomorrow?" I asked.

"Hopefully." He lifted his hand in a wave and left my trailer.

I stared after him. He was still treating me exactly like a friend. And although I did like him as a friend, it killed me that he didn't want more.

Dancing Graves

INT. LORD LUCAS'S LAB—NIGHT
SCARLETT overhears EVELIN talking to LORD
LUCAS about how Benjamin told her about
the cave full of zombies. There had been
multiple deaths in the forests lately,
and she felt she had to go to the other
zombie hunters with the information.
Scarlett steps through the window. Evelin
screams.

LORD LUCAS
It's me, darling. Your father.

Scarlett seems to shake off a fog upon
seeing her father. She cries out and runs
from the mansion.

TWENTY-SEVEN

I walked outside. We were shooting on location the next day, and the set was a hive of activity. The crew was filing out of the studio, carrying equipment and packing it away in open trailers on the other side of the lot. I made my way to the end of the row, where Duncan and Phil stood guard.

"Uh-oh, here comes trouble," Duncan said when I reached the barrier that led to Grant's trailer.

"Hi!"

"You want me to radio Grant?"

"No. I wanted to talk to you guys."

"Really?" Duncan said. "What can we do for you?"

"You two have a pretty good view of my trailer. Have you seen anyone, besides me, of course, go in there?"

"Who don't we see go in your trailer? It's like a revolving door."

"I agree. Anyone who looks suspicious though? Like they shouldn't be there?"

"Anyone on set would have made it past security up front, so no, it's all cast or crew. And that tutor of yours."

"Hmm. What about people going in there a lot when I'm not there?"

"We're not sure when you're in there or not." He looked up as if thinking. "But I'd say your most frequent visitors are probably that tutor kid . . ."

Of course. He was in there all the time.

"The director's son."

"Aaron," I filled in for him. And again, that didn't surprise me; he was always stocking my fridge and snacks.

"And Faith."

Faith might have had reason to dislike me because she'd been unsuccessful when she tried out for the movie, but it was also completely expected that she'd be in and out of my trailer. Besides, I just couldn't picture her trying to sabotage me. I couldn't picture any of the people I worked with doing that.

"What about Amanda?" Phil added. "I've seen her go in quite a bit."

Of course Amanda had been in my trailer a lot. She was my best friend on set.

"Okay, thanks." I backed away slowly. That hadn't helped at all.

Tuesday we were filming at a campground an hour outside the city. All the trailers were lined up in a gravel parking lot, and the action was taking place a hundred yards into the trees. There was a shallow cave that, with the right camera angles and lighting, would look much bigger on-screen. And today that shallow cave was the setting for the bloodiest zombie scene in the entire script.

"Cut!" Remy called. "Remember, Lacey, this is Scarlett's breaking point. Again. From the top."

I nodded and picked my way back toward the cave entrance, around fake body parts, when my foot met a human finger that was actually attached to someone.

"Ouch," the extra hissed, raising his head a little.

"Sorry," I said.

"It's okay." He put his head back down.

We had already shot the beginning of the scene where I had just discovered the carnage. Now we were mid scene, and I was covered in fake blood. It dripped from my fingers and onto the dirt floor. I made it back to the first zombie, my starting mark, and knelt beside her. Simone came over and poured more blood onto my palm.

"Thanks," I said.

She laughed a little. "You're welcome?"

I smiled, and she backed out of the shot.

"Quiet on set," Noah called. "Slate in, sound rolling, camera rolling."

"Action," Remy said.

"No!" I screamed, bringing the limp form to my chest in a hug. "No!" I stood and tripped my way deeper into the cave. "Please, no." I tried to walk again, but my foot snagged on my skirt and I fell down to my knees where I was now eye to eye with a zombie's dead eyes staring into space. I cried out.

"Cut!" Remy yelled. "Very good. I think we're done in here."

And just like that, the dead bodies lying on the cave floor stood and began talking to one another. I stood too. My hands were caked with blood and dirt, and I tried to wipe them off onto each other, which did nothing.

Grant stood just beyond the lights. I hadn't realized he was watching. He wasn't in this scene at all.

"Don't touch me," he said as I came close.

I held up my hand and lunged toward him. He let out

a funny shriek and laughed.

"Don't worry," I said. "I'm coming after you and your kind tomorrow."

"Can't we just be friends?" he asked.

I paused for a moment and looked at his smirking face. It took me too long to realize he was talking about his character. "Never," I said. It seemed I didn't trust anyone right now.

I didn't use the shower in my trailer often, but I was done for the day and there was no way I was getting into my car like this. I piled my bloodied clothes by the rack for wardrobe and went into the small bathroom. When I was done, the shower walls looked straight from a crime scene. I tried to spray them off with the showerhead, but it was pointless, they'd need to be scrubbed.

I stepped out of the shower and wrapped myself in a towel. The mirror was foggy with steam, so I wiped it with a hand towel and brushed through my hair. The sound of my trailer door shutting startled me. The little trifold door to the bathroom didn't lock, so I held it closed.

"Hello!" I called. "Dad?"

There was no answer.

"Donavan?"

Nothing.

"I'm not dressed. So don't come in here. And I swear

if that's you, Amanda, and you jump out and scare me, I will never speak to you again!"

There was a rustling noise, but then the outside door shut again. I quickly dressed and slowly opened the door that led to the main part of the trailer. It was empty. I checked my table to see if maybe it was just Faith dropping off revisions. There was nothing. My fridge wasn't newly stocked either. This was not cool.

I was not staying in my trailer today. I could do homework from home. I got my backpack and jumped down the metal steps. I turned to the left and headed for my car. Amanda's trailer was just past mine, and I slowed outside of it. I glanced over my shoulder to see a new set of security guards blocking the way to Grant's trailer. Why couldn't they guard all of us? I remembered what the other guard had said the night before: Amanda had been in my trailer a lot.

I took a determined breath and knocked on Amanda's door. There was no answer. I started to leave but changed my mind. I reached up and pulled on her door handle. It opened. I went inside and pushed myself against the closest wall.

Her trailer was dim, all the blinds closed. It smelled like rose petals, like Amanda. Anyone who smelled like rose petals couldn't be out to get me. Right? The trailer looked a lot like mine—a rack of clothes in the corner, a couch, small kitchenette, and bunk area. I wasn't sure what I was looking for. Incriminating evidence? A journal or something spelling out how she hated me? The thought made my eyes sting. She didn't hate me. We were friends. I knew that. Maybe that's why I was here, to put my mind to rest.

I closed my eyes, then pushed myself off the wall. Apparently I was doing this. I started at her cabinet in the corner. Like me, she had a script there. I riffled through all the pages, but it was just a script. Next to that was her phone. We weren't allowed to bring them on set, so it didn't surprise me that, like me, she left it in her trailer. I picked it up and pushed on the home button. It gave me the prompt for a passcode. I didn't know how to break into phones like someone on set did, so I put it back down.

I spun around and went to her bunk. I checked under her pillow and blankets. Nothing. "You are a horrible person, Lacey," I said, but that didn't stop me from moving on to the kitchen drawers. I opened each one, reaching my hand all the way to the back. On the third drawer, my hand met with something hard. I pulled it out. It was a red plastic case. My breathing hitched, because I knew exactly what this was before opening it. I opened it anyway, hoping I was wrong. I wasn't. The section of my zombie cheek that had gone missing was here. In Amanda's trailer all along. My lip quivered, and I bit it, angry at the emotion that flooded through me.

I shut the case and shoved it back in the drawer. Then I stood there, not sure what to do. Did I take it and show it to Remy? Would he think I had taken it? And if he believed me, what then? Would he replace Amanda? I didn't want him to. I liked her. She'd been my only real friend on set. But it was obviously one-sided. So I should just pretend this didn't happen? I didn't understand why she had done this, what sabotaging me did for her.

I covered my face with my hands. Did this mean she called into that entertainment site too, trying to trash my reputation with that article? Of course that's what it meant.

I pushed the drawer shut and left her trailer, walking slowly until I reached my car. At home I found an empty apartment. Not that my dad was the first person I wanted to talk to about this. We still hadn't spoken since our last fight. I had wanted an apology from him, and he'd probably wanted the same from me. We were at a standoff.

I thought about calling my mom. She'd be more sympathetic, sure, but she would also be more preoccupied.

I paced the living room several times before deciding there was only one person who might help me feel better right now. Donavan Lake.

TWENTY-EIGHT

This time when I arrived on campus it was busy. The bell must've just rung, because it felt like every student in the entire campus was now walking to their next class. I went straight for the journalism department.

"Hey, isn't that . . ." I heard as I walked by a couple of guys. I didn't linger to hear how that sentence would finish.

Before I made it to my sanctuary, two guys came up on either side of me. One said, "Are you Grant James's costar? You're way prettier than that pic they posted."

That article must've been passed around online even more than I realized.

This is not how I wanted to become famous. I wanted to earn it with stellar performances. "No," I said.

"You totally are," the other guy said. He put his arm around me, held up his phone, and leaned in. I wanted to tell him not to touch me, but I was afraid he was recording. I didn't need more bad press. I kept my head down, hoping that my face wouldn't turn out well in that picture. At this point I was closer to the building in front of me than I was to my car, or I would've turned around and left. Finally, I couldn't handle it anymore, I shoved the guy off me and they both left but not before yelling out to anyone who would listen who I was. I picked up my pace and ducked inside the building.

The journalism class that I'd been in before was halfway full and continuing to fill up. I scanned the room and the far office for Donavan. I saw him at the same desk he'd been sitting at before, his head bent over some papers. A new set of tears stung my eyes.

"Are you Lacey Barnes?" someone asked from beside me. "I'd love to get an interview."

Right, now I was in the journalism department, where good journalists would be thinking that I would make a great story. "I can't. I'm not." Why did I keep saying that when it was obvious they knew exactly who I was? I stepped around backpacks and people until I was in the office where Donavan sat. I shut the door behind me and he looked up.

"Lacey?"

"I need to get out of here."

Maybe he heard the tears in my voice or the desperation in my eyes, whatever it was, he didn't question me, just stood. He took my hand, opened the door, and dragged me through the room as several people called out his name, including the teacher.

Outside, the halls were now almost empty, but he continued to hold my hand, like I needed a guide.

"I'm sorry to make you leave class. I didn't know who else to go to," I said.

"You chose well," he responded.

The second he said those words, the tears I'd somehow managed to hold in began pouring down my face.

He clenched his jaw and squeezed my hand.

"I don't want to be here."

"I know. Where do you want to be?"

"I don't know."

He led me out to the parking lot, where I pointed out my car.

"Not spoiled, huh?" he said, obviously trying to make me laugh. The most I could manage was a smile.

I handed him my keys, and he drove us away from the school.

"Your house?" he asked.

"I want to go far away from here," I said.

"Okay." He flipped a U-turn at the next stoplight and headed for the freeway.

He drove for about an hour, neither of us saying much, before he pulled off the freeway and into the parking lot of a state beach. It was a weekday in October, so there were only a few other cars there, which I assumed belonged to the surfers I could see bobbing in the waves in the distance.

"This is the beach my parents used to take us to a lot." He put the car in park, turned it off, and got out. I followed him to a bench that faced the ocean, where we both sat down. We watched the waves roll in. One of the surfers caught one and rode it until it fizzled.

The breeze blew hair across my face, and I tucked it behind my ears. My brain wouldn't shut off, my eyes stinging with the thoughts. "Amanda hates me."

"What?" he asked.

In sobs and hiccups, I summarized talking to the security guards and searching Amanda's trailer. His face displayed the shock and sympathy he felt. When I was done, I pulled my knees up to my chest and buried my face in them. "I just want to do my job. I don't understand why people are trying to stop me from doing that. I guess I'm unlikable."

"Lacey," he said. When I didn't lift my head, he softly said, "Lace."

I turned my head toward him so that now my cheek rested on my knees. My tears dripped sideways, over the bridge of my nose, and continued down the other side of my face.

"I'm sorry," he said. He put his hand on my back, as if he had no idea what to do. I had no idea either. "You are very likable."

I shrugged. "I didn't think it was Amanda."

"I'd hoped it wasn't her."

"Back at your school . . . people knew me."

He smiled a little. "You're getting famous."

"This isn't how it was supposed to happen. People weren't supposed to know me for something negative."

"I know."

Fresh tears followed the same trail. I sat back and looked up at the sky, trying to stop them. I hated crying when I wasn't trying to. "But honestly, I don't care about that as much as I do about what Amanda did. I thought we were friends. She made it seem like we were friends. Maybe everyone just puts on an act." I looked at Donavan. "Are *we* even friends?"

He slid closer to me and took my face in his hands. He

used his thumbs to wipe beneath my eyes. "Of course we're friends."

"Maybe I've been living in this world of fake emotions for so long that I don't even know what real ones are."

He brought my face closer to him and kissed my forehead. "You know what real emotions are," he whispered.

There was something so comforting about that action that I pushed my forehead against his lips again and he complied with another kiss there. Then I lifted my eyes to his. He paused, his mouth lingering near mine, his hands still holding my face. This felt real. I was done thinking, and I didn't wait for him to analyze this either. Because I knew he *would* analyze this, and I knew he'd come to the wrong conclusion: that now might not be the right time for this. I took a breath and pressed my mouth against his.

Maybe he wouldn't have come to the wrong conclusion, because he didn't hesitate at all, he kissed me back. He kissed me like this wasn't the first time the idea had occurred to him. And for the first time that day, I was able to forget about everything but that moment—his hands, now in my hair, his mouth moving across mine, my hands, pressed against his chest, feeling his heart hammering fast. My heart sped to match the pace, taking my breath away.

He groaned and pulled back. "I'm sorry. I'm sorry."

"Please don't be. Not for that." That was the most real kiss I'd ever experienced. Amanda would've called it my first kiss. It felt that way, because nothing before it even came close.

He closed his eyes and brought me into a hug. I draped my legs over his lap and leaned my head against his chest as he held me.

"So do you think Amanda leaked that story to the press too?" he finally asked.

"Yes. I do."

He hummed a little.

"What should I do?"

"We'll figure something out."

I tightened my arms around him. "You're the best."

"How long have you thought so? Just today?"

I laughed. "At least since that time we talked on the phone and you blew me off."

"I didn't blow you off, I . . ." He trailed off like he wasn't going to or didn't want to finish that sentence.

I sat back and looked at him. I was sure my face was red and blotchy and my eyes were puffy, but he'd seen me in all stages of horrible, so I didn't really care. "You don't date actresses."

"That was part of it. And I work for your dad."

"Hey, my dad is dating my makeup artist, so he has no room to talk." Well, my ex–makeup artist now.

He smiled and shook his head. "You're Lacey Barnes. Famous," he said, using my words against me. "It's just that I shared a lot with you that day on the phone, and I was convinced you were very close to becoming bored with me."

"You're not boring."

"Not yet."

"Are you saying we're a bad match? We're a worse match than a zombie and zombie hunter. An actress and a critic."

"Yes," he said.

"Do you really think so?"

He ran a thumb along my bottom lip and then kissed it. "Yes. But apparently I've abandoned all good judgment, so I might not be a critic for long."

TWENTY-NINE

We sat on that bench for a while. The breeze coming in off the ocean was starting to make it cold. We'd outlasted the surfers and our cell phone batteries when Donavan said, "Should we head back?"

"Do we have to?" I wasn't sure what time it was without my cell phone, but going by the sun, it was probably late afternoon. I wasn't exactly an expert on telling the time from the position of the sun though.

"Your dad is probably worried."

"He won't be expecting me until ten o'clock tonight."

"Well, my mom probably started worrying the second

the attendance line called saying I missed school today."

"I'm sorry about that again."

"I wasn't trying to make you feel guilty." He stood, my legs sliding off his lap as he did. "Let's at least move to the car. You're shivering. I have a phone charger in my backpack. I can see how in trouble I am." He held out his hand for me.

I took it, letting him help me to my feet. He could charge his cell phone; I really didn't want to charge mine. I was done on set for the day, so I had nobody looking for me.

He kept hold of my hand as we walked to the car. "You still want me to drive?"

"Will you?"

"For sure." He opened the door for me, and I slid in. Then he climbed in on the driver's side and started the car, turning on the heat. He connected his phone. He put his finger up as if telling me to hold on, then reached into his bag again and pulled out a hoodie. He passed it across the center console to me. "It might smell like paper or dry-erase marker or something, but it's warm."

I had my own hoodie in the back, but I wasn't going to tell him that. I pulled it on. It didn't smell like anything but Donavan. A smell I didn't realize I knew until that moment.

He tried to turn on his phone, but it didn't have

297

enough battery power to do that.

"We can go," I said.

"Do you . . . ?" He paused, hesitating for a moment. "I mean, what if we just went back to my house? If you don't want to go home yet, I mean."

I nodded. "Sounds good."

"Yeah?"

"Yes."

"Okay, good."

I looked at the ocean as he pulled out of the parking lot. I felt tired. I leaned my head up against the window and watched the world outside pass by in a colorful blur. He must've known I was past talking, because it was a silent car ride. I didn't mean to fall asleep, but eventually my eyes drifted closed.

When I woke up, everything was still. It took me a minute to reorient myself and another minute to realize I had woken up because Donavan's hand was gently shaking my shoulder. "Hey," he said. "We're here."

I lifted my head, my neck screaming in protest at the weird angle it had been in for the last hour. I rubbed at it and looked at the house in front of me. It was a small home in a neighborhood full of houses that looked exactly the same. The yard was nice: some bright pink and purple flowers in a window box, neatly trimmed grass, stepping stones carving a path to the front porch.

KASIE WEST

It looked homey. Donavan jumped out of the car, and by the time I'd opened my door, he was around to give me a hand.

He glanced over his shoulder, up at the door, a nervous expression on his face.

"Oh, I didn't ask, are you in trouble? Had your parents blown up your phone?"

"No, I don't think my mom realizes yet that I wasn't at school."

"Do you need to go warn your parents or your sister that you're bringing company inside?" I asked, not sure what other reasons he'd have for being nervous.

"No, but I kind of need to warn *you*."

"Warn me about what? I'm pretty good with parents."

"I'm sure you are. No, my sister. She . . ." He narrowed his eyes and studied my face.

"What?" I hadn't put makeup on after my shower, so I knew my cryfest hadn't reduced me to a mess of mascara or anything. My hair might have been a bit crazy. When I brushed through it, like I had, my curls were unpredictable. I looked down at my outfit, which was just a pair of jeans, his hoodie, and flip-flops. Not fancy, but not bad either. Was he embarrassed of me?

"She's a huge fan."

It took me a second to process those words. "Of me?" I asked, incredulous.

"She loves *The Cafeteria* more than I do, and she cried when your character died."

"Your sister, the freshman?"

"Yes, Kennedy."

"She got attached after four whole episodes?"

"What did I tell you? You were very convincing."

"You didn't tell me that."

"I told you that you were brilliant. That was an all-encompassing compliment."

"Oh, really? So you can say that you told me anything in the future and it's covered under the 'brilliant' umbrella?"

"Pretty much."

"I guess I'll brace myself for this, then."

"I apologize in advance."

He headed toward the steps, up to the front door, and I stood there taking in a few breaths and attempting to shake everything that happened today. I put on my happy face. I was about to have an audience—his mom; his sister, my only fan. I needed to be on, not a pathetic mess.

He turned back, one eyebrow raised, his hair tousled from the wind, his skin a healthy glow from the time we'd spent outside. He was adorable. My heart fluttered.

"You coming?" he asked.

"I'm coming."

He was right to warn me, because even after his

warning, I wasn't expecting his sister's reaction. At first it was completely normal. We walked into the kitchen, where his sister had spread peanut butter on some bread and was now adding sliced bananas to it.

Donavan looked at me. "Are you hungry?"

Was I? I hadn't eaten all day, but my stomach felt like a nervous mess.

"Well, obviously," his sister said, not looking up. "Hence the sandwich."

"Kennedy, I wasn't talking to you."

"Then who were you talking to?" She looked up and immediately met my eyes. I didn't think she'd recognize who I was so fast, because most people took a moment to process someone out of context, but she must've known Donavan had been tutoring me or something because her mouth immediately dropped open.

"Kennedy, this is—" he started to say.

His sister interrupted him with, "I know who she is! I don't live under a rock."

I laughed a little. One didn't have to live under a rock to not know who I was. In fact, there was a very specific set of qualifications people needed to have to actually *know* who I was. Those included: be related to me in some way, go to Pacific High School, or be a rabid fan of *The Cafeteria*, apparently. Well . . . at least before the article those were the qualifications. Now . . . "Hi," I said. "Good to meet you, Kennedy."

She had stopped topping her peanut butter with bananas and was now shaking her hands out and doing a running motion with her legs. "Donavan! Why would you bring her here without warning me! Look at me. Do I look ready to meet a celebrity?"

"You look fine, Kennedy," he said, and I nodded my agreement.

"Fine? Fine! Fine is not a good compliment. If you learned this, maybe you'd have a girlfriend."

Donavan and I exchanged a quick smile.

She sighed a big drawn-out sigh. "Well, I guess it's too late now, the first impression is over. You will forever know me as the after-volleyball-hair, peanut-butter-and-banana girl."

"It could be worse," I said.

"It could?" she asked.

"The first time I met your brother . . . and the second and third for that matter . . . I was decomposing-flesh girl."

"How is that worse? My brother is not a celebrity. My brother is nobody!"

"Thanks, Kennedy. Love you, too."

She waved her hand at him. "You know what I mean."

"Well," I said. "I think you're charming. And I'm not a celebrity either so we're good."

"I love your hair," she said. "And you have beautiful skin, I see why that zit cream picked you for their commercial. I'm sorry everyone is being mean to you on the internet lately."

I sucked in a breath, her last comment catching me off guard.

"Kennedy, she's trying to forget about that," Donavan said. "Let's not bring it up again."

"I'm sorry," she said, then her eyes lit up. "You can stay here as long as you want!" She pushed her sandwich toward me. "You should eat this. And we can turn off the internet in the house and watch movies. Or *The Cafeteria*! Do you want to watch it? I have all six seasons on DVD."

"Kennedy, she doesn't want to watch herself on television."

I shrugged. "I could watch myself on television."

Kennedy laughed, and Donavan only looked surprised.

"What?" I said. "It's a good show. You said so yourself."

His eyes lit up in amusement.

I grabbed hold of his hand and squeezed. "Does that make me a diva?" I asked.

This time he actually chuckled. "Not at all. I'm glad to see your confidence back."

A gasp sounded, and I turned to see Kennedy's mouth

open again. "Wait," she said, looking at our clasped hands, then at the hoodie I wore. "Are you two . . . no. Wait, *are* you?"

I started to say yes when Donavan said, "No, we're not. Now go turn on the TV."

She ran out of the kitchen, and I dropped Donavan's hand.

"Sorry," he said. "She's usually not so excitable."

"You warned me."

He pointed at her abandoned sandwich. "Does that appeal to you at all?"

"No, thanks." I pulled my dead phone out of my pocket. "Do you have a charger I can borrow? I left mine in my trailer."

"Yes, I'll go get it."

He left, and I stood in the kitchen alone. Had I been stupid to think that the kiss on the beach meant something? He'd had an hour while I slept to analyze it over and over again. Had he decided it was a mistake? Had he just done it because he felt sorry for me? Because he was a nice guy? I didn't need his pity. I didn't want it either.

THIRTY

"I didn't say *you* could eat my sandwich," Kennedy said as we walked into the living room.

After Donavan had plugged my phone into the charger on the kitchen counter, he had put Kennedy's sandwich on a plate and had already taken three big bites.

"That was for Lacey."

"I'm okay," I said.

"Are you sure you don't want anything?" he asked around his mouthful.

My stomach was already full of nervous energy, and this new fake-happy face I was now putting on for both

Donavan and his sister wasn't helping at all. "I'm sure."

Donavan studied my face for a moment and tilted his head as if he was going to call me out on my act, but then he sat down on the center cushion of the couch.

Kennedy popped a DVD out of its case and put it in the player.

I took in the room. There were several seating options. Obviously, a cushion on either side of Donavan, but there was also a love seat and two overstuffed chairs. I thought about taking one of the chairs, but then Donavan would think there was something wrong. He didn't need to know I was more invested in him than he was in me.

A row of framed pictures along the mantel drew my attention, and I walked over and looked at them. They spanned several years and several locations—Disneyland, the beach, a birthday party. Most of them were of Donavan and his sister, his mom was in a couple, but it wasn't until the last picture that I saw his dad in one. It was taken right here in this living room. Kennedy was looking up at him in admiration, Donavan wasn't smiling, and his dad stared straight at the camera, a neutral expression. Not sure this was a picture I would frame, but maybe there weren't many to choose from.

"It's our family timeline," Donavan said as I joined him on the couch.

"You two were adorable kids."

"Are you saying we aren't adorable anymore?" He smiled over at me and then plunked his empty plate onto the coffee table, where both of his feet now rested as well. The home version of Donavan was very relaxed. It was nice.

"I'm offended too," Kennedy said, sitting on the other side of Donavan.

"You're both super adorable." I wedged myself into the corner of the couch and pulled my legs up under me. "You were just cuter two to ten years ago."

"Didn't I tell you she was rude?" Donavan said to Kennedy.

"No," Kennedy said. "You actually told me she was nicer than you expected her to be."

I gasped and backhanded Donavan across the chest.

He grabbed at his chest as if I'd hurt him.

"You should take that as a compliment," Kennedy said. "Most people don't get that glowing of a review."

"So a critic of people too?" I settled more into the corner, sliding my legs out from under me so they now took up the space between me and Donavan.

He shook his head. "No ganging up on me, you two."

"You ready for awesomeness?" Kennedy asked.

"Are we starting right with Lacey's episodes or the

beginning of the season?" Donavan asked.

"Right with Lacey's, of course," Kennedy said in a *duh* voice.

"Of course," I agreed with a wink at him.

His brows shot down with that response for some reason. "Okay, push play."

The theme song for the show sang out.

Donavan reached over and rested his hand on my ankle. I pretended not to feel it, even though every nerve up my leg sung. The episode started, and I kept my eyes glued to the television. Instead of moving his hand back to his lap, he kept it there.

When I came on the screen, I could feel both Donavan's and Kennedy's eyes shift between the television and me a couple of times, obviously curious about how I'd react. Or maybe they were just comparing the on-screen version of me to the real one. I was just trying to get through this. I was trying to sit here long enough to convince the room I was fine so that I could leave without an inquisition. Donavan's hand, still on my ankle, wasn't helping.

I heard a distant buzzing from the other room and I realized, with great relief, that it was my phone. "My phone is ringing," I said, moving my feet to the floor. "It's probably my dad."

"Do you want me to pause it?" Kennedy asked.

"No, that's okay. I've seen it before." I gave her a smirk, and she laughed.

By the time I reached it, my phone was still again. With my phone now charged, I saw three missed calls from my dad.

I took a deep breath and called my dad back.

"Where are you?" was how he answered.

"At a friend's."

"Lacey, this is information you need to tell me before it happens."

"I'm sorry, it was a last-minute decision. I'll come home now."

"Good."

We hung up, and I leaned against the counter for a moment, letting myself just breathe. Then I unplugged my phone from the charger and turned. Donavan stood in the passage between the kitchen and living room.

I jumped, my hand flying to my chest. Then I laughed. "You scared me."

"Why are you doing that?"

"Doing what?" I asked.

He took a few steps into the kitchen. "Why are you putting on an 'everything is fine' face?"

I kind of hated that he knew I was doing this. I thought I was a better actress than that. "Because everything *is* fine. I'm feeling better. I need to go." I held up my phone. "That was my dad." I took off the hoodie I wore, walked it to Donavan, then poked my head into the living room. "I have to go, Kennedy! It was nice to meet you."

She jumped up and ran into the kitchen. "It was so nice to meet you too! You need to come back and finish watching this with us. Please."

I nodded once. "I will."

She gave me a quick hug, then ran back into the living room.

Donavan smiled a little. "You made her life."

"She made mine." I walked back through his house and to the front door, where I turned around, feeling him behind me. "You don't have to walk me out."

"Lacey, what happened? What did I do?"

"Nothing. I just don't want you to feel some sort of obligation toward me."

"Obligation?"

"Can we just talk tomorrow? I'm so tired." The smile I had been doing such a good job of keeping on my face slid off, and with it, my shoulders slumped.

"Yes, we can," he said, and opened the door for me. Despite what I had said, he walked me out. When I saw my car, sitting in his driveway, I remembered he had driven it here.

"Your car," I said. "Is it at school? I can take you to go get it. Yes, let me do that."

"It's okay. My mom can drop me off at school tomorrow on her way to work. I'll get it then."

"Okay . . . are you sure?"

"I'm sure."

"Okay." I took several steps toward my car when Donavan grabbed my hand and gave it a gentle tug, turning me back toward him.

"Things will look better in the morning."

I nodded.

He kissed my forehead, again. Even though I wanted to melt into the comfort of it, I was beginning to think that was his pity move. He felt sorry for me. It was the same thing he'd done earlier. And after, I was the one who'd kissed him. Then he'd apologized for it. I turned back toward my car and took several more steps before irritation took over. I turned around. "I don't need your pity," I said. There. That made me feel better, getting that out of my head.

"My . . . what?" he asked, eyes narrowing.

"You said you don't date actresses."

"I don't."

"But you're fine kissing them?"

"No, I mean, yes. Not them, you. I'm fine kissing

you." He raked his hand through his hair as if he didn't mean what he said at all. As if he was frustrated with himself.

"You don't need to kiss me because you feel sorry for me," I said.

"You think I just go around kissing girls I feel sorry for?"

"I wouldn't know."

"Well, I don't."

"Good, because girls don't like that. Me included."

"I don't feel sorry for you."

I groaned at the sky. "Of course you do."

He closed the space that I'd created between us, took my face in his hands, and kissed me. My breath seemed to be sucked from my body, and my lips stung. I shouldn't have, but I answered back, grabbing on to his shoulders and pressing myself against him. Why did this have to feel so good? I pushed him away, panting for breath.

He lowered his voice. "Lacey, listen, I feel bad about what's happening to you, but this is definitely not pity."

"Isn't it? Because that's what it feels like. I feel like some problem you're trying to solve."

His jaw tightened. "I'm not an actor. I don't kiss people unless I mean it."

I gasped. "Well, at least when I kiss people for real, I don't pretend like it meant nothing."

He looked up as though trying to piece together the meaning of those words. I was about to turn and walk away when he said, "My sister? Is this about what I said to my sister?"

"No . . . maybe."

"My sister is your biggest fan. She'd mean well, but she'd post it all over online if her brother was dating Lacey Barnes. I didn't think you needed that complication right now. And besides, I didn't hear you rush to tell her there was something between us either."

"I was about to."

He went still. "You were?"

All the anger and irritation I felt seemed to seep out of my body. I leaned into him, putting my forehead against his chest. His hands moved up and down my back. "I'm sorry," I said.

"For what?"

"You're right. I'm not okay. I'm a mess right now. Maybe it isn't a good time to start . . . whatever this is. There's too much negativity."

He nodded. "I understand. I don't want to be another complication in your life right now."

"You aren't. You won't be. I just need to sort everything out."

He wrapped me up in his arms, holding me. I could feel the pulse in his neck against my temple.

"Will you kiss my forehead again?" I asked.

He chuckled a little. "Are you mocking me?"

"Not at all."

He pressed his lips to my forehead and I closed my eyes. There was something so sweet about this gesture. Something beyond passion, beyond lust, it felt like he cared, like he truly cared.

He pulled back, and I met his eyes. "Thank you for today. You made it bearable." With that, I got in my car and left to face my dad.

THIRTY-ONE

I slid my key into the lock at home, but my dad swung open the door before I even had to turn it.

I took several steps into the room before I saw Leah sitting on the couch. "Hi."

"Hi, Lacey."

I hadn't talked to her since the firing, and I still felt bad. "I'm sorry he fired you."

She rolled her eyes. "It's not your fault. Remy and me . . . well, I'm sure you know by now."

"I heard." I went to the kitchen and filled a glass with water.

"Why the disappearing act today?" Dad asked.

"I just . . . I needed to get off set."

"You need to tell me these things. How am I supposed to feel when I show up and you aren't there and nobody knows where you are?"

"I don't know. Worried . . . I guess."

"You guess?"

"I mean you could just not show up, then it would've been fine. I would've been home by curfew."

"That's not how it works, Lacey."

"Believe me, I know."

"You're not helping your case here," Dad said.

"If I apologize, can I go to bed?"

"Not with that attitude."

I glanced over his shoulder to Leah. "By the way, that missing zombie section. It was in Amanda's trailer. Maybe if you tell Remy, you can get your job back." Then I looked at my dad. "I will text you my every move from now on."

I walked into my bedroom and did something I hadn't done in years, I slammed the door.

Thirty minutes later there was a soft knock on my door. "Dad, I don't want to talk right now."

"It's Leah."

I didn't want to talk to anyone, but at least I wasn't angry with *her*. "Come in."

She opened the door and sat in the chair at my small desk. "So Amanda took it?"

"I found it in her trailer."

"I'm sorry, Lacey. I know you two were friends."

I sat up and leaned against the wall. "If you want to go in and talk to Remy, I'll tell him where I found it."

She shook her head before I even finished the sentence. "No, I don't. I already have another job lined up. It's not me I'm worried about."

"You don't need to worry about me. Now that I know it's her, I'll watch my back."

"I'm more worried about your future."

"Did my dad send you in here to tell me to do my homework and go to college?"

She laughed a little. "No. And even if he asked me to, I wouldn't tell you that. I mean, you should definitely do your homework and graduate from high school. But you're an amazing actress, Lacey, you're getting a lot of experience if this is what you want to do with your life."

"It is."

"Good." She clasped her hands and let out a breath. "I read that article."

I sighed. That article was never going to go away. "That's what you're worried about? Do you think people won't like me because of it?"

"It's not that. You need to be less concerned about

what the public thinks and more concerned about what Remy thinks. You need to talk to him."

"I should tell him I didn't do those things? That Amanda did?"

"Maybe. But you really need to convince him that you are a professional. He is the one other directors will call when deciding whether to give you a job. He is the one who might have a role come across his desk in the future and think you would be perfect for it. He will play a part in your career, and you have to make sure that article, that the drama on set, isn't making him think twice about your abilities."

"You're right."

"I know."

"Thank you . . . for that advice."

"You're welcome." She stood but stopped. "Can I give you one more tiny piece of advice?"

"Yes."

"Take everything your dad says and put it through the 'I'm extremely worried about my daughter who I love so much' filter."

"He's being unreasonable."

"I know. It's partially my fault because I've told him way too many horror stories. So forgive me for that. But it's also that you're growing up. That's hard for parents."

"I'll try to apply that filter, but he needs to apply a couple filters of his own."

She smiled. "Good night."

"Good night."

As I approached Remy's trailer the next day I heard loud voices coming from inside. I stopped and waited. I couldn't make out what they were saying, but after a few minutes the door was flung open and Aaron came storming out.

When he saw me, the scowl dropped off his face and his eyes went to the gravel that made up the parking lot.

"You okay?" I asked.

"Fine," he mumbled, and kept walking.

This might not have been good timing after a fight with his son, but I pressed forward. I knocked on the wall outside Remy's trailer because Aaron had left the door open. Remy sat at a desk flipping through what looked like some revisions on the script because the pages were blue. He looked as stressed as I felt. He glanced up with the knock and dropped the pages to the desk when he saw me. He beckoned me in with a wave of his hand. "Lacey, come in. You're my third visitor already this morning."

It was early. Before first call. I wasn't on the call sheet

today, but I knew I couldn't put this off. I stepped into his trailer, leaving the door open. "Third?"

"Faith, my son, and you."

"Faith was here? Did it have to do with me?"

He waved his hand. "No. It was nothing. What can I do for you?"

"Did you read the article about me online?"

"I did."

"They're talking about your movie. That's good, right?"

A toothy grin spread across his face. "No publicity is bad publicity? Is that the angle you're going with?"

"And sticking to," I said.

He let out a surprised laugh. "I'm remembering why we hired you. You're spunky. I had forgotten in all your greenness."

"I know I'm green. But I wanted to talk to you about the fact that someone is setting me up." I hadn't convinced myself I was going to use Amanda's name yet. I just wanted him to know I was professional. That I hadn't actually done all those things.

"Setting you up?"

"Someone is trying to make me look bad."

His expression that had softened with my speech went hard again. "Lacey, I don't need drama on my set."

Okay, so he didn't want to hear it; he thought I was

being immature and paranoid. I would only sound more immature if I insisted I was right. That was fine. I knew who was setting me up, and I would make sure she knew I wasn't going anywhere. "You're right. I'm done with drama. I'm here to work. I just wanted you to know that."

"I'm happy to hear it."

THIRTY-TWO

I left Remy's trailer and headed for my own. Amanda must have seen me out her window as I walked by because she came flying out the door. "Lacey!" She gave me a hug. "Don't you love it up here? I used to camp with my family all the time. We should have a campfire tonight in the trees and tell ghost stories."

I stood frozen to my spot, still not sure what I wanted to say to her.

"What's wrong?" she asked.

"Nothing. I'm just . . . tired."

"You have another day off though. Lucky." She paused,

seeming to realize what she just said. "Wait, if you have today off, why did you drive all the way up here?"

"I needed to talk to Remy about you, actually." I wasn't one to hold things in. I knew this about myself.

"What's that supposed to mean?"

"I know what you did. What you took. I'm still trying to figure out why though." A thought occurred to me. "Was it for Grant? To help him out? Were you trying to get rid of me? Hoping someone better would be put in my spot?"

"I have no idea what you're talking about."

"I found what you took. You might as well come clean." Maybe this wasn't the place for this discussion with the security guards behind us and crew members walking by.

"Found what?"

She'd probably moved it by now, but I pointed to her trailer. "I'll show you."

"Okay." She held her hand out to the side, inviting me to lead the way.

I marched up the two metal steps and to the small kitchen, where I yanked open the drawer half expecting it to be gone. She had followed behind me and stood looking over my shoulder. We both saw it at the same time, the unassuming red plastic case sitting there.

"What the—" She lifted it out of the drawer and

immediately opened it as if to verify what it was. "I did not put this here."

"Right."

"I didn't! Why would I put it here of all places? If I took this I would've put it as far away from me as possible."

That logic tripped me up. "You might as well just admit it. I just want to know why. To help Grant? To help yourself?" Maybe she'd been worried about my effect on the movie's reputation too.

"I didn't do this. I swear."

"It doesn't matter because I'm not going anywhere. You can try all you want, but I'm here to stay. I earned this part, and I'm keeping it because I'm good."

"I agree. You are and you should. I like you, Lacey. I thought we were friends. I would never do this."

It was hard to fight with someone when they seemed so concerned and sincere. I crossed my arms. "I didn't actually tell Remy, but I'm on to you," I mumbled. I fled to my trailer, leaned back against the door and let myself cry again.

Waiting in front of someone's house until they got home from school was not creepy behavior. Especially not after telling said person that I needed to sort things out, implying that lots of space was needed. He was obviously giving it to me. He hadn't called, texted, or stopped by in twenty-four hours. Scratch that, twenty hours. And eight of those hours had probably been spent sleeping. Another eight he'd been at school. So that left four hours where he hadn't called, texted, or visited me. Four hours! Okay, I was being creepy, but that thought didn't make me turn the key in the ignition and drive away.

I checked the clock on my phone. School had gotten out thirty minutes ago. I'd been sitting here for thirty minutes. Maybe he had something after school. Paper stuff. Or maybe he worked right after school. I pulled up my messages again to make sure I hadn't missed any. "You could just text him, Lacey, instead of being creepy."

There was a knock at my window, and I screamed. Very loud. Then I looked over to see Donavan standing there. I powered down the window.

"Hi," he said with a smile. "Were you talking to your-self?"

I matched his smile because I couldn't help it, see-ing him made me happy. It had been twenty and a half hours, after all. "Yes."

"Should I leave you alone to finish that out?"

"No, I think I'd made my point to myself pretty clear."

He patted the top of my car. "Did you want to come in?"

I nodded, and he opened the door for me.

"How was school?" I asked as we headed up his walk.

"Good. How are you?"

"Not great."

"I'm sorry." We stopped on the porch, and he fished out his keys and opened the door.

"Is your sister here right now?" I asked.

"No, she has volleyball." We walked inside, where he dropped his backpack and then led me into the kitchen. "Can I get you anything?"

"You have a trampoline," I said. The window over the sink had a nice view of the backyard.

"We do."

"I haven't been on a trampoline in years. My mom calls them bone breakers and won't let my sister and brother have one."

"My sister broke her wrist on it last year."

I smiled. "Don't tell my mom that. It will only make her think she's right."

I must've been staring at the trampoline longingly because Donavan said, "Do you want to jump on it?"

"Yes!"

He laughed like I was kidding, but I was already heading for the sliding glass door across the way. The trampoline had a net around it. I slipped off my flip-flops, unzipped the net, and rolled onto the bouncy surface. Then I stood and took several small practice bounces before I gave it my all.

"This is so fun!" I called to Donavan as he walked out of the house with two bottles of water. I bounced onto my knees and then to my feet again several times before I finally launched myself onto my back and stayed there until all was still again.

The trampoline moved as Donavan climbed through the opening and joined me. He must've left the water on the padded border because when he lay down next to me, his arms were free. I moved my foot over to his to see if he'd taken off his shoes. My bare foot slid over his socked one. "Just checking," I said.

"Everyone knows you take your shoes off on a trampoline."

I left my foot up against his, and we stared up at the clouds lazily making their way across the blue sky for several quiet minutes.

"Do you want to talk about it?" he asked, calling me out once again.

"No."

He reached over and took my hand.

"I talked to Remy this morning. Leah told me that directors talk to each other and I should be less worried about what the public thinks about me and more worried about what Remy thought of the article . . . about me."

"And what did he say?"

"That I'm green . . . but spunky."

"You are spunky."

"I don't know if he'd hire me again. If he'd recommend anyone else hire me. If all this on-set sabotage keeps happening, he probably won't."

"So what are you going to do?"

"I still have at least five more weeks of filming. I guess my plan is to make the drama on set stop and to change the online narrative of me."

"How?"

"I don't know yet."

"Can't Grant write some nice things about you online? He has millions of followers. That would help the online reputation at least."

"He won't. I already asked him . . . twice. I'll figure something else out. In the meantime, I'm going to jump on a trampoline, pretend everything is fine, and make out with this boy I really like." I shifted onto my side and propped my head up with my hand so I could see his cute face. "As a well-known critic, what are your thoughts about this plan?"

"What are my thoughts about denial?"

"I was thinking more the making-out part."

He smiled, still looking up at the sky. "As a critic, I think this plan is flawed," he said. "It could make things muddled while someone is trying to sort things out."

"That's a good word, *muddled*. That feels like a writer word."

"Yes, it's descriptive." He finally looked over at me, and I could see the smile in his eyes. He stared at me for a long moment. "On second thought," he said. "Muddled isn't a bad thing, is it? It always makes for a more interesting plot." His hand went to the side of my neck, and I met him halfway in a kiss. It was almost as if we hadn't just kissed the night before, it felt just as good this time. I tangled my legs up with his and pulled myself closer.

"You always seem to talk me into doing things I know I probably shouldn't do," he said against my mouth.

I smiled but didn't pull away. "This didn't take much convincing."

He gave me a small peck, then another before pulling back. He squinted his eyes as if studying me. "You're right. We better try that again, so I can figure out why that is the case."

Before I could laugh, his mouth was on mine. I closed my eyes. There was nothing to figure out. Things may have been muddled with my parents, with Remy, with Amanda, but in this aspect of my life, everything was perfectly clear. I didn't need to sort anything out here. It was no mystery why I liked kissing Donavan Lake.

"By the way," I said, pulling back and propping myself

up on my elbow again. "I talked to Amanda."

He matched my position, his brow immediately showing his worry. "And?"

"She's denying everything. Says she has no clue how my zombie face got in her trailer."

"Do you believe her?"

"I want to believe her. I like her. I've always liked her. She's nice. She seemed sincere. But she's an actress. That's kind of her thing."

"What's her thing? Being sincere?" he asked.

"No, making people believe what she wants them to believe."

"Is that your thing too?" he asked, running a finger down a vein on the back of my hand.

"No. I don't think so. Not with you."

His eyes softened, and he tugged on one of my curls.

"What about you? What's your thing, Donavan Lake?"

"My thing?" His brown eyes held mine.

"Yes," I said. "Your thing."

"I'm kind of into *you* right now," he said.

My heart skipped a beat. "I'm kind of into you, too."

He jumped to his feet and began bouncing around me on the trampoline, causing me to catch some air. "What was the order of things we were going to do today?" he asked while bouncing. "Jump on a trampoline, pretend everything is fine, and . . . ?"

I squealed as a bounce sent me higher. "Make out with a boy I really like!" I yelled.

He fell forward, catching himself by his hands on either side of my head. "That sounds like the perfect day to me."

I reached up and pulled him down to me. "Me too," I said as our lips met.

THIRTY-THREE

That night my name was on the call sheet and my determination was strong. I was going to catch my saboteur in the act. I'd thought of a plan: I'd leave my phone and a couple prop pieces on the table in my trailer. Then I'd set up my laptop to record. I'd do this for several days if I had to.

The next morning, as I was getting ready to head out, my phone rang and Abby's name flashed across the screen. I picked it up. "Hello?"

"Guess what?" she asked as a greeting.

"What?"

"I'm coming to see you this weekend. You get to show me around a set, I get to meet famous people. It will be awesome."

I swallowed. Was this a good thing or a bad thing? I wanted to see her. So bad. I needed a friend right now. But the timing was off.

"You don't want me to come?" she asked.

"Of course I do. It's just . . ." I filled her in on everything that had been going on.

"Lacey! Why haven't you called me? Talked to me?"

"I don't know. It all just happened at once and I've been overwhelmed."

"I am definitely coming this weekend. I can help you. I'll be your spy or something."

I laughed, but she was right. More eyes on set wouldn't be a bad thing. "Okay. That would be great, actually. Oh, also, I need to introduce you to a boy I really like."

"What!" she screamed so loud I had to pull the phone away from my ear. "You like a boy?"

"I do."

"Then I'm in," she said. "Even more in than I was a minute ago."

"I can't wait to see you," I said.

"Me too!"

We hung up, and I grabbed my toothbrush. My dad stopped in the open bathroom doorway.

"Who was that?" he asked, which didn't sound at all like an apology. Not even close to one.

"My friend Abby from home. You don't know her."

"You're still mad at me."

"Dad, I'll be eighteen in five months."

"I know."

I put my toothbrush down and faced him. "I know you worry about me. I know you wish I would never grow up. But what I'm doing makes me happy."

"You've been happy this last week?"

Leah must've filled him in on everything. "So you're saying every day of your life you've been happy at your job?"

He grimaced. "I wish you weren't so good at arguments."

"It's a gift."

"One that works against me."

"Dad, don't you see, this isn't about you. It's about me. It's about my life, my future. It's about what I want to do and how you've made me feel like you don't care about that at all. Like you don't care about me in the least."

His face went slack. "Oh, Lacey. No. It's that I care too much."

"Too much to listen? Too much to pay attention or make me feel like you support me?"

"That's how you've felt?"

"More than you know."

"I'm sorry. I didn't mean to make you feel like I didn't support you. I moved down here for you. I thought you realized how I felt."

"I thought you moved down here so that you could control every aspect of my career."

"I made it hard to think otherwise."

I nodded.

He held up a book I hadn't realized was in his hand. His finger was holding his place about halfway through. "I'm reading it."

"Reading what?"

He turned the cover toward me. "*Dancing Graves.*"

"What do you think so far?"

"It's good."

"Did you buy that? I have a copy in my car, you know."

"I bought it. And it just occurred to me that I'm going to have to buy another when they redo the cover with the movie edition." He dropped his hand back to his side. He looked a little defeated.

"Dad, I promise I'm not going to go wild and crazy."

"You can't promise me that."

"Will you stop loving me if I do?"

"No. I'll always love you."

I smiled. "Then either way, we're good, right?"

He laughed a little and opened his arms. I stepped into his hug.

He kissed the top of my head. "I'm not going to let you stop doing your homework."

"Don't worry, Donavan won't let me stop either, so I think we're good there."

"I chose a pretty good tutor, yes?"

I bit my lip and looked up at him. "If I told you that I'm dating him now would that count as going wild . . . or crazy?"

He tilted his head in thought. "Really? I thought he'd be too straitlaced for you."

"He is. But there's this weird thing I learned: apparently I can't plan everything that happens. That's a good lesson for you to learn too."

He let out a single laugh. "It is. And I'm learning it."

"Good."

"Well, I approve of Donavan, not that my approval matters for much with you right now."

"It does, Dad. That's what I'm trying to tell you. It matters a lot. It's all I've wanted these past couple of months."

"You have it."

I gave my dad one last squeeze, then said, "I'm going to be late."

"Good luck with the drama. And just to be clear: this is something you don't want me to get involved in?"

"Dad," I said with a sigh.

"Okay, so no. See, I'm learning."

If I thought my dad would be able to do anything about this, it might be something I wanted him involved in. But I'd already talked to Remy. He didn't believe me. Having my dad swoop in was not going to make Remy want to hire me again or give me a good reference. Plus, I had a plan.

Dancing Graves

INT. LORD LUCAS'S LAB—NIGHT
SCARLETT perches on the windowsill
outside her father's lab, the place she
had seen BENJAMIN sneaking into. He pulls
a small leather pouch from his belt,
looks around, and dumps the contents
into the vials on the table, damaging
any chance one might have been the cure.
Scarlett growls and he turns.

                    SCARLETT
You betrayed us.

                    BENJAMIN
No. I'm trying to help.

                    SCARLETT
I don't believe you.

SCARLETT lunges at him with a rusty metal

fence post and drives it through his
shoulder. She stands over him as crimson
blood spills onto the marble floor.
EVELIN appears in the doorway and gasps.
Scarlett yanks the post from Benjamin's
shoulder and turns slowly, blood dripping
off the tip.

                    EVELIN
It's me, Scarlett. Don't do this.

SCARLETT advances on her.

THIRTY-FOUR

As I pulled down the dirt road that led to the camp, I saw the first set of security guards up ahead. They were stationed at a row of barricades. I stopped, powered down my window, and waved.

"Hi, Lacey," the one on the right said as he moved a barricade for my car to go through.

"Hi. Thanks."

I drove through and parked in the first small lot next to a black car with duct tape on the bumper. I narrowed my eyes. I'd been in it only once, but I knew that car. It was Donavan's. Why was he here? Especially when he should've been at school. I jumped out of my car and walked quickly to my trailer. He wasn't there.

Past the trailers, before the path that led to the filming in the trees, was a small amphitheater surrounding a fire pit and stage. That's where I saw two guys standing and talking. Grant and Donavan.

Was Donavan "interviewing" him? Did he think Grant was a suspect, after all? I looked at my phone. I was supposed to be sitting in a makeup chair right now. I sent Simone a text: *Give me ten minutes.*

I knocked on Amanda's trailer door. She answered, and when she saw it was me, a hopeful expression took over her face.

"You want to help me with something?" I asked. If she was being truthful about not trying to sabotage me, she could prove it to me now by backing me up with Grant.

She hopped down the two steps and shut the door behind her. "With what?"

"Follow me."

As we got closer to the guys, I heard Donavan speaking in slow, measured sentences. He had his notebook out and was holding his phone up too, as if he was recording the conversation. "And do you feel others have helped you get to where you are today?"

"Absolutely. I wouldn't be here without a long list of people."

He was conducting the interview.

Donavan's back was to me, so Grant saw me first. He smiled. "Lacey, Amanda, hey. Say hi for the recording."

"Hi," I said as we reached them. I tried to catch Donavan's eye, but he was focusing all his energy on his notebook and phone.

"You look hot, Lacey," Grant said, and Donavan's jaw twitched.

"What are you guys doing?" I asked.

"Your tutor wants to know about acting. He's going to write a piece for his high school paper."

"I just have one more question," Donavan said.

"Okay, shoot," Grant said.

"How would you feel if I shared the following statement on my social media?" He cleared his throat. "'Grant James, helped by many over the years, doesn't believe in helping others. He watched from the sidelines as his costar's reputation got trashed'?" Donavan's face showed no emotion. He had asked the question in the same measured calmness he had asked the one before.

Grant's face, on the other hand, became stone.

Amanda let out a startled cough and I just stared at Donavan. I couldn't believe he was doing this, and doing it so well. I knew it must've been hard for him.

"That's a great question," Amanda said.

Grant crossed his arms over his chest. "What do you expect me to do? I'm not exactly in a good position to help anyone else."

"You still have millions of loyal fans," Donavan said. "A few nice posts about Lacey online would go a long way."

"My publicist tells me exactly what and when to post."

"I don't believe you."

Grant didn't respond, meaning Donavan was right, Grant wasn't told what to post. At least not all the time.

"Nobody tells me when or what to post either," Donavan said. "So I guess I know what I'll be posting today."

"I'm sure you and your hundred followers will find a post about me shocking."

"Between all my platforms, I have two hundred thousand followers," Donavan said.

"What?" I asked in shock.

"I had a review go viral," he said. "So most of my followers are very specific ones. Ones who would appreciate this new bit of information about Grant James."

Amanda laughed a little next to me. "Let me guess. Can I guess?"

Grant looked at her. "Am I missing something?"

"'Grant James Goes Down in Flames,'" she said.

Grant's head whipped back to Donavan so fast that I was surprised he didn't black out. "That was you?"

Donavan handed his phone to me as if he knew what was coming.

I stepped in front of him. "Don't do anything stupid," I said to Grant.

"Are you all blackmailing me?" he asked.

"Just giving you a little motivation to be a good person," Donavan said. "I have a different, much better statement I'd rather share with my followers: 'Grant James breathes the life into Lacey Barnes's career and revives his own along with it.' Together they are power."

"You'd say that?" Grant asked. "To your mob of Grant James haters?"

"And I would actually mean it. I could throw in something about how Lacey said you were an excellent kisser too, if you'd like."

I almost scoffed at that, because I said nothing of the sort, but I clamped my mouth shut. Donavan was seconds away from succeeding at this.

Amanda chimed in. "Can you imagine the praise you'll get forever if you help launch a career? Lacey will do big things after this, mark my words. And it will be because of you."

It was obvious that everyone in this group knew that the way to appeal to Grant's mercy was through his ego. Except him, maybe.

"It's not that I don't like you, Lacey," he said. "You're cool. It's just that I need to prove myself with this movie, and if you don't hold up your end, I kind of want to distance myself from you."

"I know," I said. "I'm not a fan of things going wrong either." I looked at Amanda, waiting to see if she was willing to confess yet.

"It wasn't me," she insisted. "And if it wasn't me. And I'm assuming it wasn't you," she said, pointing at Grant. He shook his head. "Then whoever it was is still out there trying to ruin things."

"Hopefully, I can work around that. I want this movie to be successful just as much as you do. And I think if we work together as a team, it will only help all of us." I met Grant's eyes.

His eyes went down to the phone that I realized I was still holding out, recording. "I turned it off." He let out a long sigh. "Fine. I'll post some awesome things about you."

"You will?" I asked.

"And . . . ," Grant said, "I can expect a viral campaign about me breathing the life into Lacey or something? You can help me win over some Grant haters?"

"Yes," Donavan said.

Grant pointed between himself and me. "We good?

You still going to be able to work with me after this? We have lots of time left."

"We're good," I said. "And thank you."

Grant put his arm around Amanda. "Are we good?"

"You're completely selfish, but I might be willing to overlook that. We'll see." She steered him back toward the trailers.

I watched the two of them go, then tried to hand Donavan's phone back to him but he sank onto the nearest bench of the amphitheater.

"You okay?" I asked.

His hands were shaking and his face was pale.

"You're not okay," I realized.

"I'm fine," he managed to get out. "Just give me a second."

"You are a rock star. Thank you for that."

He nodded, but his eyes were still on the ground in front of him.

"You have more online followers than I do, by the way, which I am insanely jealous about."

He smiled a little. "You'll pass me soon, I'm sure."

I put my hand to his forehead, which was cold and slightly damp. "Come on, let's go get you some water and some sugar. I have both in my trailer."

He let me lead him to the trailer, where he laid on my couch. "I feel so stupid right now," he said.

"Please don't. You just suppressed your flight instinct to face down someone you'd skewered on social media and who totally would've punched you in the face if I hadn't been there. That wasn't supposed to be easy, but you did it brilliantly."

"Brilliantly?"

"That's the right word, yes? The one we use when we are completely in awe of someone?"

"Yes," he said. "That's the all-encompassing compliment."

I retrieved a water from the fridge and brought it over to him. He scooted toward the back of the couch and pulled on my hand so I'd sit on the small bit of space at the edge. I complied.

"I did it for you," he said.

I stretched out alongside him, laying my head on his chest. "I know, and I love you for it. I just hope you don't hate me after you have to actually compose and post that statement on all your social media."

I could hear his soft laugh through his chest. "I could never hate you. And if all it takes is a couple of showdowns with some enemies for you to love me, just make me a list and I'm on it."

I propped my chin on his chest and looked at him. "I think you're set for a while."

"So are you."

I smiled, happiness coursing through my chest. "You know, I always thought this is what being famous would feel like. This happy, content, amazing feeling."

"Yeah?"

"Maybe it's even better," I said.

"Let's not get crazy." He twisted one of my curls around his finger.

"You're right. Let's wait until I'm actually famous and then I'll decide."

His eyes traveled over my face. "You are beautiful."

"So are you."

"What now?" he asked.

"Now I work hard and set a trap."

"You don't think it's Amanda anymore, do you?"

"No. I don't."

"Neither do I."

"Okay, I need to go turn this face into a zombie's."

"You make a pretty good zombie."

I bared my teeth and lunged for his neck.

Dancing Graves

EXT. FOREST—NIGHT
SCARLETT hunts her former friends and
family one by one. BENJAMIN, who she
thought she had killed in the lab several
nights ago, knows she's out of control
and he must take her down. He stalks her,
weapon at the ready, hoping he can do
what he knows he needs to do. He comes
upon her after her latest kill.

                    BENJAMIN
Scarlett, what have you become?

                    SCARLETT
Exactly what I was meant to.

There is a fight between them, Benjamin
is weakened from his recent injury, but
eventually he overtakes her. He watches

her die, mixed emotions taking over.

EXT. CEMETERY—MORNING
Scarlett is lowered into the ground, and
Benjamin—the only surviving mourner—
watches, then drops a bloodred rose on
top of her casket before she is covered
with dirt.

EXT. CEMETERY—NIGHT
Camera, pointed at Scarlett's headstone,
slowly zooms out. The loose dirt over her
grave begins to shift. A hand emerges
from the soil. The formula she took
minutes after being bitten has made her
nearly invincible.

THIRTY-FIVE

The campgrounds were dark. We had filmed today's scenes in the early evening and night. Scarlett's hunting scenes. Hazy lights had been set up, so I didn't realize how dark it was until I was several hundred feet beyond the lights. My phone sat on the table in my trailer, bait for a troublemaker, but not helpful for me in this moment. I slowed my walk, trying to stay on the foot-worn path. The voices behind me faded with the lights, and soon I found myself in the middle of a group of trees unable to see more than three feet in front of me.

Crickets chirped, and a flapping noise sounded from

above. I put my hands out in front of me so I wouldn't hit anything and kept walking. If I just walked straight, I'd eventually emerge from the trees . . . if I remembered right.

It sounded like another set of footsteps joined mine, so I stopped to listen. The other noise stopped as well. Maybe it had just been an echo. Or someone farther down the path. I proceeded, only to hear it again.

"Hello?" I called. "Grant? Is that you?"

Nothing.

I picked up my pace, and after ten steps my hands met a tree, forcing me to stop. I turned a full circle and pressed my back up against the trunk. I'd somehow gotten off the path. Time to swallow my pride.

"Hello!" I yelled. "I'm stuck out here and need a flashlight!" I waited, but nobody answered. I cupped my hands around my mouth and yelled the same thing again. This time in my silence I heard the footsteps, as clear as day. And they were close. Obviously the person had heard me yelling, and if they were purposely not answering, then their intentions weren't good. I felt around on the ground for something. Anything. My hand met a decent-size rock. I picked it up.

"What do you want?" I asked.

"Justice," a voice whispered back.

I screamed and chucked the rock I held toward the

sound of the voice. A light appeared down the path to my right, and the rustle of someone running away rang out to my left.

"Lacey?" That was Grant holding the light.

"Over here," I said, and then the light was shining on my face, in my eyes.

He let out a small grunt, then laughed a little. "You shouldn't hide in the dark with zombie makeup on. You look extra creepy right now."

"Someone was just out here, telling me they wanted justice."

"Who?"

"I don't know. I couldn't see them."

"Are you okay?"

"No!"

He walked to my side and held out his elbow. "Can I walk you to your trailer?"

"Yes. And pick up a rock or branch. Your fake sword won't do anything for us."

"It's actually pretty sharp."

"Rock!" I demanded.

He laughed and aimed his light at the ground, where he found a large rock. "Is that good enough?"

"Yes. I'll hold the light."

"Wow, you're spooked."

"Of course I'm spooked. There is someone out here."

"Who do you think it was?" he asked, picking up the rock.

"I have no idea. It was too dark to see anything."

"Was it a guy or a girl?"

"A guy . . . I think. They were whispering, it was hard to tell." We took several more steps. "I might be able to find out though. I was recording my trailer today. I'm going to go watch the footage now."

"You were recording your trailer?"

"With my laptop, to see if I could catch someone messing with my things."

"I'm totally there for that. Let's grab Amanda."

"This is so boring," Amanda said as she, Grant, and I sat huddled around my computer, watching a recording that so far consisted of my cell phone sitting on the table undisturbed. I'd sped up the video but it had been recording all day, so it was taking forever. I didn't want to risk missing something by skipping forward.

"Look!" Grant said, tapping the screen. A figure had come into the shot.

I tapped on the play button so it went back to normal speed, then skipped it back thirty seconds. We all watched as Faith came into my trailer carrying some green pages. She dropped them on my table, then left.

"So it's not Faith," Grant said.

"That doesn't prove it's not her," Amanda said. "That just shows she comes into your trailer when you're not there."

"Like everyone else," I said.

"I don't come in when you're not here," Grant said.

"I do," Amanda said. "To hide in your shower."

"You're still evil," I said, and sped up the video again.

We all proceeded to stare at it. I wasn't sure how much time had passed, but there was a knock on the door. I jumped, and Grant laughed.

"Come in," I called.

Donavan poked his head inside.

I smiled. "I didn't think you were coming back today."

"I got done at work early." He looked between the three of us. "What are you doing?"

"We're watching the video of my trailer."

"Any activity?"

"None."

Grant didn't give up his seat next to me, so Donavan slid into a chair at the table. We stayed this way until the recording ended.

"Huh," I said. "Guess I'll have to set it up again tomorrow."

"I will not be watching that again tomorrow," Grant said.

I stood and set my laptop on the table. Donavan

grabbed my hand and gave it a squeeze.

"You know what we need to do?" I announced. "We need to set a trap."

"What do you mean?" Amanda asked.

"Someone intercepted me in the woods earlier, tried to scare me."

"They did?" Donavan asked. "Are you okay?"

"I'm fine. But maybe they'll try again tomorrow night."

"Why would they try again?" Grant asked.

"Because they succeeded. I was terrified, and they knew it. If I give them the opportunity to do the same thing tomorrow, I have a feeling they would. I'll make a big deal about forgetting my light. I'll ask you to walk me, Grant, and you'll say no."

"That would make me seem like a jerk," he said.

"You are sometimes," Amanda commented.

"Thanks," he said.

"And then I'll walk down the same path I did tonight and hopefully draw the person after me, and you'll all surround them."

"The three of us will surround them?" Donavan asked.

"You're right. We need more recruits we can trust." People not involved with this movie in any way. "I'll take care of that part. You guys just get ready to catch the culprit."

Amanda let out a low laugh.

"What?" I asked.

"Did you just use the word *culprit*?"

"Shut up."

Grant stood and stretched. "This is like a real-life movie. Except that whole watching an hour's worth of video on your computer would've been edited out."

Amanda stood as well. "Good thing we have America's favorite action hero, Heath Hall," she said, taking Grant's hand and leading him to the door.

"I'm not America's favorite right now, but I will be soon." He winked at me, and they both left my trailer.

I turned to Donavan. "Hi."

"Hi." He pulled me down onto his lap and into a hug. "Is this the exciting life I can hope to lead when dating an actress?"

"No, most of the time it will be really boring. Just me. And occasionally you needing to fake a British accent to help me with my lines."

"Sounds perfect to me."

"Give me one second. I need to text my friend, and then we are going to make out."

He laughed. "I like how you give me warnings when

we are going to make out as if I need to prepare myself."

"You do."

I grabbed my phone and texted Abby. **Are you still coming to see me tomorrow?**

She responded almost immediately. Yes!!

Will you bring Cooper?

I can see if he's available. Why?

We're taking down a bad guy.

THIRTY-SIX

We were on our dinner break the next day, and I had gathered my band of vigilantes in my trailer. I didn't want too many people in on this or suspicions would arise, but I needed enough to trap the perpetrator. Hopefully five was the lucky number—Donavan, Abby, Cooper, Amanda, and Grant.

"Thanks, everyone, for coming. For believing me."

Abby kept giving Grant sideways glances. I'd introduced both her and Cooper to him earlier, and both of them were beyond starstruck. Especially now, with him in full costume, leaning against the wall, hair perfectly coiffed, neck scarf neatly tied, and sword dangling from his waist.

"What's the plan?" Grant asked.

"After our final scene of the day, I'm going to start walking back, just like yesterday. I'm going to say something about how I forgot a light again. I'll pause and pretend like I'm going to turn back but change my mind. Donavan, Amanda, Abby, and Cooper will be hiding ready to intercept from the far side. Grant, you'll come up from behind, since you'll have been on set with me."

"And if the person never shows up?" Amanda asked.

"Hopefully they will."

"Let's catch the bad guy!" Amanda said, standing up.

I smiled. "T minus two hours to take down."

"Can I eat now?" Grant asked.

"Yes, go eat."

Grant waved to the room as he left.

"Me too," Amanda said. "I'll see you later." She shut the door behind her, and Abby let out a little squeal.

"I know I shouldn't think this is cool, because someone has been screwing you over, but . . . ?"

"It's fine, you can say it," I said.

"I just met Grant James," she said.

"You were right," Cooper joined. "He is very attractive."

I laughed. "You all okay to hang out here for the next two hours while I'm on set?"

"Yes, we have your boyfriend to grill," Abby said.

I raised my eyebrows at Donavan, and he said, "I'll survive."

"Good. I need to go eat, and next time I see you, hopefully you'll be surrounding my tormentor."

I had stepped onto the gravel outside my trailer when Donavan said, "Hey."

I turned.

"You okay?"

"A little nervous," I admitted. As much as I wanted to figure out who had been sabotaging me, I also kind of didn't want to know.

"You don't think this person would hurt you, do you?"

"I don't think so. . . ." Although I wasn't sure. I hadn't felt safe at all the night before.

"Be careful, okay?"

"I will." I hugged him.

He moved to kiss me, when I took a step back. "You really want to kiss this?" I pointed at my zombie makeup.

He smiled. "Hey, I started liking you in the middle of you wearing all that."

I patted his cheek. "That's sweet, but you still can't

kiss me. I can't risk you messing it up."

"Fair enough." He gave me another hug. "See you later."

The tip of Benjamin's sword pressed against my throat. It was cold, and Grant was right, a little sharp.

"Do you know how many people you've killed? I can't let this go on," Grant said as Benjamin.

"Then don't," I growled.

We walked a slow circle, the camera following us.

"Scarlett, what have you become?"

"Exactly what I was meant to."

He pulled his arm back and thrust the sword forward. I dodged, and we got into our choreographed scuffle. Then Grant stabbed his sword to the right of my neck. The angle of the camera would make it look like it went straight through. I put my hands to my throat, breaking the packets of fake blood I'd been holding. I collapsed to the ground. Grant stood over me, then brought his sword down again. He paused, staring down at me for several moments before Remy called, "Cut!"

I stood, and Simone came forward and cleaned up my neck, then fixed the makeup for another take.

I let my eyes scan over the group of people in the hazy light surrounding me. Remy studied the monitor and pointed out a few things to the cameraperson. Noah was just beyond him, looking over his shoulder. Simone was now talking to Audrey, the hair person. Faith was looking at the script. Next to her, standing alone, was Grant's agent. We locked eyes for a moment, and he shook his head slightly. I wasn't sure what that meant. Everyone else was a crew member I'd seen around but had never really conversed with.

My heart picked up speed as I thought about walking through the dark alone.

"You want to take my sword?" Grant whispered from beside me as if he'd read my mind.

I smiled.

Grant's eyes were now taking in our surroundings as well. "Do you think the person is here right now?"

"I don't know."

We ran the scene two more times before Remy said, "That's a wrap."

I took a steadying breath. Grant reached over and squeezed my arm. It was a sweet gesture that bolstered my opinion of him.

"I'm right behind you," he whispered.

I nodded. "Hey," I said loudly. "Will you walk me back to the trailers? I forgot my light."

"I need to talk to Remy and watch some raw footage.

You'll be fine," he said, playing the role I assigned him.

"Fine."

He smirked and headed over to the monitors. I went for the path. And just like that I was alone in the dark. Just beyond the set I was leaving behind, I stopped and looked back, acted nervous. I took one step back toward the set, but then shook my head and turned back to the path.

I walked slowly to provide plenty of opportunity. The problem was, I really couldn't see. I should've remembered this small detail from the day before. I'd shown the others which path to wait on, but after several more minutes of walking, I wasn't even sure I was on that path. Especially not when I tripped over a large root. I didn't remember there being roots on the walking path.

"Crap," I grunted under my breath. Each step I took forward after that, I used my foot to feel the ground in front of me. This was going to take all night.

Then I heard it. The footsteps behind me again. I looked over my shoulder but saw nothing but blackness.

"Grant?" I knew that wasn't the plan, but maybe he'd followed me when I got off course.

No response.

"Hello?"

"Are you scared?" a voice whispered.

I let out a scream, hoping my friends would hear it, and took off running. I'd made it only ten steps before

I tripped on a root and went down hard, scuffing both palms. I flipped over and scooted backward while looking all around me.

"What do you want from me?" I said.

A rustling sound to my right launched me to my feet again. I should've taken Grant's sword. "I'm over here!" I yelled. My voice bounced off the trees, which wouldn't help with locating me at all.

Silence.

And then the loudest footsteps yet. Fast. Running toward me. I should've run. I needed to run. But the thought of tripping again and having my back to someone coming at me had me doing the exact opposite. I held my ground, and when I saw a dark form reach my field of vision, I launched myself forward, wrapping my arms around it. We both fell. I landed on my back, knocking the wind out of me. The figure rolled off me and bolted. I caught my breath, lying there while I assessed the damage. I seemed okay. I'd probably have a few bruises.

I heard a shout behind me and then several others. I picked myself up off the ground and made my way to the noise.

My friends were there. Donavan was shining a light on someone who was struggling against Cooper's arms. Grant ran up from a different direction, joining the scuffle.

Abby came to my side. "Sorry! We got to you just as you fell over."

"Who is it?" I asked.

"I don't know."

I reached the small knot of people.

"Aaron?" I said.

He pushed against Cooper's arms one more time but then gave up, a defeated look coming over his face.

"Why?" I asked.

"I didn't mean for you to fall. You were supposed to run." His voice sounded panicked, and his eyes darted all around, even though I knew he couldn't see much of anything with the light shining on him.

"But why did you do all this? Why were you sabotaging me?"

"I wasn't," he said, but it wasn't convincing.

"I know you were, so you might as well talk."

"I just want to go. Let me go." There were tears in his voice, even though there were none in his eyes.

"Tell me why first, and then we'll let you go."

"Because my dad is a jerk. He traded our year of plans for this stupid movie. He deserves for it to fail epically."

My eyes went to Donavan, who was still holding his light to Aaron's face, so I couldn't really see him. I wondered if Aaron's bitter feelings toward his dad were something he could relate to.

"And you thought targeting *me* would make it fail?" I asked.

"I wasn't targeting you. I was just trying to mess up the movie in general."

"They all related to me . . . ," I started to say but then realized they really didn't. When the light fell over and the headstone was damaged, I just happened to be in the wrong place at the wrong time. And my zombie face section going missing reflected badly on Leah, not me. The other things seemed directed at me, but I wondered if there were more things that he'd done that I hadn't even realized.

"That article felt really personal," I suddenly remembered.

He shook his head. "I didn't do that. At all. That was probably just crew members talking to the press or something."

Cooper let go of Aaron, and he just stood there, staring at me, looking miserable. "Are you going to tell my dad?" he asked.

"Of course we're going to tell your dad," Grant said.

I held up my hand. "You have two choices. You can stop coming to the set. Or you can keep hanging around and tell your dad yourself."

"I'll stop coming," he said quickly.

"We're not going tell?" Amanda asked.

"No . . ." I held Aaron's gaze. "We're not."

He gave me a single nod, wiped at his eyes with the back of his hand, then said, "I'm sorry."

"I know," I responded.

He pushed his way through the group, head hanging, and disappeared into the dark.

"What a little punk," Amanda said.

Donavan came up to my side. "Did he hurt you?"

I looked at my palms, and he shined his light on them. "Just a few scrapes. I'll be fine. I'm just glad it's over." It was over. I let that sink in. Now I could do my job without distractions.

"This calls for a campfire!" Amanda said.

THIRTY-SEVEN

It had been several weeks of highs and lows, but this, *this* was definitely the high point—sitting around a camp-fire, with a movie star, my best friends, and my boyfriend on location at the movie I was filming. I'd taken off my makeup and changed into street clothes. We'd rounded up some chairs, but I preferred the ground, leaning up against Donavan's knees behind me. He pulled on the ends of my hair as I held a stick over the flames.

"Do you think craft services has marshmallows?" Amanda asked.

"I think they're gone for the day," I said. It was close

to eleven. My dad had given me permission to stay out late since Abby was in town.

"I think I have some in my trailer," Grant said.

"You have marshmallows in your trailer?" Abby asked.

"Probably. That Aaron kid always kept me stocked up with treats. I'm going to miss him."

Silence followed his statement.

"Too soon?" he asked.

We all laughed.

I poked at the logs in the fire with my stick. "I don't think you have marshmallows in your trailer."

"I'll bet you a thousand dollars."

Amanda threw a small piece of bark into the fire, sending up a few sparks. "Grant, most people say, I'll bet you five bucks or maybe twenty bucks."

"What?" he asked.

"Just trying to keep you relatable."

He gave her a slow smile. "Whoever said I wanted to be relatable?" He stood. "I'm going to get those marshmallows."

Amanda climbed to her feet. "I'll come with you, so I can verify that you owe Lacey a thousand bucks."

I laughed as they walked away.

"I left my phone in your trailer, Lacey," Abby said. "We'll be back too."

"Okay."

It was just Donavan and me. I leaned my head back on his knees and looked up at the stars. They were so bright up here away from the city lights.

"Thanks for helping today," I said.

"Any time." He played with my hair some more before he asked, "Why did you let Aaron off so easy?"

"I don't know. Not that it excuses his behavior, but I sort of understood his motivation. He's feeling neglected," I said. "I've been there before."

"Me too," Donavan said. "It was nice of you."

"I know. I'm brilliant."

Donavan gave a soft laugh. "Yes, you are."

"I don't have zombie makeup on anymore," I said.

"I noticed."

"That means you can kiss me now."

He leaned over to where I was still resting on his knees and kissed my forehead.

"That's nice," I said, turning around and moving up on to my knees. "But I need more." I pressed my lips against his.

EPILOGUE

One Year Later

I knew it wasn't going to be a blockbuster, but that didn't mean I hadn't dressed up like I was some world-famous star for the premiere of *Dancing Graves*. They had rolled out the red carpet, after all. I was pretty sure they did that for every movie premiere, or just whenever the carpet needed airing out, but whatever. It was red, and I was walking on it.

My dad and mom were bypassing the carpet and meeting me inside. But I had a handsome date decked out in a tuxedo on my arm and was owning every second of this experience.

"Lacey, Lacey! Look over here!" A photographer called, and Donavan and I paused for a moment to pose for a shot.

"Is this more what you had in mind when you thought of people yelling your name?" Donavan asked quietly from beside me.

"Yes, actually." I squeezed his hand. "Is this what you had in mind when you banned yourself from dating actresses?"

"This part hadn't even occurred to me. It should've gone on the cons list for sure."

We continued walking, the same scene playing out with the photographers until we were inside.

Amanda and Grant were there, looking amazing. They'd come together, but I didn't think they were still dating. They'd been on again off again for the last year. I didn't see them much. I ended up finishing out the school year at the school that had hosted my independent study, surprising both my dad, my mom, and myself. I missed my Central Coast friends, but I wanted to spend more time really connecting with my dad. And the fact that Donavan was there didn't hurt at all. I also decided I wanted to wait to film another movie until high school was over. It was my senior year; I wanted to experience it. And I had. And now I had my first audition the following week.

Amanda rushed over to give me a hug. "How are you feeling? Are you ready to see your face on a huge screen?"

"I've never seen it on one quite so big, so I'll let you know later."

Grant sauntered over. "You brought a critic for your date?"

"I'm only *your* critic," Donavan said to Grant.

I laughed. "He's teasing you, Grant." When he still didn't laugh, I asked, "How is your shoot-'em-up movie going?" He'd been hired again for his reoccurring role as Heath Hall, the teenaged spy. The role he thought he'd lost.

"Very well," he said. "There are loads of special effects."

"Are you trying to say there aren't any in the movie we're about to watch?"

He smirked, finally loosening up a bit.

"See you guys later," I said. "I see my parents."

My mom and dad had come together as well, even though they were, of course, not together. My mom was still happily married, and my dad was single again. He and Leah had dated only a few months, and last I heard she was back together with Remy. I wondered if I'd see them here tonight. I wondered if that would be awkward. Dad smiled as Donavan and I approached.

"How are you feeling?" Mom asked, sounding like

she was the one who might not be able to contain her excitement.

"Excited and kind of terrified."

"We're proud of you," Dad said.

"For what?" I asked. "Getting dressed up and coming to a movie premiere?"

"For seeing it through, even when it got hard." That was big coming from my dad. He was part of the reason it had been so hard. But he had let go a lot in the last year. My mom was still as busy as ever, but I knew she was happy for me.

"What do you mean? It was never hard," I said.

Donavan smiled beside me. He looked so good in a tux.

"So really?" I asked Donavan. "Are you going to review this movie? I know you're done with the school paper and everything, but maybe for your first piece at college?" Donavan had been accepted at Berkeley, majoring in journalism and communications, and my plan was to be as close to him as possible when I wasn't filming.

"I'm just going to be your boyfriend tonight," he said.

"Good answer." People starting filing into the theater. "Are you all ready?" I asked.

"It doesn't matter if we are," Donavan said, kissing the back of my hand. "Are you?"

"More than ready."

ACKNOWLEDGMENTS

This book was so much fun to write!! One of the things I did in order to prep myself for it was visit a movie set. My friend was directing a short film and allowed me to come and snoop around the set for a day while they were filming. It was a blast. So thank you, Brock Heasley (with Tremendum Pictures), for the education. And thanks, Ciara Daniel, for allowing me to follow you around like a puppy dog and for answering all my really naive questions. And thank you to actress Ema Horvath for the interview where I became an awkward, unorganized fan. And thanks as well to Nicole Spate and the rest of the cast and crew. You were all awesome. I'm sure I still got things wrong in the book, things that would probably never happen on a set but that I needed to happen for the book, but I hope it at least feels more authentic.

As always, thank you to the readers! You make this possible and I have so much fun meeting you and hearing from you. You are awesome! I'm sure a lot of writers say this, but I think my readers are the absolute best kind of people!

I also want to thank my family. They are such fun people and I love them dearly. So to my husband, Jared, and my kids, Skyler, Autumn, Abby, and Donavan, thanks for the support! I know you have to give a lot of it, and you are all so good at it.

Next, I'd like to thank my agent, Michelle Wolfson. I am always so happy that my green little writer self somehow had the good sense to know you were the right one for me! I have never regretted that decision a day since.

Thank you, Catherine Wallace, my awesome editor. You are awesome and so easy to work with. It really helps a busy writer out. I appreciate all you do for me and my books, I know they wouldn't be the same without you. And thanks to the rest of the HarperTeen team and all you did—my cover, edits, marketing, and on and on.

I have some of the best friends ever. Friends who read my books and give me advice. Friends who cheer me on. Friends who get me out of the house and away from my computer when they know I need it. Those people in my life are: Stephanie Ryan, Candi Kennington, Rachel Whiting, Jenn Johansson, Renee Collins, Natalie Whipple, Michelle Argyle, Bree Despain, Elizabeth Minnick, Brittney Swift, Mandy Hillman, Jamie Lawrence, Emily Freeman, Misti Hamel, Claudia Wadsworth.

And last, but definitely not least, thanks to my family, who have always been there for me no matter what. It's so fun to have a big family! It has helped me to write big authentic family relationships. So thank you: Chris DeWoody, Heather Garza, Jared DeWoody, Spencer DeWoody, Stephanie Ryan, Dave Garza, Rachel DeWoody, Zita Konik, Kevin Ryan, Vance West, Karen West, Eric West, Michelle West, Sharlynn West, Rachel Braithwaite, Brian Braithwaite, Angie Stettler, Jim Stettler, Emily Hill, Rick Hill and the twenty-five children and the [I lost track of the amount] children of children that exist between all these people. I love you all so much.

TURN THE PAGE FOR A SNEAK PEEK!

ONE

I moved my arms in a windmill as I stared out over the pool in front of me. The water had calmed from the last race and the still night made it look like glass. I couldn't wait to break through its surface. I rotated my head side to side to the beat of the music blasting through my headphones. My music was loud but I sensed a hush come over the watching crowd. That wasn't normal. I brought my brows together, determined not to think about it. I needed to stay in the zone. No distractions.

The shrill sound of microphone feedback cut through my music. I tugged out a single earbud and looked up.

The first thing I saw was my dad. He sat in the middle of the bleachers with a goofy grin on his face. He waved. Mom was next to him, typing something into her phone.

The feedback sounded again and then someone cleared their throat into the microphone. The noise wasn't coming from the booth, where the announcer was looking around, just as confused as the crowd.

"Ladies and gentlemen," the voice said. "May I present Heath Hall."

"What the—?" I mumbled. "No."

A low buzz of chatter rippled through the audience.

"The guy from the movies?" someone behind me asked. "Is he here?"

I knew the real Heath Hall wasn't here. Well, obviously. Heath Hall was a spy hero character played by the actor Grant James. But the person about to appear was neither the character nor the actor. The person about to appear was some attention-seeker who I'd successfully ignored until this point.

The coaches and officials moved around the pool, searching for the interruption. That's when a guy in a Speedo and rash guard emerged from the locker room across the way, hands in the air. He was wearing a Heath Hall mask. Not one of those cheap, plastic, fake-looking masks but a high-quality, very realistic version of Heath Hall encased his head. The same exact mask I'd seen in online pictures classmates had posted over the years of him causing public disturbances. If I were closer I would've seen the electronic eyepiece and scar running along his right cheek that some mask maker had painted on so we wouldn't mistake this mask for another one of Grant James's characters.

The impersonator let out a guttural yell and charged straight for the pool. My mouth dropped open. The coaches rounded the pool but weren't fast enough to catch him before he jumped in feetfirst. The voice over the rogue microphone said, "Go, go, go!"

The crowd soon joined in as fake Heath Hall swam the length of the pool and crawled out right next to my starting block, mask still concealing his entire head. He gave me a thumbs-up, water flicking off his hand and onto my arm, then took off at full speed toward the open gate. I wiped off my arm and watched the coaches attempt to catch him. He was too fast. A few moments later they walked back, defeated.

"Okay," the real announcer said. "That was interesting. Are we ready for an actual race? One hundred free, take your places."

What? No. My chest tightened in a panic. My goggles were still pushed up onto my forehead, very much not in place. The other racers were heading toward the starting blocks. I swallowed my protests about needing more time, realizing none of the officials seemed to care, then quickly tugged out my other earbud, dropped it on top of my parka at my feet, and pulled down my goggles, pressing them into place.

Less than thirty seconds later I dived into the pool. I was glad this was my last heat of the night; my body was tense. The lines on the bottom of the pool were there just like they always were, but as I fell into my rhythm, the image of the guy wearing a Heath Hall mask seemed to take over my vision.

Stop, I told my brain.

My shoulders burned and my eyes stung with the pain. I winced and pushed through, forcing my arms to make the rotation even though they tried to tell me as loud as possible that they didn't want to. I touched the wall and then flip-kicked off it. Just one more length of the pool. The adrenaline masked some of the pain. I stretched out and with one final kick, touched the wall.

My eyes went straight to the results board. I was three seconds slower than my normal time, putting me in fourth place. I hit the water in frustration. It was the first race I'd lost in weeks.

Coach stood over my lane so I pulled off my cap and goggles.

"Hadley, how are the shoulders?"

"Okay."

He raised his eyebrows. "Go have DJ ice them." Coach reached down and gave me a hand out of the pool. He didn't say anything else. He didn't have to.

After rinsing off in the shower and pulling on my T-shirt and sweats over my still-wet suit, I went to the trainer's office.

DJ sat in a chair, his feet on the desk, reading a book. There were some who faked injuries just to get in front of him. His dark eyes were so concerned as he'd check out any ailment. And yes, he was cute. I wasn't interested, but I wasn't blind either. With his light brown eyes and loose dark curls he looked like the sweet best friend in movies who always ended up with the girl.

I knocked on the glass of the open door and he looked up.

"Are you busy?" I asked.

He held up his book but the title was in Spanish so I couldn't read it.

"For school?" I asked.

"Sort of," he said. "And to make my mom happy. Apparently language can be lost in as little as one generation." He set the book aside and sat forward. "What can I do for you?"

"Ice."

He jumped out of his seat. "Shoulders?"

I was only ever in here for one reason: my shoulders. "Yes."

"Come in." His hands were gentle as he guided me to the seat he'd just abandoned. "Your races go okay? You seem upset."

"I'm fine," I said, not wanting to talk about the only race I lost tonight and how irritated I was about the distraction. Apparently my face had already done the talking for me. I changed the subject. "I didn't think you'd be here tonight."

"I'm here so the real trainer can be poolside." He scooped ice into two large ziplock bags. Only half of his last scoop made it into the bag, the rest spilling on the floor. He fumbled with trying to clean it up. I bent down to help him and he waved me off and left it there scattered across the floor. He returned to my side.

"I know you don't take this pain very seriously, Hadley, but if you're not nicer to your shoulders, this could get serious soon. You need to rest them more."

"I'm nice to my shoulders."

He gave a grunt of disagreement and placed a bag on my right shoulder. "Hold this."

I did and he grabbed the plastic wrap, then began to secure it down. As his hands worked their way around my shoulder, his shirt brushed my cheek. It smelled so good that it relaxed me a bit. He moved on to the other shoulder and I looked away to control my urge to sniff him.

"Okay, you're all set."

"Thanks."

"Maybe for a while, until your joint pain settles, you could work on your form."

I smiled. "Yes, Coach."

Amelia, my best friend, was applying mascara when I joined her by the lockers. After she put it back in her bag, she turned and poked one of the ice packs attached to me. "Nice. You're all suited up for some football."

"Funny."

"How was DJ? As dreamy as ever?"

"Yep. Still the cutest nerd I know."

"Do you think he'd date a high school student?" Amelia often set her boy-sights high, determined to land guys that were mostly unavailable to her. I liked her confidence, even though her plans almost never worked.

I always supported her unrealistic hopes because I knew that she knew they were just that. "He only graduated last year, right?" I wasn't exactly sure because he'd gone to a high school across town.

"Yes, but I feel like college years are like dog years

compared to high school years."

I opened my locker and pulled out my towel and bag. "Dog years?"

"Yes, for every year you're in college, you're like seven years older than a high school student."

"You're weird."

"And proud of it."

I opened my bag and stared inside blankly. "Were you out there for my last race or were you already in here?" Amelia swam the race right before mine so she was often changing when I was up.

She scrunched her nose, looking guilty. "I'm sorry, did you want me to watch? Are your parents not here tonight?"

"No, it's not that. Heath Hall was here. He jumped into the pool."

"What? And I missed it?"

"He completely distracted me . . . and probably all the swimmers."

"That sucks. So . . . did you get a good look? Who is he?"

"What?"

"That's the online debate. He's obviously someone from around here because most of his public appearances—"

"Public disturbances," I interrupted.

"Have happened within, like, a hundred-mile radius."

"How do you know this?"

She turned one way and then the other as she looked at herself in the long mirror on the inside door of her locker. "Someone did a map of them."

"People have too much time on their hands."

She shut her locker and leaned her back against it. "By the way, did I ever tell you that my brother met the real Heath Hall last year? I mean the guy who plays him— Grant James."

I rolled my eyes. "Yes, only a million times."

"That's because it's cool! And Grant James is hot."

I shoved my towel into my bag and zipped it up. "Is that what Cooper said?"

"Yes, actually, he did. Was this guy hot?"

"What? No, I mean, I don't know, he was wearing a mask."

Her eyes went wide. "Just a mask?"

"Yes, just a mask." I shoved her shoulder. "No! He had on a Speedo and a rash guard too."

"So . . . did he have a nice body?"

"I don't know. I wasn't paying attention. He jumped into my pool!"

Amelia raised her eyebrows. "*Your* pool?"

"Well, my lane, whatever. He spread his bad mojo all over it."

She laughed and slung her backpack over one shoulder. "You and your rituals."

"I don't have rituals, I have routines." Routines that made me win races and today that routine was wrecked by a wannabe Heath Hall. If I ever found out who he was, I'd have some words for him.